Praise for the Novels of Nancy Martin

Murder Melts in Your Mouth

"Hilarious repartee and zany characters move the story along. . . . Martin is an outstanding mystery author."
—*Library Journal* (starred review)

"A witty, wonderful offering."
—*Romantic Times* (top pick)

"The long-awaited reunion between the sisters and their parents will satisfy longtime fans." —*Publishers Weekly*

A Crazy Little Thing Called Death

"A window [to] a moneyed world that the author skewers and spotlights with equal fun."
—*San Antonio Express-News*

"Why can't the perfect little black dress serve for interviewing benefit hostesses and dodging bullets? Of course [it] can, darling. The proof's right here."
—*Pittsburgh Magazine*

"Martin's wicked observations about the horsey set enhance another fine-feathered mystery."
—*Publishers Weekly*

"A delightful lighthearted satirical tale that jabs at the pretentiousness of the upper class."—The Best Reviews

Have Your Cake and Kill Him Too

"Martin, a master of one-liners and witty repartee, mixes the zany lives of the Blackbird family with posh Main Line Philadelphia society and comes up with another winning mystery." —*Library Journal* (starred review)

continued . . .

"Charming and funny."   —*Publishers Weekly*

"Sassy, exciting, and impossible to put down."
                                         —*Midwest Book Review*

"Martin's fabulous offering is peppered with witty dialogue, oddball characters, and a clever plot that blends two separate mysteries into one delightful tale of murder and the unusual relationships between sisters."
                                         —*Romantic Times* (4 stars)

Cross Your Heart and Hope to Die

"Nora Blackbird has humor, haute couture, and sexual heat, and *Cross Your Heart and Hope to Die* has me hooked on the Blackbird sisters."
                                         —Harley Jane Kozak, author of *Dead Ex*

"A laugh-out-loud comic mystery as outrageous as a pink chinchilla coat."   —*Booklist*

"The right mix of humor ... but like the best writers in this subgenre, Martin keeps the story grounded in reality."   —*South Florida Sun-Sentinel*

"A blend of fashion-forward romance and witty suspense ... Martin's wicked tongue-in-cheek satire will appeal to fans of Jennifer Crusie ... and Janet Evanovich."   —*Publishers Weekly*

"Wide-eyed sleuthing, sisterly antics, and humorous dialogue will have readers panting for more."
                                         —*Library Journal*

"Vividly drawn and immensely entertaining ... an absolute delight."   —*Romantic Times*

Other Books in the
Blackbird Sisters Mystery Series

MURDER MELTS IN YOUR MOUTH

A BLACKBIRD SISTERS MYSTERY

Nancy Martin

AN OBSIDIAN MYSTERY

OBSIDIAN

Published by New American Library, a division of
Penguin Group (USA) Inc., 375 Hudson Street,
New York, New York 10014, USA
Penguin Group (Canada), 90 Eglinton Avenue East, Suite 700, Toronto,
Ontario M4P 2Y3, Canada (a division of Pearson Penguin Canada Inc.)
Penguin Books Ltd., 80 Strand, London WC2R 0RL, England
Penguin Ireland, 25 St. Stephen's Green, Dublin 2,
Ireland (a division of Penguin Books Ltd.)
Penguin Group (Australia), 250 Camberwell Road, Camberwell, Victoria 3124,
Australia (a division of Pearson Australia Group Pty. Ltd.)
Penguin Books India Pvt. Ltd., 11 Community Centre, Panchsheel Park,
New Delhi - 110 017, India
Penguin Group (NZ), 67 Apollo Drive, Rosedale, North Shore 0632,
New Zealand (a division of Pearson New Zealand Ltd.)
Penguin Books (South Africa) (Pty.) Ltd., 24 Sturdee Avenue,
Rosebank, Johannesburg 2196, South Africa

Penguin Books Ltd., Registered Offices:
80 Strand, London WC2R 0RL, England

Published by Obsidian, an imprint of New American Library, a division of Penguin
Group (USA) Inc. Previously published in an Obsidian hardcover edition.

First Obsidian Mass Market Printing, January 2009
10 9 8 7 6 5 4 3 2 1

MANY THANKS:

Meg Ruley and the Rotrosen dream team

Wendy Garofalo and Ted Pence

Elizabeth Tierney

Ramona Long

Sarah Martin

La Sweeney

The Tarts at www.thelipstickchronicles.typepad.com—
Harley and Sarah and Michele and Elaine and Rebecca.
(And you, too, Margie.)

Without Ellen Edwards and the whole wonderful team
at NAL, the Blackbirds wouldn't be the characters
I love so much.
Thank you!

Chapter 1

While yakking into her cell phone with her massage therapist, my sister Libby walked out into traffic and got herself hit by a Rolls-Royce.

It happened during a heat wave so unbearable, a dozen water mains had burst all over Philadelphia, and cabdrivers reverted to their native languages to scream at one another. Libby decided her recovery depended on her moving from the hospital into the peace and quiet of a luxury suite at the Ritz-Carlton. The mysterious owner of the Rolls insisted upon paying, and the suite was full of flowers and restorative chocolate when we arrived.

"Nora, you'll take care of my children while I recover, won't you? I'm sure they'll be no trouble at all."

Struck dumb by the terror her hyperactive monsters could cause during a heat wave, I watched while Libby stripped off most of her clothes, slipped into the fluffy white robe provided by the hotel and arranged herself on the king-sized bed like a determined Vegas gold digger awaiting a randy billionaire.

She looked nothing like a woman with a head injury. In fact, I still wasn't sure she'd actually suffered any injuries at all. I had arrived at the hospital too late to hear an official diagnosis, but she seemed indecently robust at the moment.

She poufed her auburn hair, opened the first box of chocolate truffles and deeply inhaled their seductive aroma. "You don't mind babysitting, right? I need serenity. The charming neurologist was adamant about that. You heard him, didn't you?"

I had indeed heard rest prescribed for my sister by a doctor who seemed interested in palpating more of her as soon as his shift ended. But perhaps I was the one who needed to have my head examined, because I agreed that her five children could stay with me at Blackbird Farm until she felt better.

"But only until Friday," I said firmly. "I'm supposed to cover the Chocolate Festival Gala that night, not to mention four parties for the Fourth of July on Saturday. I can't miss any of them. I'm serious, Lib. I'm still on probation at the newspaper. If I blow these assignments, I could lose my job once and for all."

"That awful job! It was so much more convenient when you were unemployed, Nora."

"And broke, you mean?"

"Details, details!" She caught sight of my expression. "Oh, all right. I'll be good as new by Friday."

"Promise?"

She looked good as new already. Maybe better. Being half-naked always gave her a glow. She said, "I promise."

I checked my watch. "I was supposed to meet with my editor an hour ago. Maybe he's still in his office."

"Yes, run along." She yawned prettily. "Just remember, Maximus is at a crucial developmental stage. So keep the binky out of his mouth and practice his language skills. Even though I'm opposed to formal education, it can't hurt if he gets into Yale someday."

"Libby, he's eight months old. His favorite toy is his own penis. He's a long way from Yale."

"I know several Yale graduates, and their favorite toys are still their penises. Just sing the ABC song once in a while, please? Or conjugate some verbs." She collapsed against the mound of pillows. "I need a nap. It's impossible to get any rest in a hospital. Before you go, will you slip down the hall and bring me some ice, darling? And pull those curtains? Do you think this hotel has a masseur on staff?"

Because I was actually happy to see her alive after the Rolls-Royce scare, I drew the draperies, filled the ice bucket and gave Libby a cool cloth to press to her not-so-fevered brow. When I slipped out the door, I distinctly heard her pick up the phone and say, "Room service? Will you send up a bottle of chilled champagne right away? And two glasses, please!"

Only Libby could find a date in a psych ward.

I took the elevator down to the sweltering street and pulled out my cell phone to contact my editor. He was out until three, I was told. A slight reprieve. So I tried calling our sister Emma for the third time since I'd been summoned to spring Libby from the hospital. But Emma didn't answer her phone. Again.

I hadn't seen my little sister in ages, and such an extended absence didn't bode well. Left unsupervised a few weeks ago, she had run off to Atlantic City with Jon Bon Jovi's roadies. Heaven only knew what kind of trouble she could get into during a heat wave.

With Emma on my mind, I began the arduous trek back to the Pendergast Building and my job at the *Philadelphia Intelligencer*. I had my weekly column to finish and phone calls to make to finalize arrangements for all those Fourth of July parties. But the intense heat that radiated up from the sidewalk nearly melted the soles of my Kate Spade sandals, and after four blocks I lost my determination. The city smelled of hot asphalt and garbage, and the howling of horns and enraged drivers started my head pounding. I was wilting faster than cheesesteaks on a griddle.

And besides, I suddenly had an idea where I might find Emma.

So I stopped at a trendy Broad Street oasis.

It was an upscale restaurant, popular with theatergoers in the evening, but crowded with bankers and lawyers from the financial district during the lunch hour. A sizable contingent of reporters hung out there, too, ears to the ground. Several tables hummed with the low-pitched rumble of wheeling and dealing.

A very married news anchor sat at the bar, sucking down his first scotch and water of the day. Beside him, a pretty summer intern spun on the barstool, showing off her legs. A tableful of bankers leaned their heads together as if plotting a financial coup.

I ordered an iced tea and snagged a seat at the end of the bar, near the window so I could keep an eagle eye out for Emma.

"Nora? Is that you?"

Crewe Dearborne got up from a secluded table and came over to the bar.

Rich enough to be a dilettante, Crewe had instead turned an appreciation for the finer things in life into a career as the restaurant critic for the city's most respected newspaper. His opinions on food and drink made him a tastemaker for readers and restaurateurs alike. Today he had a sheaf of notes in his breast pocket and a dish of mixed berries in one hand. His thinning fair hair spilled over an aristocratic forehead and the regal Dearborne nose.

He also wore a false mustache, wire-rimmed glasses and a light seersucker suit.

"Good heavens, Crewe, you look like a nephew of Colonel Sanders."

"I'm in disguise. I understand the chef has my picture on the refrigerator with a target drawn on my forehead. Mind if I join you?"

He set his dish on the bar. The berries were drizzled with a vintage balsamic vinegar, dark as chocolate. It was the sort of piquant treat enjoyed by sophisticated palates on a hot afternoon.

I avoided contact with his bristly mustache as I gave Crewe a kiss on the cheek. "Your identity is safe with me. How on earth can you look so cool on a day like this?"

"Restaurants are the new theater, Nora, and I've got

a front-row seat. I've been here in the air-conditioning for hours. You look lovely today, by the way. You have quite a glow."

Desperate to dig something cool out of my closet that morning, I had slipped into a Lilly Pulitzer sheath printed with ladybugs—inappropriate dress for the workplace, but infinitely more comfortable than a business suit during a heat wave. "That's sweat, darling." Using a cocktail napkin, I dabbed my forehead. "I thought my sister Emma might be hiding out here this afternoon. Have you seen her?"

"Quite a bit of her, in fact. Emma just stepped into the ladies' room."

"Good. That gives me time to cool off before we have a public fight."

Crewe's brows rose. "What's going on?"

"A lack of family communication, that's all. She bought several ponies to teach riding lessons at Blackbird Farm, then disappeared and left me the keeper of the animal kingdom." As the bartender arrived with my iced tea, I said, "Thank you."

While I drank deeply from the glass, Crewe watched me with his smile fading to concern. "How are you, Nora? Besides riding herd on the pony farm. Tell the truth."

He kept his tone casual, but I knew his question was genuine. The two of us had been embroiled in an unfortunate business just a few weeks ago, and I still hadn't quite recovered. I took a sip of my drink and forced my voice to sound steady. "I'm fine. Or giving my best impression, at least. I'm focusing on work. If only I can hike back to the office through all this heat."

He smiled down at me. "Isn't the Pendergast three blocks from here?"

"Today it feels like twenty miles. I'm thinking of hiring a camel."

He laughed as he leaned against the bar beside my stool. "You'll have to fight the tourists. With the Chocolate Festival going on, it's gridlock all over the city—with or without camels."

Although Crewe made small talk, he rested his hand on mine for an instant and squeezed, communicating how he sympathized with my rocky mental state. Between a couple of restrained blue bloods, his gesture was tantamount to a violent emotional display. My throat tightened abruptly.

I squeezed him back, then slipped my hand from Crewe's touch and took another thirsty gulp of the cold drink. "How's Lexie?"

I expected Crewe to smile. He had been dating my best friend, Lexie Paine, for over a month, and I thought their relationship had blossomed despite her long-avowed reluctance to venture into a meaningful affair with any man. Lexie was happiest when dealing with financial transactions, not matters of the heart, but Crewe seemed to have melted her reserve. I thought they were on their way to becoming a blissful couple.

But Crewe's expression clouded.

"What's wrong?" I asked.

"I'm not sure," Crewe said slowly. "You've known her longer than I have, Nora. Maybe you can tell me."

Lexie and I had met while still in diapers, and we'd grown up together. Our parents shared a Hamptons summerhouse, and we spent several hot Julys roaming the dunes and playing dress-up in her mother's closet. If I closed my eyes, I could still conjure up the mental image of skinny Lexie racing barefoot across the sand in her mother's best Vionnet nightie. We'd been playmates first, then roommates in boarding school, confidantes for years ever since. I knew Lexie better than my own sisters, really. And for Lexie, I was the sibling she never had.

"Let's see. I last spoke to her—oh, dear, it's been over a week," I said. "Come to think of it, she seemed a little distracted then."

"She's more than distracted now. She had her assistant cancel our dinner date last evening—couldn't even make the call herself because of a problem at work. And when I telephoned later to say good night, Lexie acted like I was a telemarketer trying to sell time-shares."

That was a surprise. Even on dire days when the stock market behaved like an Alpine skier plunging off an icy slope, Lexie always took the extra second to be unfailingly polite. I asked, "What kind of problem at work?"

"She didn't say. She's very secretive."

"That comes with the territory, you know."

Lexie had inherited a vast financial empire from her father and his various curmudgeonly business associates. Now she was the controlling partner in a firm that represented more billionaires than some of the biggest houses in New York. Wall Street bulls stopped snorting and listened carefully when she spoke. Her clients included ruthless tycoons, a handful of peripatetic European royals and a fair number of idiotic heiresses, who all depended on Lexie's know-how to keep their investments secure and growing.

Crewe pushed his dish of berries away. "Yes, I know discretion is part of her job, but she seems genuinely upset. I thought the two of us had reached the point where we could confide in each other, but . . ."

"You've been very patient, Crewe."

He allowed a rueful smile. "It hasn't been easy."

No, I was sure it had been excruciatingly difficult to convince Lexie to trust him. Their relationship had grown only in tiny increments. Lexie was too skittish to enter into an impulsive love affair. As a young teenager, she had been sexually assaulted by a cousin, and since then she had been unwilling—unable, really—to have a man in her life. Only Crewe's gentle persistence had nudged Lexie toward a relationship that could be considered almost normal for her age.

"If something's wrong at her office," I said, "she'll find a way to fix it. Then she'll get back to you. Don't give up on her. She's worth it, you know."

"I've been in love with her for ten years, Nora. I'm not quitting now, not when I'm this close."

I raised my glass to him. "Good for you."

"And how are you? Now that you and Mick are ...?"

"As good as can be expected. I've had my heart ripped out and handed back to me. So I'm a free woman. If you have a scholarly cousin, Crewe, or a friend who has a spare theater ticket, or maybe just a nice man with a few boring habits, why don't you fix me up?"

"Nora."

"I'm not kidding. I'm looking for a man who's as dull as beans, please. Someone dependable and quiet. A Mr. Nice Guy."

Quietly, Crewe said, "Mick's not exactly a knight in shining Armani, but he's good for you."

I had fallen head over heels with the most unlikely man my friends could imagine. In fact, I'd taken a stroll down lover's lane and gotten myself mugged by Michael Abruzzo, the son of a New Jersey crime boss. He maneuvered his way into my life and made a wreck of it. No—that wasn't quite true. It had taken two of us to do the wrecking. I'd managed to live through my husband's murder, but even that emotional upheaval didn't compare with the earthquake Michael had caused.

"I can't be with Michael," I said.

"Baloney," Crewe said just as gently as before.

I drew my fingertips through the cool condensation created by my glass on the surface of the bar. "He's not like us, Crewe. His opinion of what's right and wrong . . . isn't mine."

"Are you worried that he's some kind of criminal?"

"I know he's a criminal. It's in his blood. And even though he fights it, it's like cocaine was to Todd." Seductive. And eventually all-consuming.

My first husband had gotten himself addicted to drugs while working in a research hospital, and his death—

he'd been shot one horrible winter night by his coke dealer—had rocked my world. If it hadn't been for good friends like Lexie and Crewe, I might still be wallowing in the aftermath.

And then I allowed myself to get involved with Michael, whose addiction was different. And yet the same.

I said, "Anyway, he's the one who broke things off this time. Usually, he does that when there's something going on in his family."

"I heard his brother got arrested for stealing a tractor-trailer."

"Really? That hardly seems terrible enough, but how would I know?"

"I'm sorry, Nora." Crewe looked genuinely dismayed. "I like Mick."

I gave up pretending. "I do, too."

Most of the time, I loved him with all my heart. At other times I wondered along with a lot of people if perhaps Michael wasn't some kind of psychopath—a man who could be charming one minute and a cold-blooded crook the next.

All I knew for certain was he kept many secrets.

From the back of the restaurant, we heard a door bang, and seconds later my little sister sauntered into the bar, blowing I-don't-give-a-damn cigarette smoke.

One of the bankers sitting at the corner table stiffened at her approach, prepared to be electrocuted if she came too close. The rest of the men at his table suddenly quieted, as if a scene had already taken place before I arrived. I saw frowns cast my sister's way.

Emma wore flip-flops, a black T-shirt and a schoolgirl's plaid skirt with the hem ripped out—an outfit that somehow had a certain streetwise chic, but also conveyed how much more spectacular her naked body could be. Her long, lithe thighs—tickled by the fringe of her skirt—glistened with a golden tan no doubt acquired by nude sunbathing.

She flicked the banker's ear as she walked past him.

He winced and ducked in case Emma decided to hit him with something more painful. But she caught sight of me and grinned.

Crewe said, "She looks amazingly like someone I saw behind a window in Amsterdam the summer I finished prep school."

I said, "Don't give her any ideas."

Pushing through the patrons along the bar, Emma came toward us, running one hand through the stiff tufts of her short auburn hair. Her slate blue eyes flickered with humor and malice. "Hey, Sis. Long time no see. How's life in the slow lane?"

"Faster than usual. I tried to telephone you earlier."

She shrugged and reached past me to surrender her cigarette to the bartender, who pointed out the NO SMOK-ING sign. She said, "I threw my phone off a bridge."

"Along with the rest of your clothes, I see. Can that skirt get any shorter?"

Emma laughed. "Since when did you become part of the Puritan Patrol? Hey, Crewe. Have any luck selling ice cream in that getup?"

Crewe smiled, unfazed. "Hello, Emma."

With a nod of my head, I indicated the group of men at the corner table. "Since when did you start hanging out with bankers?"

"I'm not hanging out." She took my iced tea and slugged it all in three gulps. "I'm adding to the ambiance." She used her fingers to fish the slice of lemon from my drink.

"I tried calling you. Libby was hit by a car last night. You'll be relieved to hear she was discharged from the hospital this morning."

"Into your capable custody?" Emma put the empty glass back on the bar and proceeded to suck on the lemon.

"Yes, as a matter of fact. I checked her into the Ritz-Carlton just an hour ago."

"Who's paying that bill? You? Or has Libby met another rich nutcase to support her luxury living?"

"A mystery man," I said. "I haven't met him, but he's obviously trying to keep her from suing him. He's the one who hit her with his car."

"She going to be okay?"

"She seems better than okay. The prospect of a new boyfriend always gives her a new outlook on life. I was hoping you might lend a hand with the kids for a few days, though. The twins listen to you. How about it?"

"Sorry." She chewed the sour pulp of the lemon without flinching. "I have a new job."

Knowing that she had recently found work as the bouncer in an S and M club, I asked cautiously, "Doing what? Training horses, I hope?"

Emma's true gift was training and riding Grand Prix show jumpers. But she shook her head. "I'm working the Chocolate Festival. Temping as an industrial model."

"A what?"

"Like that gig I had at the auto show last year. Except I stand around handing out candy instead of pointing out the antilock brakes. I've never made so many people happy at one time, believe me. Everybody loves chocolate."

"Well," I said, "I'm glad to hear you're employed."

"Yeah, it seems I need the money." She tossed the lemon on the bar.

"You mean, to feed all those ponies I'm looking after?"

"That. And I've got another little problem I need to solve."

"What kind of problem?"

She smirked. "I'm suing Trojan."

I saw the mad gleam in her eye, but still didn't understand. "What are you talking about?"

"The rabbit died. Except they don't use rabbits anymore. I got a test kit from Rite Aid. And guess what?

There's a bun in my oven. A—oh, hell, I'm knocked up. It was bound to happen eventually, right?" She laughed at my expression and pulled a tiny paper strip from the waistband of her skirt. She threw it onto the bar. "I found out this morning. Don't look so shocked. Even I slip up once in a while."

"Emma," I said, hardly able to speak at all. The idea that my feral little sister was pregnant made my head spin.

And so soon after my own miscarriage, it felt like a knife in my ribs, too.

"Yeah, big mistake, right? I mean, what am I going to do with a kid? So it's off to the clinic for me as soon as I can raise some cash." She grabbed my wrist to check my watch. "I gotta run, as a matter of fact, or I'll be late."

"Late for what? Oh, Em, please—"

"I gotta get to work." She tweaked Crewe's cheek. "Good to see you, Crewsie. Stop by the Chocolate Festival, Nora. I'll hook you up with some nice desserts."

She strolled out into the heat without a backward look, leaving me to stare at the crumpled strip of paper on the bar.

Crewe said, "Is she drunk?"

"Loaded, I imagine." I picked up her test strip. Two pink lines.

I shook my head. Once again, my sister managed to shock me with her behavior. Emma's drinking had started in her teens and escalated during her brief marriage to her party animal husband. But it wasn't until after Jake's death that Emma started drinking as if competing in the vodka Olympics. I thought she'd managed to cut back, but clearly I was wrong.

And now she was expecting a baby.

Crewe said, "It's hard to imagine somebody like Emma being a mother."

I could barely summon my voice. "Yes, it is."

"There ought to be some kind of entrance exam before you can become a parent."

"Emma's SAT scores were very high. We think she found a way to cheat."

Crewe tapped the pregnancy test strip. "Well, this is one test that's hard to outsmart. I wonder who the father is."

"Hard to say."

But I hadn't failed to notice that the faded T-shirt she wore advertised the Delaware Fly Fishing Company, owned and operated by Michael Abruzzo. I knew exactly where her shirt had come from. And where I could learn some answers.

Crewe misinterpreted my thoughts. "Take it easy, Nora. Emma couldn't terminate a pregnancy. Give her some time to think it through."

I stuffed the test strip into my handbag. "I hope you're right."

"Of course I am."

I wasn't so sure. There was no telling what Emma might do in a crisis. Her usual response was to dump her problems on somebody else. This time, that option wasn't possible.

"Your sister sure knows how to liven up a place." Crewe turned sideways and leaned against the bar to look at the patrons of the restaurant. They were all going back to their salads while exchanging grins and wise-cracks. "She made all these lawyers and bankers forget about their business."

"That's her specialty."

"What's the story with those guys at the corner table? She had a dustup with them earlier. And they've been arguing hot and heavy among themselves all day. Do you know them?"

I figured Crewe was only trying to distract me from the latest Blackbird bombshell. I did a quick head turn to accommodate him and spotted four men just getting up from the coveted corner table. Three of them were smooth businessmen wearing gray business suits. One of them had been the target of my sister's ear flick.

The fourth one—much younger and decidedly un-happy—was ridiculously handsome in a white dress shirt unbuttoned at the throat and folded back from his forearms to show off a dark tan. His hair was long and brushed back from his face as if by sea breezes.

Crewe said, "Who's Heathcliff? Do you know him?"

As we watched, the younger man stood up and shook hands grimly with his dining companions, then turned and strode away. His backside drew a few appreciative glances from women around the room. But the hard set to his face clearly said, "Hands off."

As he came closer, I murmured, "He looks familiar."

"I saw him brooding at the opening reception for the Chocolate Festival. You know everybody, Nora. Is he—"

"Tierney Cavendish." I kept my voice low as he drew nearer. "Yes, I knew him when we were children. Our families were friends. But he went off to boarding school early, and I don't think he ever came home."

Crewe was nodding. "I thought so."

"He joined the Peace Corps. Didn't he end up helping farmers somewhere in South America?"

"Cocoa farmers. Now he provides raw cocoa to choco-late manufacturers here in the States. Very politically correct, too—partnering with family farmers in some godforsaken place instead of using those big cacao plan-tations that run on slave labor."

"How dashing," I murmured.

At that moment, Tierney Cavendish walked past and caught me looking at him. Our gazes met, and I couldn't help staring into his face. He had gray-blue eyes marked with fine brows, and a full-lipped, almost feminine mouth. Only the stubborn edge of his jaw saved him from look-ing absurdly beautiful. He was only slightly taller than me, but with a body that looked strong—and capable of pulling a knife if the need arose.

Like an idiot, I bumped my handbag off the bar, and it tumbled to the floor at his feet.

For an instant, he was going to pass by without a word. But only a lout would have stepped over my fallen handbag. Tierney Cavendish checked his walk, then stopped and bent to retrieve my bag.

"I'm so sorry," I said. "I'm not usually so clumsy."

"Sure," he replied, his voice laced with sarcasm.

I felt myself flush as I accepted the bag. "Thank you."

"Anytime."

But his tone said, "Don't try that trick again."

He brushed past Crewe without another word and left the restaurant.

"He thought I did that on purpose!"

"Didn't you?"

"Crewe!"

"I'm sure it was only some kind of Freudian accident." Crewe grinned at me. "Women always fall for the handsome guy with the machete. Why is that?"

"Our primitive instincts are always at work," I said, still blushing. "Why did you ask me about him?"

"I couldn't place him. Turns out, he's the guy I've been trying to catch for an interview. He owns Amazon Chocolate, which is very hot in the foodie world right now. Besides the star chocolatier, Jacque Petite, Tierney Cavendish is the biggest story in the festival. But he hasn't learned that free publicity is golden, I guess. He's been dodging me. Who are the guys he was talking with?"

"Bankers, I think. Isn't that Hart Jones?" I was pretty sure I recognized the man Emma had flicked as one of Philadelphia's up-and-coming financiers. I remembered seeing him at a charitable event a few months earlier. I wondered how my sister knew him. "He invests millions in businesses—a kind of hedge fund, I believe."

"You're right, of course. Think he's going to invest in chocolate?"

"That's the logical assumption. But judging by the look on his face just now, Tierney didn't get the money he was asking for."

"I think you're right."

Handsome Tierney's bad mood was unmistakable as he stormed out of the restaurant and disappeared up the street as briskly as a man putting an unpleasant scene behind him.

"Seems strange, doesn't it?" Crewe asked. "That Tierney was asking Hartfield Jones for money? Isn't Tierney's father one of the semiretired partners in Lexie's firm? Why isn't the chocolate hero borrowing capital from his own father?"

We didn't have a chance to discuss his question. The bartender came back to ask if I wanted a refill on my iced tea. I accepted gratefully, and Crewe took a moment to pay his luncheon check. He gallantly paid for my drink, too, and he was just starting to explain more about Jacque Petite and the Chocolate Festival.

I listened, smiling, although my mind buzzed with Emma and her current situation. I felt as shaken as I had the time she threw a cherry bomb into my bedroom when we were kids.

Minutes later, a teenage boy slammed against the restaurant door and pushed inside, gulping cool air as if he'd run a mile across a blazing desert. At that exact moment, a police car went *whoop-whoop*ing down the street, so heads turned to see what the commotion was. The newcomer caught himself as he realized he'd made a show-stopping entrance.

"Who's that?" Crewe asked.

Chapter 2

The kid wasn't really a kid, but only dressed like one. He wore long shorts and huge sneakers in the latest street fashion. Everything else about him said spoiled suburban white boy. His shirt sported an expensive logo and a Japanese anime drawing. In his ears he wore the latest high-tech earphones. His sideburns had been expertly trimmed, his eyebrows waxed. His immaculate baseball cap was worn sideways, hip-hop-style, but he removed it instinctively. He'd been raised where good manners were taught young.

To me, Crewe said, "Wait. Isn't that—?"

"Chad Zanzibar," I murmured. "The actor previously known as Scooter."

"I bet he couldn't wait to get rid of that nickname."

"I think his agent insisted."

The other restaurant patrons went back to their drinks and conversation, dismissing the arrival of this very short and badly dressed young man in their midst.

But Chad Zanzibar was no frat boy hoping to score a cold beer on a hot day. I knew he was a Main Line rich kid who rode some family money into show business. He'd started in commercials, then hit the big time wearing a loincloth and elf ears in a made-for-teenagers movie that spawned action figures and posters suitable for the walls of teenybopper bedrooms.

"Scooter," I said, waving. "Over here."

He blinked, and for a strange instant I wondered if the flash of confusion on his face meant he was in some kind of trouble. But then he recognized me and came toward us, pulling his earphones out. "Nora, right?"

"Yes, hello."

"I thought I recognized you. I was your cousin Farley's roommate at Choate. Not for long, of course." He shook my hand very hard. "I bailed early to jump-start my career. I'm called Chad now, by the way."

"Of course, sorry."

But he would always be Scooter to me—a kid who reminded me of Mighty Mouse—all upper body on short legs. He had been a nonstop talker with a lisp. Now, though, his speech was impeccable and his dark hair had been highlighted with white-blond tips. His teeth were impossibly bright. With a very broad chest and long, muscular arms, he had the stunted look of a circus strong man.

He gave me a not-so-subtle once-over, then released his crushing grip on my hand and tried to be suave. "How is Farley?"

"Still in college," I said. My cousin was finishing Harvard in record time, but I didn't say so. Instead, "This is my friend Crewe Dearborne. I think your fathers were good friends."

Graciously, Crewe shook the boy's hand. "Yes, members of the golf club, I think. Do you play?"

"Hell, no, dude." Chad twitched as he glanced around the restaurant. "Waste of time. What does it take to get a drink around here?"

Crewe summoned the bartender with a mere glance and raised eyebrows.

"I need a mineral water," Chad snapped. "No ice. Two slices of lime."

"Certainly. Do you have ID? You have to be twenty-one to sit in the bar."

Chad sighed heavily and flipped his driver's license onto the bar with a practiced motion. No doubt with his boyish looks, he was asked to prove his age everywhere.

The bartender picked up the license and gave the face and numbers a long study. At last, he handed the license back politely. "Thank you, sir."

When the bartender stepped away, I said, "What a miserable day to be in the city, isn't it?"

"Yeah." Chad climbed onto the stool I had vacated and proceeded to play with a coaster. "Gramma made me come to a meeting with her. But I don't let anybody keep me waiting, especially not the money men. So I walked."

"Money men?" Crewe said politely, for Chad had clearly wanted to be asked to explain.

He drummed his knuckles impatiently on the bar. "Yeah, Gramma's bankers. She's going to be a producer for another of my flicks, and we need to get some money in the pipeline."

I had heard that his grandmother, Elena Zanzibar, the cosmetics queen, plunked down a small fortune to get Chad a role in the elf movie. What luck for everyone that the movie became a blockbuster and launched Chad's career.

"What's the new movie about?" I asked.

"I can't really talk about it. It's in early development. But it's going to be very big." He craned to see what had become of the bartender. "Turns out, the bankers didn't even want to talk about the movie, though. They wanted her to rat on somebody who stole a bunch of money. It's going to be a big stink in the papers tomorrow."

The bartender returned with Chad's mineral water with lime. Chad said, "What took you so long?"

"Sorry, sir. Consider the drink on the house."

Chad shrugged, all forgiven. "Peace out, dude."

Crewe and I exchanged a glance over Chad's head. We shared the same thought: His grandmother, an Old Money aristocrat, undoubtedly kept her riches safely stashed with Lexie Paine's financial firm. All the Main Line grandes dames did.

Suddenly Crewe's concern that Lexie had problems at work seemed real.

But Chad didn't pause in his discourse about his favorite subject. He slugged his mineral water and set the glass on the bar. "Meantime, I got a recurring role on *Law and Punishment.* It's more than a guest shot. Real meaty. Something for me to sink my teeth into. I'm in town to research the part, in fact."

"How interesting," I said. "How does an actor conduct research?"

Another shrug. "Just talk to people. Soak up the vibe."

Crewe couldn't hide a smile. "Whose vibe did you soak for the hobbit role?"

"I wasn't a hobbit, man. I was an elf. Big difference." He spotted Crewe's dish of berries and pulled it close. "I met some midgets. Wow, this fruit smells funky."

Crewe steered Chad back to the subject of bankers. "Who wanted to talk to your grandmother about the stolen money?"

"A bunch of people. They're pissed off about some old dude. Cavendish."

"Hoyt Cavendish?" Crewe couldn't hide his surprise. "Lexie's partner?"

"Yeah, him. You know him?"

"Lexie's former partner," I corrected. "He's semiretired now."

And his son, Tierney, had left the restaurant just minutes earlier.

"Yeah, well," Chad said, "Cavendish is going to get retired to jail from all the yelling at that meeting. That dude is in real hot water."

Another police car roared past the restaurant, followed by an ambulance with lights flashing. Some people stood up from their tables to peer out the windows.

"What in the world is going on?" Crewe asked, his reporter instincts on alert.

But Chad's story intrigued me more. Of course, I had known Hoyt Cavendish since my childhood. He'd been a longtime partner in the Paine financial empire, a friend of my father, an active member of my social circle.

And just a few months back, I had been in one of the concert halls at the Kimmel Center the night Hoyt had stepped onto the stage carrying a Stradivarius violin. It was a gift he had purchased at great expense for a deserving musician. Hoyt wore a fine tuxedo for the occasion, and his white hair, cut short but brushed up from his face with pomade, gleamed as he stood in the glowing spotlight as the audience rose to applaud. He had bowed his head in a show of humility. A diminutive man made large by the stage lighting and his own act of philanthropy.

The violinist had come onstage in her concert black gown and stood at his elbow until the applause died away. But Hoyt had withheld the violin for an instant— long enough for the whole audience to inhale a deep breath. The violinist began to weep silently, and then Hoyt had slowly extended the instrument to her. The glowing light gleamed on the violin and on the tears on her cheeks. When her hands closed on the Stradivarius, and Hoyt released it at last, the audience went wild. I had never seen a charitable act so dramatic.

"Crewe," I said, "were you at the Kimmel Center the night Hoyt Cavendish gave the violin?"

Crewe turned to me, the street noise forgotten. "Why, yes. I sat just a few rows behind you, remember?"

"Yes, that's right. This is an odd thing to remember, but did you get the feeling—I don't know—that Hoyt was—oh, never mind. It's ungenerous of me."

"I know what you're thinking," Crewe said. "And I got the same impression. That Cavendish was onstage for his own gratification."

"I can't believe he's in any kind of trouble at the firm," I said. "But . . ."

"Judging by all the ticked-off people I saw this afternoon," Chad said, "he'll be lucky if he walks out of that office alive."

After the concert, I had met Hoyt Cavendish in the receiving line at the reception.

"Mr. Cavendish," I'd said, shaking his thin, almost feminine hand, "your gift will mean so much to the community as well as Miss Ling."

His fine-boned face was pink with pleasure. His voice had an odd, reedy timbre. "I hope my charitable giving will encourage others to be just as generous."

I had not introduced myself, but the next person in line said, "Nora Blackbird, how nice to see you!"

And Hoyt's expression froze. He remained gracious, but turned away from me quickly. We hadn't spoken since I was a child, so he hadn't recognized me. But he certainly knew my name.

Crewe was frowning out the window again. "I wonder what's going on."

My own instincts finally kicked in. I said, "Crewe, we should go up to see Lexie."

"Now?"

"Yes, now."

Crewe's gaze met mine, and his eyes widened. Without saying good-bye to Chad, we bolted.

The wails of police cruisers echoed against the tall buildings around us. We hurried up Market Street to Lexie's office. As we drew closer, I felt a weight of dread start to build in my chest. In front of the Paine Building, two cars had pulled up on the sidewalk, blocking pedestrians. Several officers milled around, shouting at one another.

"Oh, no," I whispered.

Beside the hood of the first car, a stern-faced cop unrolled some yellow crime tape.

Crewe asked him, "What's going on?"

"Oh my God," I said.

The only thing that kept me from falling to my knees was Crewe's arm as he wrapped it around me.

A small man lay crumpled on the sidewalk in front of the Paine Building. His gray suit obscured the tortured position of his body, but it was clear he was dead. A pool of blood widened around his head. One black shoe lay at the curb.

Crewe looked up at the Paine Building above us. "Dear heaven," he said. "I think he jumped!"

With the afternoon sun ablaze overhead, I could barely make out the penthouse balcony. A gauzy curtain blew outward from the open window.

I heard Crewe's voice, but the whole world tilted around me.

I knew the figure on the sidewalk. Hoyt Cavendish.

A police officer stood over the body. To the crowd of people gathering, he said, "Move along. This isn't a freak show."

If a partner in her firm had just committed suicide, Lexie might need us. Crewe whisked me past the police. We left the awful scene on the sidewalk, ran across the small terrace and into the building.

We made it through the security checkpoint in the lobby only because one of the guards recognized me. Although he was yelling into a phone and trying to communicate by hand signals with a belligerent police officer at the same time, he saw my stricken face and waved me past. Then I heard him say, "This building is locked down! Nobody gets in or out from now on, understand?"

An instant later, the elevator arrived in the lobby. The door opened, and a gaggle of elderly ladies rushed out. Some were weeping. One was irate.

"How dare you chase us out of there? We might have been helpful! I was a triage nurse once!"

A police officer gripped her elbow. "Fifty years ago, maybe," he snapped. "Move it, ladies. Over to the desk so I can take your names and addresses."

Crewe flattened me against the wall as the police officer brushed past us. Then he pulled me into the elevator and punched a button.

But on Lexie's floor, another police officer planted his hand on Crewe's chest as soon as the door opened. "Sorry, buddy. Come back tomorrow."

"What's going on?"

"You hear what I said? Beat it, bub."

"Sure, sure. Sorry."

Crewe pressed the button, and the door began to close.

I said, "Crewe—"

"Don't worry. I'm not giving up."

He hit the panel of buttons again, and the elevator dropped only one floor before it stopped again. We stepped off and quickly found the emergency staircase.

Crewe turned to me. "You okay, Nora?"

"Yes, let's hurry. I want to be sure Lexie's all right."

We started up the echoing stairwell together, Crewe leading the way.

Coming toward us down the stairs, though, came Tierney Cavendish.

He was in a rush, white-faced and silent. He clattered on the steps, one hand gripping the handrail to keep him from plunging headlong down the stairs. He didn't say a word. I'm not sure he even saw us.

Crewe and I stood aside to let him pass.

"Oh, Crewe," I said, thinking of the scene on the sidewalk. "He shouldn't see his father like that!"

"Even the two of us couldn't stop him," Crewe replied, just as hushed. He grabbed my arm, and we raced upward.

On the top floor, the heavy stairwell door was locked from the inside. Crewe pounded on it. When the door opened, we slipped into a rear hallway.

The woman who had let us through the emergency door was Brandi Schmidt, the last person on earth I expected to meet at that moment. A local television personality, she was pretty at thirty-something, although thick makeup and false eyelashes created a kind of mask of vacancy on her face.

For an instant, I thought she'd been sent to cover the story of Hoyt's death for her news station.

But in the next second, I knew it was impossible for any news to travel so fast.

She backed her wheelchair up the hallway to allow

Crewe and me to enter. Normally, her chair was discreetly hidden behind her on-camera desk, so it was a jolt to see it in reality, although the whole city knew she used one. The story was she'd been injured as a child and couldn't stand or walk, although she had partial feeling in her legs.

But her disability was not Brandi's most distinguishing trait. She had an unfortunate propensity for malapropisms. If unrehearsed, she often mispronounced the names of rivers and politicians. During a prison riot, she had unfortunately read a story about the state's "penile" system off the teleprompter, which made for hilarious commentary in the newspapers for weeks afterward. After a series of verbal gaffes, she was rarely seen on programs with high ratings anymore. She appeared on the occasional weekend morning show when her frequent mistakes could be covered up by a smooth-talking cohost.

Today Brandi looked nearly incapable of any speech whatsoever.

I guessed she had maneuvered the chair into the service hallway to grab an illicit cigarette during the emergency. She blew a nervous stream of smoke at us from her chair.

"Oh, my God, Nora," Brandi said. "Poor Hoyt!"

Crewe murmured he'd be back as soon as possible. He ripped off his mustache and dropped his Colonel Sanders jacket on a chair. Then he disappeared down the hallway, leaving me alone with Brandi.

"Are you all right?" I asked. I knew her from a few months ago when she'd acted as the honorary chairperson for a charity ball, and I'd interviewed her for my column.

Holding her cigarette, Brandi's right hand trembled, spilling ash onto the carpet. "It's so awful!"

From the hallway, I could see that the suite of offices was jammed with shaken employees and hysterical clients. Police officers were starting to organize the chaos, but it would be several minutes before order could be established in the confusion of the reception area.

The darkly paneled domain of Lexie's father and his staid partners had once smelled of stale cigars and musty paper. But when Lexie took over the firm, she refurbished the whole building to an architectural wonder full of light and color. Dazzling sunlight streamed through the skylights and cast a dappled light through the huge Calder mobile that swooped majestically overhead. The gloomy portraits of Lexie's esteemed relatives had been replaced by an enormous Rauschenberg that graced the wall behind the main desk.

But today, Lexie's personal art collection went unnoticed by the noisy melee of people.

"Okay, everybody," shouted a police officer. "Step this way, please."

Brandi dropped her cigarette on the carpet and rolled her wheelchair over it in a practiced maneuver. Then she used the electronic switch to motor up the hallway. I followed until we reached the main reception area. There, Brandi suddenly swayed in her chair. She put one hand to her face.

I sat down next to her on the edge of a glass-cube coffee table. Still shaken myself, I tried to focus on helping her. "You're not well. Can I get you a glass of water? Shall I call someone for you?"

She shook her head. "I can't leave yet. They told me to wait here. I suppose they'll want to question everyone. Do you think we'll be segued?"

"Sequestered? I doubt it. But the police will certainly question everyone."

"Well, that's the least I can do for—for dear Hoyt." Her eyes overflowed with tears.

"I'm so sorry, Brandi." I handed over my handkerchief.

She used it to mop her eyes. "Did you see him? Down there? Was he on the street?"

"I didn't see much. But he is—he's definitely gone."

"Dead?"

"Yes. I'm very sorry."

She slumped in her wheelchair and burst into tears. "I can't believe it!"

I tried to suppress my own emotions and patted her hand. "What went wrong?" I asked. "What happened?"

Brandi blotted her face, but succeeded only in smearing her makeup. She blurted out a disjointed explanation. "I don't know. We—everyone had been arguing in the boardroom, and Miss Paine finally insisted we go to different offices to calm down. Then I heard—we all heard Miss Paine shouting with Hoyt, but I—next thing, someone rushed in and said he jumped from the balcony."

"He killed himself?"

Brandi dabbed her blotched mascara and blew her nose. "He hasn't been the same since his wife died. He was so devoted to Muriel!"

Hoyt's wife had passed away at least three years ago. It hardly made sense that he'd be overcome with grief today of all days. I wondered if Brandi was trying to gloss over the financial trouble Chad had mentioned.

Brandi babbled. "He's never been the same since her death. I know—he confided in me often. We were—I tried to give him the companionship he craved. But everything must have overwhelmed him at last."

"But—why today? What happened here?"

Brandi had worked herself into hysterics. She drew a breath and tried to calm down. "Miss Paine called the meeting. She made it sound like an emergency. We're all clients of Hoyt's. She said there was a—a situation. I can't believe it was true, though. Everyone began shouting. It—it was a personal attack on poor Hoyt! And then Hoyt—he punched the Vermeer!"

I thought I had heard wrong. "He did what?"

"He put his fist through the painting in Miss Paine's office!"

The destruction of a work of art hardly seemed as devastating as the loss of life, but I knew Lexie's reaction to Hoyt Cavendish destroying her best-loved painting would be extreme. In recent years, she had sublimated much of her emotional life into her intellectual pursuit of fine art. And the Vermeer meant more to her than nearly the rest of her whole collection put together.

Brandi said, "After he ruined the painting, Lexie blew up. She sent us to different rooms. But Hoyt stayed in Lexie's office, and they argued some more. He must have been more upset than we thought."

Steadying myself, I said, "Where's Lexie now?"

"With the police, I suppose." Brandi blinked her doe eyes tearfully at me. "Do you think I should call the station? I suppose this is an important story. I just—I'm not sure I can pull myself together enough to be coherent on the phone. I was very fond of him. He was such a special person."

Perhaps I should have stayed with Brandi to calm her down. But I cared about Lexie more than whether a television station got first dibs on a morbid death on Market Street.

I said, "Take a few deep breaths while you think about how to handle it. I'll be back as soon as I can."

"Thank you, Nora. You're so emphatic."

I left Brandi in the lobby and went looking for my friend.

Chapter 3

I managed to slip past Lexie's support staff who stood around the cappuccino machine answering the questions of a middle-aged policewoman. She jotted rapid notes. Everyone looked very serious.

In a doorway, Lexie's administrative assistant, Carla, wept uncontrollably. One of the secretaries put her arm around Carla to calm her.

It was still only minutes since Hoyt had fallen. The police were just starting to take control of the scene. I knew it would be a short time before the offices would be in total lockdown.

A burly uniformed officer at the door shook his head at me. "Sorry, miss. You can't come in here."

Beyond him in the office, I saw another officer standing at the French doors that led to Lexie's balcony. He held aside the diaphanous curtains and peered over the wrought-iron railing at the street below. A wave of vertigo caught me, but I fought it down.

On the primary wall of Lexie's office, the Vermeer hung crookedly. Even from the doorway, I could see a gaping hole in the canvas. The serene woman depicted in the picture had presided over Lexie's day-to-day business for so long I had almost become unaware of her presence. But at seeing the horrible puncture in such an exquisite painting, I reeled back from the doorway, sick all over again.

Where was Lexie?

Behind the public spaces of the firm lay a labyrinth of

smaller offices where less-important employees toiled.
I went down the hallway to the door of Lexie's private
bathroom. It adjoined her office but also had this door
that opened into the hall. The door was locked, but I
tapped on it and said softly, "It's Nora."

Crewe opened the door to me, and I slipped in. It
was a spacious retreat with plenty of marble, a heavily
framed gold mirror and a brass tray on the counter con-
taining a collection of soaps, lotions and sprays.

Lexie stood leaning against the wall, head bowed,
arms folded on her chest. I crossed the marble tiles and
hugged her hard. She felt thin, but not fragile. She rowed
on the river every morning, and her body showed it. But
she shivered as if she'd just spent a day in the Arctic.

"Oh, Lex," I said. "This is terrible."

She might have been crying minutes earlier, but she
had pulled herself together now and simply looked
white-faced and tense. Her black hair was still neat in its
ponytail. Her suit—an impeccably tailored silver Armani
jacket paired with a black skirt that further emphasized
her slim figure—showed no evidence of the catastrophe.
Her mouth quivered, though. She was barely in control.

Standing as far away as possible while still in the same
room, Crewe said, "The police want to talk to Lexie in a
minute. I told her she needs an attorney."

"I do not," she snapped. "I can make perfect sense on
my own."

"This situation is complicated," Crewe said. "I'm not
saying you're guilty of anything—"

"Of course she's not," I said.

"But this thing is going to get ugly."

"How much uglier can it get?" she demanded. "A
man is dead. Not to mention my wonderful Vermeer
violated."

"Oh, Lex."

She shook off my touch as I reached for her. "The
Vermeer will never be the same. Can you believe the
bastard did it? He punched my painting!"

My heart went out to her. Lexie wasn't herself. I could see she was redirecting her emotions, and I ached to hug her.

"Lexie," Crewe said, "you've got to calm down. If Hoyt jumped, there will be questions, probably lawsuits—"

"Lawsuits!" I said. "What does that matter now?"

"He didn't jump," Lexie said, her voice flat. Crewe and I both stared at her.

"He didn't." She used both her hands to smooth her hair back from her face, but she ended up pressing the sides of her head as if it might explode. "He wasn't suicidal. He was angry and defensive, but wasn't going to harm himself."

"Don't say that to the police," Crewe said. "Don't try to explain. Just say what happened."

I said, "Brandi Schmidt said it was suicide."

"Brandi Schmidt," Lexie snapped. "What does Miss Malaprop know?"

"Did Hoyt fall? Was it an accident?"

"Don't be a fool, Nora. He didn't fall through a closed door and over the railing."

"What are you saying?" I asked, undaunted by her cold sarcasm. "That somebody pushed him?"

"What else?" Crewe said. "Someone must have barged in there and wrestled him out onto the balcony."

"Who?" I said, astonished.

"Stop it, both of you!" Lexie clamped her hands on her ears. "The son of a bitch is dead. Just shut up and let me think!"

In the short silence, Crewe said, "Hoyt Cavendish has been called a lot of things, Lexie, but never a son of a bitch. Have you gone crazy?"

"Take it easy," I said, trying to soothe both of them. "Lex, we're just trying to figure out what happened here."

Harshly, Lexie said, "We argued, and he punched my painting. I left Hoyt in my office and told my assistant to call the police."

"Why?"

"Because I wanted him arrested for vandalism! When I went back into my office—look, just let me explain it all to the police. I can have the whole thing settled in a few minutes."

Although she was struggling to hang on to her composure, I had never seen Lexie so agitated. I could see her pulse beating in a vein on her temple.

"Crewe is right," I said quietly. "Why not call an attorney before you start making statements?"

She swung on me, furious. "Do you think I killed him?"

"Stop it," Crewe said. "You know she doesn't. You're in shock, Lexie. You're not thinking straight. We're trying to help you see the seriousness of the situation."

"This is none of your business. It's a firm situation, nothing you need to know about. There are privacy issues at stake. I've got clients to protect!"

"Will the police see it that way?" I asked.

Lexie's eyes blazed. "This is not the time for you two to gang up on me!"

"We want to help," Crewe said. "You're in no shape to defend yourself."

I tried to remember exactly what Hoyt Cavendish's relationship to Lexie's financial firm was. He'd been one of her father's early partners in the venture. Chances were, he still handled a few loyal clients who didn't trust anyone else to manage their investments—probably that swarm of elderly women we'd seen in the lobby. In recent years, Hoyt had primarily appeared in public in his role as a prominent philanthropist. It was hard to imagine how he might have caused trouble for the firm. But Crewe had said Lexie was dealing with some kind of financial problem.

"Lex," I said, "if you and Hoyt were at odds, and you were the last person to be with him—you definitely need a lawyer."

"This is ridiculous!" She cut around me and seized the brass handle of the door.

"Lexie, wait—"

She stalked out of the bathroom. I felt like crying, but I held Crewe back as he started after her.

Crewe's face was tense and worried. He said, "She needs to calm down, but she's right—we shouldn't gang up on her. Why don't you stay here, Nora? There's a murderer around here somewhere. Lock the door behind me. You'll be safe until I get back."

"Don't worry about me. Try to make her see reason!"

I watched him hustle after Lexie. I wanted to go, too. But tag-teaming her had only made matters worse.

I hesitated in the doorway, daunted by the thought that a real killer might be hiding in the maze of offices. But I remembered my promise to return to Brandi Schmidt. By now, she might be even more upset than when I'd left her. It would take only a few seconds to return to the lobby, and I knew the route.

As I stepped out of the bathroom, the toe of my sandal struck a small object caught on the threshold of the door. I bent down and picked up a silver compact. Lexie must have dropped it in her turmoil. Without thinking, I slid it into my handbag to return to her later.

Then I left the private bathroom and headed back down the hallway in the direction of the lobby. I could hear voices ahead of me. My sandals made little noise on the thick carpet underfoot. The heavy oak paneling muffled all sound from inside the offices I passed, making me realize that in any one of them, a killer could be lurking. I quickened my pace.

When I'd nearly reached the open door to Lexie's office, I heard the voice of the newly arrived plainclothes officer as she barked orders.

"I want a list of everyone who's on this floor. And who the hell are all those old biddies in the lobby? Check with the security desk downstairs first, and double-check with the receptionist by the elevators up here. We've got at least forty people to interview—and half of them are still wandering around unsupervised! I want this scene secured right now."

I turned toward the lobby, but suddenly spotted a puff of cigarette smoke. The small trail of blue vapor seeped out between the closed doors of the coat closet located halfway down the hall.

Brandi, I thought. She must have gone into the closet to have one more calming cigarette.

I put my hand on the doorknob. In that brief instant, I recognized that the smell of the smoke was distinctly not tobacco but marijuana.

Without thinking I might be surprising a murderer as he smoked his last joint, I opened the closet door.

And I froze. In shock.

From inside the closet, a startled man stared back at me. He held a smoldering, hand-rolled cigarette between two fingers and looked anything but furtive.

I stifled a scream before uttering the first word that came into my head.

"Daddy?"

Chapter 4

My father grabbed my wrist and pulled me inside the closet. "Thank heaven it's you!"

He pulled the door behind me with a slam, then groped for the light switch. When the bulb popped on overhead, I got the first good look at my father in two years. Through a cloud of marijuana smoke.

"Daddy! *What are you doing here?*"

"Shhhhh! They'll find me!"

For a man of sixty, he still cut a dashing figure—tallish and thinnish with perfect posture and a tennis player's tan. He wore his hair longer now—white and flowing over the faded collar of his Bermuda pink shirt. To hide a few wrinkles, he had knotted a jaunty silk ascot at his throat, and the insignia of a long-defunct yacht club glowed on the breast pocket of his threadbare blue blazer. Holding the joint elegantly between two long fingers, he looked like a slightly seedy gentleman who'd just walked away from the captain's table on a cruise ship.

I grabbed the joint from his grasp and threw it onto the floor. I crushed it with my sandal and frantically waved my hand to dissipate the pungent smoke. "What do you mean, they'll find you? The police? Oh, my God! Daddy—"

"Shh!" He put one forefinger to his lips and bugged out his eyes to command my silence. "Do you want me to get in trouble?"

"You're already in trouble," I hissed. "I thought you could never set foot in the United States or the IRS would slap you into jail! And now you're smoking dope with the police just ten feet away?"

His eyebrows were already suspiciously high—perhaps the work of a South American cosmetic surgeon—but they lifted even farther. "Good heavens, Muffin, you haven't seen me in ages, and all you want to do is throw insults?"

"It's not an insult if it's true!"

"Is that all you can say to your father? I've missed you, Muffin!"

"Don't call me that. When you call us Muffin, it makes us think you can't remember our names."

"Of course I remember your name. You're Eleanor, and you've always been my favorite. And don't you look beautiful!"

Still the handsome con man. Still the silver-tongued devil.

"Daddy," I groaned. "Please tell me you didn't do something foolish here today."

"Foolish? The police getting upset about a gentleman enjoying a little harmless smoke—that's what I call foolish!"

"Hoyt Cavendish is dead. He just fell off a balcony."

"Yes, I know. Poor old Hoyt. He never did know which way was up."

"Daddy!"

My father had inherited the Blackbird family fortune and managed to spend every penny—and more—in less time than a starlet could blow her millions on a shopping spree in Dubai. He had done it generously, of course. As a child, I often woke up to elaborate gifts on my bedspread. Toys from FAO Schwarz, rare books from shops in Paris, prayer flags from Kathmandu and beaded jewelry from Africa—I never knew what treasures he might bring home before he flitted off again. But by the time I finished college, all the money was gone.

He'd had every right to spend it, of course. But when the cash ran out, he'd committed the ultimate social faux pas of gouging his friends for more. On the brink of social exile, he threw one last party before fleeing the country with my mother. Since then, they had run up debt in luxury resorts all over the world, skipping out in the nick of time just as local gendarmes came knocking on their doors.

I said, "Don't make jokes about Hoyt. It's possible he was murdered."

"Of course he was murdered. Why do you think I'm hiding in a broom closet? There's a stone-cold killer on the loose!"

I stared at my father. "Did you see something?"

"I saw plenty. And heard even more."

"Then you've got to talk to the police! You could help figure out what happened. You could—"

Again, he motioned for me to keep my voice down. Then he whispered, "I'm not exactly in a position to assist the police, Nora."

"What do you mean? If you—"

"I'd rather keep my presence a secret."

"From whom?"

"Everyone. But especially from the police. I'm here on a mission, you see. An important government assignment. And Hoyt taking a swan dive from the balcony has thrown me a curveball, if I might mix my sports."

"What are you talking about?" If my father had been recruited to be some kind of secret agent, the whole world was doomed.

"It's very complicated. But if all goes well, I'll buy freedom for your mother and me. There might even be a presidential pardon for both of us!"

I felt a thunk in my stomach. "Mama's here, too?"

"Not *here* here, but nearby. I'd tell you more, Muffin, but it's all very hush-hush."

"How long have you been smoking that stuff, Daddy?"

He drew himself up tall and straight. "I use a medicinal amount of cannabis, young lady, not enough to cloud my judgment. I'm telling you the absolute truth. I'm here in Philadelphia at the behest of the Treasury Department. And maybe a few more federal agencies."

I had no clue what he meant. But experience told me I should assume he wasn't entirely telling the truth.

"What's going on, Daddy? Does Lexie know you're here?"

"Not yet. I was waiting to be called to the inner sanctum to give my testimony when everything went haywire."

"When Hoyt died, you mean?"

"Exactly. I'm here to shed light on a situation he caused."

"Hoyt caused a situation? Was he in some kind of trouble?"

"Not anymore," my father said. "Now that he's dead. But things may just have gotten more complicated for everyone else. Your friend Lexie most of all."

"Daddy, you really need to come outside and talk to the police."

"No, Muffin, not until I'm sure I won't end up in one of those country-club prisons where the inmates play shuffleboard all day. You know I have a low tolerance for shuffleboard. And prisons don't serve wine with dinner, if you can imagine such savagery."

"But—"

He spun me around. "Run along, dear. Before the police cordon off the whole block, I need to make my escape."

"Where will you go? How will you get out of here?"

"I know all the secret exits." His eyes twinkled. "Don't forget, I used to borrow money from this establishment. Many's the time I needed to make a quick departure."

Another flood of dread nearly overcame me. "Daddy—"

"Shh. I'll find a way to keep in touch."

"You're leaving the country again?"

"Not if I can help it." He winked. "Your mother wants

to see her hairdresser. Do you have any idea how difficult it is to have good hair in Argentina?"

He pushed me out into the hallway before I could ask more questions. And I had plenty of questions. What the hell was he doing back in Philadelphia? And with the help of the Treasury Department? The whole story was beyond belief. And if I knew my father at all, he was plotting something that would likely end in disaster.

I spun around to yank open the closet door and confront him one more time, but the plainclothes police detective hailed me from the lobby.

"Hey," she said. "You. Come here and give me your name."

I leaned on the closet door. "Me?"

She gave me a hard look. "Yes, you." She made a hook of her forefinger and beckoned me closer.

I obeyed. She wore a gun on her hip and didn't look as if she'd hesitate to use it.

Her name tag was nothing but consonants. I squinted and tried to imagine how to pronounce her name. "Wylcnck." She wore a tan polyester business suit, unbuttoned to show a flesh-colored T-shirt. On her belt hung a city police detective's shield. Tendrils of her hair had escaped the plastic clip at the back of her head. Her makeup consisted of a brownish lipstick she had partially chewed off.

She gave me a disapproving up-and-down look and said, "Are you some kind of candy striper in that getup?"

"No, I—"

"Never mind. Stay here with this lady for a minute, will you? I'm no damn nanny."

Sprawled out on the couch beside her lay an elderly woman in a suit and pearls, holding a wet paper towel against her forehead. I recognized Elena Zanzibar by the electric pink powder generously spread on her cheeks. She moaned softly from beneath the paper towel.

"Mrs. Zanzibar?" I knelt down on the carpet and

grabbed Elena's hand. "It's Nora Blackbird. Are you—should I call a doctor?"

"Nora? Nora, is that you?" Elena gripped me hard. "Don't leave me alone, dear child. I feel so faint!"

I looked up at the police detective. "I'll take care of her."

Wylcnck nodded shortly and strode away, leaving me alone with the hyperventilating cosmetics queen.

I had known Elena Zanzibar before she'd become one of America's great contributors to the world of beauty. Decades ago, Elena made her fortune by rolling a small inheritance—her father's share of a South African diamond mine—into the production of an eyebrow wax. The wax caught on with her friends and quickly spread to Hollywood. Soon Elena began dabbling in other beauty products and even more lucrative fragrances, and a cosmetics empire was born.

A friend of my late grandmother, she had once brought her powders and potions to my family's estate and practiced various techniques on my sisters and me while we were still in primary school. Years later, her business took off, and she became a tycoon. Today, however, she appeared old and collapsed with shock.

I patted her hand. Wylcnck's footsteps faded away.

Abruptly, Elena snatched the paper towel off her face and threw it on the floor. She sat up on the couch. "I thought that woman would never leave!"

"Are you all right?"

"Of course I'm all right!"

Sixty-something Elena Zanzibar, in a hot fuchsia suit with black piping and a triple strand of pearls around her neck, wore her hair in a Texas-sized pompadour. Numerous diamond rings sparkled on all of her plump fingers. Her papery eyelids were weighted down with false eyelashes. Her makeup was as colorful as if it had come from a child's paint box.

She said, "It's bad enough getting stuck with a police officer, but I'm always offended by people who obviously don't take proper care of their skin. And she must have chosen her lipstick in the dark!"

Elena's cosmetics, called simply Zanzibar, were sold in upscale department stores all over the world. Elena herself was past the age of wearing her own products, but that didn't stop her from slathering them on as if preparing for a Technicolor close-up.

"I must look like a fright." Elena had noticed my startled expression. "But tell me what's going on. What are the police saying? What happened to Hoyt?"

"I'm sorry, Mrs. Zanzibar, but Mr. Cavendish—he didn't survive."

Her breath caught in a sob, and her made-up eyes began to swim with tears. She groped into a pocket and came up with a handkerchief that was spotted with the colors of a rainbow. "Dear me," she said.

"I'm sorry," I said, trying to soothe her.

"It can't be true!"

"I'm very sorry."

Her mascara began to track down her cheeks. "Hoyt should have known I'd solve any financial problems he had. Surely he—he understood how generous I could be!"

"Hush," I said. "You'll make yourself sick, Mrs. Zanzibar."

She hiccoughed. "What are friends for?" she implored. "I could have given him millions!"

"Can I call someone for you?" I feared she might give herself a stroke. "A relative, perhaps?"

"Where are my ladies?"

"Your ladies?"

"Yes, my fans. The ladies who follow me wherever I go. They're such dears. I couldn't get along without them. I gather strength, just knowing they're nearby!"

Suddenly I realized who the mob of women downstairs had been. Elena Zanzibar hardly set foot out of her house without a crowd of adoring fans. For years, a cadre of elderly women took the Zanzibar skin care system so seriously that they seemed to have pledged an undying worship for Elena herself. They followed her everywhere, even chasing her distinctive pastel Mercedes in traffic.

A few cynics believed she issued her schedule a week in advance of any public appearance to guarantee a good crowd.

I said, "I believe they're all downstairs. They're perfectly safe."

"Oh, I'm so relieved! But they must be worried about me."

"Would you like me to find one of them? Perhaps if one of your friends came up here to—"

"No, no, I'll just hop downstairs myself in a few minutes, as soon as I can manage. Are you sure—I mean, is Hoyt really . . . ?"

"Yes, I'm afraid so."

She took an unsteady breath, but fought down the urge to weep. A proud aristocrat, she took command of her feelings. "You're very pretty these days, Nora. You look so much like your grandmother."

"I—thank you."

"Although maybe you should consider a frosted lipstick. Don't you love a frosted mouth in hot weather? Aren't you working for a newspaper these days?" Tears trembled on her false eyelashes.

"Yes, I took over Kitty Keough's social column for the *Intelligencer*. I report on charity events, mostly."

"Why, yes, I saw you at that measles gala last April. Why don't you come to lunch someday, dear? I could use the publicity. I'm launching a new spa line this week."

"Well—"

"At lunch tomorrow, Hoyt and I were going to announce our—dear me," she said, tearing up again. "I'm not making much sense, am I? Could you get me a glass of water, dear?"

"Certainly. Will you be all right if I leave you alone?"

"Of course," she said, abruptly calm again. "A sip of water will put me right."

As accustomed as I was to handling the eccentric women in my own unpredictable family, I wondered fleetingly if Elena was trying to pull a fast one. But I dutifully dashed down the hallway to the bathroom once again and ran a splash of water into a cut-crystal glass.

When I returned, however, Elena Zanzibar was nowhere to be seen.

Detective Wylcnck was herding the staff of the Paine Investment Group into the boardroom. The detective stopped each individual at the door and jotted his or her name in a black notebook. She caught sight of me as I tried to slip past her.

"You again." She pointed her pen at me. "Do you work here? Or are you a customer?"

"Neither, actually. I'm a friend of Miss Paine."

Her glare intensified. "So this is a social call?"

"Sort of. Look, I seem to have lost Mrs. Zanzibar."

Wylcnck snapped her notebook shut. "Where'd the old broad go? Oh, hell, why do I get stuck with all old ladies who think they're above the law? She's probably waiting for an elevator. Stay here. Don't move."

The detective hurried off in the direction of the elevators.

As soon as she was out of sight, I disobeyed. I rushed back to the closet and yanked open the door, hoping to help my father make his getaway.

But the closet was empty.

Where in the world had he gotten to? And how?

Chapter 5

By the time the police got fed up and dismissed me, my editor had left the *Intelligencer* offices for an appointment to get his annual colonoscopy. So I sat at my desk for a few minutes to pull myself together.

The whole afternoon seemed a blur of one awful encounter after another. And the mental image of Hoyt's lifeless body on the city sidewalk was going to give me many sleepless nights. I flipped on my computer to check my e-mail, but the words danced in front of me without meaning. Except the terse message from my editor telling me to phone him first thing in the morning.

I guessed my job was still in jeopardy.

But I couldn't think. Couldn't work. I kept flashing back to the grisly scene on the sidewalk. And Lexie's cold and shaken anger. Elena's ditzy confusion. Brandi's twisted vocabulary. I tried to sort all the snail mail invitations that had been delivered to the office, but I was too distracted to make many decisions. I placed two phone calls to respond to the most pressing invitations and used the computer to e-mail several more RSVPs. One invitation came with a box of cookies. I sampled one, then put the box in the break room to share with my colleagues. Unable to concentrate properly, I finally stuffed the rest of the envelopes into my handbag and called my driver for a ride home.

My original employment contract—dictated by an old family friend who owned the newspaper—allowed me the services of a town car with driver. In the first few weeks on the job, I took it for granted that other reporters enjoyed the same luxury, but I was quickly hooted at. Now I used the car very rarely. I figured I was due a quiet ride home tonight.

Reed Shakespeare, part-time student and part-time driver, preferred to keep his own counsel. Early in our relationship, I'd tried to draw him out, but he made his preference for silence known. I still thought he didn't like driving around a gussied-up white woman who went to a lot of fancy parties. But I'd also come to realize he was simply shy.

In the backseat of the town car, I remembered Tierney Cavendish racing down the stairs of the Paine Building. I was certain he hadn't managed to reach his father in time for a final good-bye. Then, oddly enough, I wondered if Tierney had been in the room when Hoyt went off the balcony.

And Daddy? He had been close by, too.

My stomach rolled over at that thought.

By the time we reached Blackbird Farm, I had a thumping headache.

Despite the blissful cool of the car's air-conditioning, I felt sticky when I got out of the car. I thanked Reed and I went into the house hoping to draw myself a bubble bath to help forget about the day's trauma.

Instead, I found my teenage nephew Rawlins sitting at the kitchen table and feeding his baby brother a bottle of formula. The two of them were a sight for sore eyes.

Rawlins frowned at the screen of my laptop computer. The teenager had gotten a buzz haircut and wore a clean T-shirt advertising the ice-cream parlor where he worked for the summer. In an obvious effort to join the working world, he'd even removed his eyebrow stud and nose ring. Only one hoop earring remained from his once extensive collection of body piercings.

I ran my hand across the boot camp coiffure. "*Semper Fi*, Rawlins."

"Hey, Aunt Nora. Sorry, but I can't fix your computer. It's really fried this time."

I dropped my handbag onto a chair. "Just like the rest of my life."

He grinned. "I guess you don't want to hear the plumber quit, too, then?"

I groaned at the news. "No, thanks. Did your mom call you? She was discharged from the hospital and went straight to the Ritz-Carlton."

"Nope, she didn't call." Rawlins seemed unfazed by the lack of communication in his family. "But that's cool. Who's she staying with?"

Although Rawlins appeared to accept the possibility that his mother wasn't alone that evening, it didn't feel right to speculate on Libby's latest conquest with any of her children.

In all honesty, I said, "I haven't a clue."

Rawlins leaned closer to me and sniffed. "What's that smell? If I didn't know better, Aunt Nora, I'd say you were smoking a fat one today."

I flushed, remembering my father. "I did no such thing. And how do you know what marijuana smells like?"

He laughed. "I'm in high school, that's why."

From under the kitchen table came Toby, the Brittany spaniel we had inherited a couple of months back. The shy dog had attached himself to my sister Emma, but in her absence, he greeted me with a wagging tail and a cold nose on my kneecap. I fondled his silky ears and found myself thankful not to be alone this evening. Hoyt Cavendish's death, Libby's brush with mortality, Emma's hormonal news bulletin, my father's inopportune home-coming—all at a time when I was feeling emotionally delicate—it was too much to bear in an empty house.

"You okay, Aunt Nora?"

"I feel better every minute." I smiled at my nephews. "Thanks for trying to fix my laptop, Rawlins. Where's the rest of the crew? Did you get any dinner?"

"I got takeout for everybody from Boston Market.

You'd be proud—we even had green beans. There's an extra meat loaf dinner in the fridge, if you want it." My nephew hooked his head in the direction of the living room. "Lucy's sacked out on the sofa with her imaginary friend. And the twins are out in the barn doing their homework."

"Homework? In July?"

His twin brothers, fourteen-year-old Harcourt and Hilton, were a pair of budding psychopaths whose activities in my barn were probably better left uninvestigated. But with his free hand, Rawlins tossed me a printed brochure.

I read the large print on the brochure's colorful cover. "An online mortuary school?"

"The twins got their first assignment this morning."

"Heaven help us," I said, meaning it.

"They haven't enrolled yet. They're supposed to complete some kind of aptitude test first."

"If anyone has an aptitude for death, it's your brothers. No offense."

"Hey," Rawlins said with a shrug, "if they're interested in embalming, I'm just glad they're seeking professional guidance."

I read aloud from the brochure. "Our graduates learn to think outside the box."

Rawlins laughed. "Who writes that stuff?"

"Good grief!"

"Let's hope the curriculum is better than the PR."

I gave him a long look over the top of the brochure. "You're very forgiving of the twins, Rawlins. Weren't you the one they wanted to practice on when they weaseled their way into that phlebotomy course?"

"I'm a fast runner. Anyway, their assignment is to find some animal bones to work with, so they're digging out in the barn."

"There aren't any bones in the barn."

"I think they're looking for dead mice or something. Then they boil off the skin and—"

"Mice, I have," I said dolefully. "Plenty of mice. Just don't tell me what happens to them."

He pointed at the kitchen counter. "The plumber left you a Dear John letter."

"I suppose that's better than a bill." Before I dared to read the plumber's note, I found a bottle of Excedrin and popped two tablets.

"He forgot his wrench, though, so maybe he'll be back."

"I doubt it."

I ran a glass of tap water and sipped it as I picked up the piece of paper left on the counter beside an industrial-sized wrench. The plumber gently informed me that the leak under the kitchen sink was only the tip of a very large iceberg. It was more than he could fix, and he suggested I contact a company that specialized in expensive historic restorations—a company that had already given me estimates big enough to revitalize New Orleans.

I sighed. My household emergencies were always more than I could fix. Some of them—like the leaking gutter over the library—were never going to be repaired unless an incredibly wealthy software magnate chose Blackbird Farm as the recipient of his endless financial support.

Rawlins watched my face. "The plumber seemed real sorry."

I tossed the note onto the table and affected nonchalance. "I have that effect on repairmen."

Baby Maximus finished off his bottle and gave it a barefoot kick. "Da!"

Rawlins obligingly heaved the pudgy infant onto his shoulder.

I said, "Your mom says she's trying to improve your baby brother's chances of getting into the Ivy League."

"Yeah, she told me. I'm supposed to chant the periodic table to him. Trouble is, I never learned the periodic table myself. *C'est la vie*, huh?"

There had been a time when Rawlins suffered from

all the worst characteristics of teenagers. For a long time, he'd been sullen and uncommunicative and entirely lacking in humor. But he'd grown up lately, and I was happy to see him so relaxed and confident. Of all my immediate family members, he was the closest to an adult, and I was going to miss him terribly next year when he went off to college.

Rawlins handed over a sticky plastic gizmo. "Here's his binky. Don't let it out of your sight or he has a tantrum."

"But your mother said—"

"Yeah, I know what she says. But she lets him have it all the time. She wants somebody else to train him not to need it."

I washed the plastic pacifier with soap and hot water at the sink. "Are you going to stay in tonight? Or do you have a date?"

Rawlins might have blushed as he patted Maximus on his back. "Well, I thought I'd cruise back into town. You know, to see if anyone wants to hang out."

I reached for the baby and gathered him up in my arms. Max was a hot, sticky bundle, and his shock of black hair was plastered to his head. He yawned in my face and let out a soft burp.

"How's Shawna?" I asked.

At the mention of his girlfriend, Rawlins pretended an intense interest in the empty formula bottle. "She's— you know, getting ready to go to school."

"Will you keep seeing her once she gets to college? Or are you two going to give each other a little space?"

Rawlins shrugged. "I dunno."

Rawlins had been seeing an older woman—a girl who planned to go to college in a few weeks, leaving my nephew behind to finish his last year of high school unencumbered.

He stretched his arms over his head and put a spin of manly stoicism on the situation. "I'm kinda hooking up with this new girl. Regan. She works at the ice-cream shop."

"Oh, really? Is she nice?"

He shrugged again. "She's okay. But she calls me on my cell phone all the time. Even when we're at work. She sends me text messages when we're standing, like, ten feet apart."

"What does she text about?"

Another shrug. "Nothing much. She wants to know where I am every minute. I mean, is it a crime to want to take a leak undisturbed once in a while?"

Sorry I'd brought up a sore subject, I said, "Well, come back here tonight, okay? I don't want to lie awake wondering if you've driven yourself over a cliff. When's your curfew?"

"Mom doesn't care when I get home."

I poked his shoulder. "I doubt that. How about midnight?"

"Sure, okay."

While balancing Maximus on my shoulder, I rooted an extra house key from a drawer. "By any chance you didn't see Emma this evening, did you?"

"Nope."

"I wonder if she bothered to feed her ponies."

Rawlins heard my tone. "There's plenty of grass."

"What about water?"

"I checked. The barrel is full."

I eyed him. "Did she ask you to do her chores?"

"Nope, I just checked the water, that's all."

With some irritation, I noticed Emma had gotten her riding school off to a rocky start, then departed without letting anyone know what to do in her absence. Her job at the Chocolate Festival was more lucrative, perhaps, but we were left looking after her livestock.

But, of course, I was really concerned about the latest development in her life. If she couldn't take care of her animals, how was she going to raise a child?

"It only takes a minute to check their water," Rawlins said, watching my expression. "They're out in the pasture eating their heads off. No big deal." He dropped the house key into the pocket of his loose khaki shorts. "They'll be okay. Don't worry so much, okay? Everything's cool."

Everything was not cool.

But I decided not to tell him about Emma's big news. Or Hoyt Cavendish's gruesome death. Rawlins's needy girlfriend was probably enough stress to cope with in his young life.

After Rawlins gave me a peck on the cheek and shambled out the back door, I checked my answering machine to see if Emma had left any messages. Nothing. If she'd decided to do something about her pregnancy right away, she wasn't letting me in on her plan.

From the porch, I called to the twins, Harcourt and Hilton, who came outside holding flashlights ghoulishly under their faces. They told me they'd brought their sleeping bags and would remain in the barn until morning. They were catching mice, but they hoped for bigger prey. I decided not to brave the darkness to see what doomed vermin they had in mind. Although I didn't want to be alone, the twins weren't exactly comforting company.

In the living room, Lucy lay sprawled out on the sofa in a bathing suit, sleeping soundly. There was no sign of her imaginary friend, but I found myself peeking into the other chairs just the same. My niece had an unnerving ability to convince everyone of her friend's existence.

I pulled a Spider-Man comic book from Lucy's sticky hands and turned off the reading lamp. Toby came in and threw himself down on the floor beside Lucy. Leaving a cashmere throw nearby in case she got cold in the night, I took Maximus up the stairs to my bedroom.

It felt cozy having Libby's children around.

The events of the last few years had me starting to believe I wasn't meant to be a parent. A miscarriage in the spring had devastated me, and any minute my biological clock was going to start ticking. Loudly. Maybe, I thought, I needed to learn to make myself happy by playing surrogate mom to the children of my sisters now and then.

I left the chandelier turned on in the front hall just in case Lucy woke in the night and wanted to find me. I noticed another bulb had burned out. The steps creaked ominously under my feet, and I wondered if the crack in the hallway plaster was a little longer than it had been this morning. The old place was falling apart faster than I could afford to fix it.

I'd inherited the farm when my parents took a powder. While they avoided extradition in the Southern Hemisphere on the beaches of one luxury resort after another, I struggled to pay their back taxes and keep the old Bucks County farmhouse from crumbling into a heap of stones, frayed wire and rusting pipes, not to mention the rampant mildew in the cellar. Emma had inherited the Blackbird art collection, and Libby received all the good family furniture, so I had moved the furnishings from my Philadelphia condo to the farm. The result looked a bit sparse in the big, rambling house, but at least the few rooms I did use were comfortable.

It was hotter upstairs, so I opened as many windows as I could. Old paint had sealed some of them permanently closed, but I managed to get some cross-ventilation going between my bedroom, my bath and the large dressing room I used as a closet. I could hear a soft breeze whispering in the oak trees as I shoved up the sash on my bedroom window.

The baby was teaching himself to stand by holding on to the furniture, but tonight he was cranky from the heat and didn't feel like playing. A bubble of drool seemed to constantly quiver on his lip, and I wondered if he might be teething.

I gave him a quick bath in my tub to cool him off, then put on a fresh diaper and pulled a clean cotton shirt over his head. The shirt was imprinted with the message, MOMMY'S LITTLE DEMON.

I hugged Max. To me, he was an angel.

Earlier in the summer, I'd brought an old playpen upstairs for the weekends when Libby needed a break and sent Max to stay with me. He seemed content to bed down in his home away from home for another night. I gave him his binky.

"I don't know the periodic tables, either," I told him.

From around his mouthful of pacifier, he said, "Da!"

With a smile, I turned off all the lights except the bedside lamp and left him alone. I heard him babbling and kicking at the musical mobile while I ran a bath for myself and undressed.

I flipped off the light and lit a lemon-scented candle. Usually, I read a book in the claw-foot tub, but tonight I didn't have the concentration. I dropped the novel onto the rug and tried to let the water ease the heat and tension out of my body. It didn't work, of course. As soon as I closed my eyes, I began to stew.

How had it happened? How had Hoyt Cavendish gone over the railing of Lexie's office balcony? I tried to imagine the scenario—all the various employees and clients moving through the offices like bumper cars in a chaotic carnival ride.

Tierney Cavendish rushing down the stairs. Scooter Zanzibar blundering into the restaurant, looking suspiciously rattled.

And I tried to remember who I'd seen in Lexie's office as the police established their crime scene. Brandi Schmidt in her wheelchair, yes. And the eccentric Elena Zanzibar. But who else had attended that shouted meeting in Lexie's boardroom? My father?

And Lexie herself, of course. But who else?

I heard a scraping noise and opened my eyes.

"Max?" I called.

The baby crooned some nonsense back to me, but he sounded sleepy.

I closed my eyes again.

Downstairs, Toby gave a halfhearted bark. Then I

heard another sound. A bump on the porch roof. And a noisier thump.

Just outside my bathroom window.

I sat up in the tub and reached for my towel. In five seconds, I was out of the water and dripping on the rug.

The curtains twitched and a familiar voice spoke from the porch roof. "Are you decent?"

"No," I replied. "As a matter of fact, I'm not."

"Great," said Michael. "I'll be right in."

He climbed through the window—quite an operation for a long-legged man with big shoulders. When all six feet four inches of him arrived in the bathroom, he grinned—a vision of curly black hair, a beaten-up face and a body most women would give up their shoe collection for. Then he leaned back out through the curtains and stretched to retrieve a package he'd left outside. When he dragged it in, he said, "I brought dinner."

"I'm not hungry."

"I am," he said, with a smile that turned his eyes very blue.

He leaned down and kissed me.

Michael Abruzzo never failed to take my breath away. I closed my eyes, felt my toes curl and my belly contract with the kind of desire that wasn't decent in the least. The kiss was meant to be a cursory greeting, I knew, but it lasted just a half second too long to be taken lightly. I wanted to fling my arms around his shoulders.

But that meant dropping my towel.

Chapter 6

Michael broke the kiss as if he'd suddenly remembered we weren't supposed to be on a kissing basis anymore. He all but wiped it off his mouth with the back of his hand. He said, "Sorry."

I pulled my towel tighter and tried to act as if ex-lovers dropped through windows every day. "I thought you decided we were history. Why are you climbing my downspouts at this hour?"

"Because Rawlins is on the back porch talking mushy on his cell phone. I didn't want him to think I had come to compromise his aunt. Plus those creepy twins are in the barn, aren't they? I'm still afraid they'll throw a net over me and use me for evil experiments."

"Michael—"

"Relax," he said. "This isn't a change of heart. I thought you could use some company tonight. I heard somebody important died today."

"How did you hear that?"

"I have my sources."

Michael had unsavory contacts on both sides of the law. His information was usually more accurate than the local newspapers, but in my worst moments I imagined his reports came from dirty cops and gangbangers—people he saw in the course of his everyday life of crime.

With a wry smile that told me he guessed what I was thinking, Michael tucked a loose strand of my hair behind my ear and lingered there, searching my face—perhaps to decide if he should stay or go.

He made a choice and said, "Put on some clothes. I brought Chinese."

"I don't think this is a good idea."

"Dinner, you mean? Did you eat already?"

"N-no."

"I figured. So we'll eat. And we'll skip the dessert, I promise."

If I was not mistaken, I heard a six-pack of beer jingle under his arm, too, as he went out to my bedroom, leaving me to dry off and slip into a soft T-shirt and loose boxer shorts. As I hung up the wet towel, I took a quick look at myself in the mirror. My cheeks glowed pink— whether from the summer heat or his kiss, I wasn't sure. I shook my hair out of its clip, then changed my mind and wound it up into a tight bun instead. If he truly wanted our relationship to be over, the drowned-librarian look was best tonight.

I tiptoed into the half-light of the bedroom and found him bending over the playpen. The baby spit out the binky and smiled up at Michael, gurgling with delight to see his familiar playmate.

"He stinks," Michael said.

"I just changed him!" Exasperated, I leaned down and checked. Yes, Maximus needed another diaper. "For heaven's sake," I muttered.

Like most men, Michael suffered instant ignorance once a nearby female had been notified of the stinky diaper. He went over to the bedside table, blithely opened his brown paper bag and began to pull out various white cardboard containers of Chinese food.

Grumbling, I located another industrial-strength Pampers and the packet of supersized wipes, then plunked the baby on the bed. Max wriggled around to get a better view of our visitor while I cleaned him up. When I turned to reach for the fresh diaper, he managed to kick himself over onto his stomach and made a break for the edge of the bed.

I grabbed Max and flipped him on his back just

in time to get a spray of baby pee up the front of my shirt.

Michael laughed, and Max let out a triumphant giggle at his new trick.

"Just what I need tonight," I said. "A couple of troublemakers."

"That's us." Michael scooped up the baby once he was freshly changed.

I dug a clean tank top out of a drawer and went into the bathroom to change out of the wet T-shirt. I washed my hands and took another look at my hair in the mirror. I decided I didn't want to feel like a drowned librarian after all. I shook out my hair and combed it fast.

When I returned, Michael was tucking Max back into the playpen. The baby gave one howl of protest and then rolled onto his stomach, binky forgotten. He rubbed his nose and went to sleep.

"How do you do that?" I asked. "For me, he'd be awake for hours."

"I promised him a beer later. Want one?"

Actually, a cold beer sounded heavenly. Michael read my thoughts and pulled a bottle of Yuengling from the six-pack. He twisted off the cap and handed over the beer, giving me an involuntary glance up and down.

I did the same to him. For some reason, he didn't look wrung out with heat exhaustion like everyone else I'd seen that day. In fact, he appeared to be comfortable in his jeans and the well-worn dark T-shirt that clung to his muscled chest and very touchable shoulders. But then, Michael was more at ease in his own skin than anyone else I'd ever known.

It was one of the things I appreciated most about him. I had a long list. But we seemed to be capable of sustaining only a few weeks of happiness together before one of us decided we weren't compatible.

This time, it had been Michael who decided we needed to be apart. For reasons I hadn't figured out yet, he said we should go our separate ways.

I had misgivings about the reliability of Michael's moral compass, of course. And the local newspapers always breathlessly reported innuendo about his family. Loan-sharking, illegal gambling, stolen cars and a tangle of other felonious crimes in New Jersey and Philadelphia were always being linked to the Abruzzo family. His cousins were in jail. One of his brothers disappeared a couple of years ago and was presumed murdered. And Michael seemed to slip in and out of police custody with catlike ease, while the press predicted it was only a matter of time before he went back to jail for some crime or other.

My resolve to distance myself from him always crumbled to the complex sort of attraction between us, however. The pull of lust was strong. It was the magnetism between the broken parts of our souls that truly drew us together, though.

The lost baby had bound us more tightly than I could have imagined.

Maybe this time our split was for real, however. Michael seemed to have mastered his self-control.

He gave me a gentle push to sit down on the bed and made his voice sound casual. "I like spicy food on a hot night, don't you? What'll it be? Shrimp? I got some of those sesame snow peas you like so much, too. The plastic fork is for me. I still can't use those damn chopsticks of yours. And here are some noodles."

I hitched myself to the middle of the bed and sat cross-legged while he sorted through the food. When he kicked off his shoes and climbed up beside me, I found myself tamping down a smile. He crossed one long leg over the other, relaxed into the pillows and dug into the spicy noodles.

"Thank you, Michael."

"Hey," he said with a shrug. "The first thing you do when you get upset is stop eating."

I wanted to shove the food aside and climb into his arms. I wanted to bury my head in his chest and listen to the steady rhythm of his heart. Tonight I needed some human contact. But I kept my distance. His body language told me to stay away.

In the silence, we heard a car start outside, and crunch slowly out the gravel driveway. Rawlins, going to see his new girlfriend.

Michael said, "Tell me what you know."

Startled, I said, "What?"

"Who's the dead guy?"

Michael enjoyed talking about crime the way most men discussed baseball scores. And since neither of us wanted to talk about our relationship, murder made a much safer dinner conversation.

"Hoyt Cavendish," I said. "He is—he *was* a philanthropist. He gave away millions. He's been very generous these last couple of years."

"Is he another one of your blue-blooded relatives? Did his grandfather make a fortune exploiting the working poor?"

"No," I said tartly. "Hoyt came from California, I think, and married one of the Slossen heiresses, who were very Old Philadelphia. Their great-uncle invested in some kind of farm implement, I think. The Slossens descended from the *Mayflower*, so Hoyt's background is unimportant."

Beneath his lazy eyelids, Michael's blue eyes gleamed with amusement. "Her pedigree trumps his, huh?"

"Yes. It was probably thanks to her connections that he became a partner in the Paine Investment Group, working with Lexie's father, helping people take care of their investments."

"That sounds more lucrative than farm equipment."

"Hm," I said. "Well, he was part of our—a part of the social scene. After his wife died, he announced he was semiretired and became a philanthropist. He presented a Stradivarius to a violinist just a few months ago. It was a very moving gesture."

"He started giving his wife's money away?"

I frowned. "I don't think she was quite that wealthy. He must have done well investing. He's been giving away monster sums of money."

Michael forked some Chinese food. "How did he die today?"

"A fall from a balcony. Brandi Schmidt—a woman who'd been with him shortly before he died—said he committed suicide. But I think he was murdered. Pushed off the terrace outside Lexie's office."

"Anybody else around when he took the swan dive?"

"Yes, of course. Lots of employees. And clients. It was a Who's Who of Philadelphia. Even Elena Zanzibar was there."

"Who?"

Of course Michael wouldn't know a woman famous for perfume and makeup. "She owns Zanzibar, the cosmetics company. She's astronomically rich. And it's possible her grandson, a movie actor, might have been in the office, too. He's Chad Zanzibar."

Michael shrugged, indicating he'd never heard of Chad, either. "How well did you know the dead guy?"

"Hoyt? Only a little. He and my father were friends a long time ago."

Michael slurped some spicy noodles and spoke around the mouthful. "Was Cavendish one of the chumps your father fleeced before he took a powder?"

I used the chopsticks to finagle a snow pea from the cardboard container. It was no secret that my parents alienated many of their former friends when they fled the country. They had begged, borrowed and essentially stolen money from many generous people to fund their flight from assorted tax collectors.

"Maybe," I said uncomfortably. "But it's even worse than that. Daddy had an affair with Hoyt's wife."

Michael choked on his noodles.

I tossed him a paper napkin. "It wasn't just a one-night stand, either, but a long-term, very adulterous relationship."

"Wow." He rubbed his chin with the paper napkin. "I didn't think people climbed out of your family tree to do that kind of stuff. What did your mom have to say about it?"

"Nothing. The affair was acknowledged, but never discussed."

With a grin, Michael shook his head. "I'm the bastard son of a mobster and an Atlantic City showgirl. Believe me, growing up, I heard a lot of discussion about affairs. Mostly at high volume and with dishes flying. Once my old man put a whole lasagna through a television during *The Price Is Right*. My mother knocked his front teeth out for that one."

I knew Michael had been raised by his father's wife, in fact, not his own mother. But Michael's upbringing had been very different from my own. That subject was old news.

I said, "Mama looked the other way. After all, Daddy wasn't going to leave her. And Hoyt's wife wasn't going to drop everything to be with my father, either."

"How did it end? A duel with swords and blindfolds?"

"Of course not. It was over as quietly as it started. Except Hoyt stopped speaking to Daddy, of course. It was a terrible shame, because they'd been good friends until then. Members of the same clubs, that sort of thing."

"And now Cavendish is dead."

"Yes."

And my father was back in town. Once again I wondered how he'd disappeared from the coat closet. My father had probably made a lot of fast getaways in his lifetime, but this one looked highly suspicious.

Before I could decide whether to tell Michael about my father's return to American soil, Michael spoke first. He helped himself to a shrimp and passed the container to me. "Tell me about the picture. Somebody punched a painting?"

"You're very well-informed, aren't you?"

"That part was on the news. Even made CNN."

I doubted the news media was Michael's only source of information, but I accepted the shrimp container. "Yes, the Vermeer in Lexie's office was damaged. It was so shocking to see, Michael. Vermeers are extraordinarily rare. I still can't believe a man who gave away a Stradivarius would do such a thing. He must have gone crazy."

"How valuable is the picture?"

"All the pieces in Lexie's collection are worth a fortune. But the monetary value isn't the real issue. Not to Lexie. Yes, it's astronomically valuable. And—it's important to her. I guess that's why Hoyt defacing it was all the more horrible. Lexie was devastated."

"Why is this one such a big deal to her?"

"I'm not sure I can explain, exactly. Lexie loves art, and she understands it in ways I don't. This Vermeer is a study—a sketch that was only partially painted. Which is probably why it's not in a museum. It's a woman sewing. Dutch paintings always have lots of symbolism. There's a dead swan in the background. And the woman depicted—her expression is almost Madonna-like. At peace. I always felt Lexie wished she could be as serene."

"Lexie's cool on the outside," Michael observed, "but she's wired tight."

"Yes." I had sometimes wondered if Lexie's affection for that particular painting stemmed more from the mutilated swan than the contented expression of the woman.

Without thinking, I chose a piece of shrimp with my chopsticks and held it out to Michael. Also out of old habit, he opened his mouth and took it. Then our eyes met, and neither of us moved in the tick of that intimate moment.

"Sorry," I said.

"So the dead guy ruined her picture," Michael said once he'd swallowed the shrimp. "I guess it's pretty much a lousy investment now?"

"Well, it has certainly lost value in the marketplace. A Picasso was similarly spoiled a few years ago, just as it was being sold for over a hundred million dollars. The seller had to withdraw the painting. But as I said, Lexie would never sell her Vermeer."

"Never say never," Michael said.

I frowned. His tone meant he knew more. "How did you really hear about the painting?"

He gave up eating and set his noodles on the nightstand. "Look, I know this is hard on you. And I wish I could make it easier. But to tell the truth, it's going to get worse."

For the first time since the heat wave started, I felt suddenly cold. "What do you mean?"

"You're going to hear this as soon as you turn on the television, so I figured I'd break the news myself. Lexie called me."

"You? Why?"

"Because she needed a lawyer."

Relief swept through me. "Oh, thank heaven she came to her senses! We tried to convince her this afternoon, but she was adamant."

"That attitude changed. Tonight she was taken in for questioning."

I nearly dropped the shrimp. "The police think Lexie had something to do with Hoyt's death? No!"

"Take it easy. It's not an arrest. Not yet. The cops started to pressure her, so she decided she wanted somebody on her side. She called me." He checked the time on my bedside clock. "And I fixed her up with Cannoli and Sons. They should get back to me soon. If anyone can spring Lexie tonight, it's them."

Michael's lawyers were adept at freeing their clients, even when the evidence against them seemed irrefutable. But Lexie's decision to telephone Michael for help when she had the resources to hire the very best money could buy surprised me. Had she felt she needed someone practiced in protecting the guilty?

I said, "Lexie didn't do it, you know. She would never have pushed anyone over that balcony, not even over a priceless work of art. And Hoyt was a treasured partner in her firm. They've been colleagues for years."

"What were the treasured colleagues yelling about, then?"

"I don't know. Some business thing. But she wouldn't hurt him. Or anyone, for that matter."

"Not even in the heat of a big moment?"

I stared at him in surprise. "You know Lexie. Do you honestly imagine she could have killed someone?"

"I can imagine a lot of things, Nora. People do crazy stuff."

"Not Lexie. It's ridiculous to even suggest she'd hurt a soul!"

"Lots of witnesses heard their argument. Maybe forensics will reveal other evidence from the body, too. Fortunately, that takes a lot more time than most of us think it should from watching TV. But meanwhile, Lexie's not helping herself. She's pissed off, and making no secret about it."

"Of course she's angry! Somebody murdered her partner, and she's furious!"

Michael shook his head. "If she's furious, she'll make mistakes. She needs to think about the impression she's giving the cops."

Unsteadily, I handed the container of food to him. "Did you tell her that?"

"She didn't ask me."

I thought of my friend and how she had behaved that afternoon. She'd been tense, angry, shaken. Perhaps more upset than I'd ever seen her, which said a lot. But the idea that she was in police custody was too much.

I put my face into my hands. "How can this be happening?"

Gently, Michael said, "Nora."

Tears stung my eyes, but I dashed them away. "I hate

to think of Lexie in jail. Not even for an hour. I hate that a good man is dead. It's all so awful!"

Michael put the food on the nightstand and reached for my hand. I turned my face away, but gripped him hard. He hesitated, and then pulled me closer. I tried to resist. For about a tenth of a second, I held firm. We had to take turns being strong. But my resolve crumbled, and I allowed him to draw me into his arms. I let my head rest against the warmth of his shoulder and relaxed against him.

He said, "She's in good hands, I promise. By tomorrow, the situation will be under control."

"Maybe not," I said.

I thought of my father, hiding from the police in Lexie's coat closet.

But I shoved the dreadful possibilities out of my head. It felt good lying there in bed. I didn't want to bring up my father's return just then. My mind was jumbled with thoughts of my friend, my family, a terrible death—and yet all the whirling mess seemed to slow down the longer Michael held me.

His hand ruffled through my hair. "Don't worry, okay? The cops will figure it out."

"Are you sure?"

He laughed shortly. "I have firsthand experience."

"Let's not talk about that."

He sighed. "I'm sorry. I never wanted you to know anything about my family's business."

I said, "It's not like my own family isn't colorful."

A laugh rumbled in his chest. "What's going on with the Blackbird sisters these days?"

"Libby got herself knocked for a loop by a Rolls-Royce, and now I think she's shacked up with the driver at the Ritz-Carlton. And Emma, of course, is knocked—"

"Wait, back up. Is Libby hurt?"

"Minor injuries, I believe. Otherwise, she's ecstatic. A

new man does that to her. And I'm in charge of the zoo until she comes home. Thank heaven for Rawlins. He's been taking care of the baby." I let my fingers slide between Michael's.

He didn't resist, and we lay together for a long moment, listening to each other breathe on the bed where we'd made sweet, hot love, sometimes losing our heads, sometimes so intensely aware of each other it was magic.

At last, I said, "I miss you."

"I know."

"I miss talking to you like this."

"I do, too. Being with you, my head gets quiet."

I wondered about the subtext of that statement.

Nearly all my friends had warned me I was playing with fire. When Michael and I had toyed with the idea of getting married, I had phone calls from people I hadn't seen in years—all of them asking if I was making a big mistake. In the next breath they wanted to know what it was like being with a dangerous man.

And an alliance with an impoverished heiress didn't exactly make sense for Michael, either. His enemies had used me against him, and neither of us wanted to be in that position again.

But until now we couldn't help ourselves. Whatever we saw in each other seemed to reflect a need we both felt inside. Perhaps one of Libby's crackpot cosmic forces had brought us together, and as much as fate tried to pull us apart, we weren't quite capable of making a clean break.

I said, "Usually you keep your distance if there's something wrong in your family. I can handle it, you know. Whatever has driven you away this time. Is there something going on with your father? Or is it about your brother stealing a tractor-trailer?"

Another short laugh, this one sounding unamused. "That was in the papers, wasn't it? Yeah, the moron stole a truck full of microwaves. Why would you want a truckload of heavy things you can buy at Wal-Mart for under a hundred bucks? But he doesn't think. Then he drove the truck across a couple of state lines, so now the idiot's in really deep shit."

"Are you involved?"

"In fixing things, yes. Talking to the lawyers, that kind of thing."

He slid his thumb under the strap of my tank top. "Let me take care of my own problems, okay? You've got all the kids depending on you right now. And God knows what's going to happen with Lexie. I don't want to add to—"

"Is it dangerous? What you're doing?"

Sounding reluctant, he said, "It's complicated."

I said, "And Emma? Is she making things complicated, too?"

Michael didn't move, didn't answer.

"I saw her today," I said. "She was wearing one of your shirts."

Michael said, "Look, I'm sorry."

It was better that we weren't looking into each other's faces. I didn't want to read his expression now. I steeled myself and said steadily, "So something's going on with you two?"

Michael was silent for a time. At last, sounding reluctant, he said, "I ran into Em a few weeks back at a bar. She was in bad shape, and coming on to every guy in the place. I figured I'd better do something before she got into trouble."

"And?"

"I took her back to my place."

I disentangled myself from his arms and sat up.

Michael said, "She's been staying with me. We should have told you before."

"Okay," I said, taking a deep breath. "I see."

"She was shit-faced, and—look, I'm not saying what I did was right. But she needed help, and the two of us decided—"

"I don't need to hear the rest."

"Nora," he said.

If he wanted to break up with me permanently, he'd finally found the way to do it. Emma was the sexy one, the sister who knew how to handle any man she cut out of the herd. And she'd been watching Michael from the first moment I'd brought him home. Perhaps she'd made passes at him all along.

Emma's idea of acceptable behavior in a significant other was totally different from mine, too. Maybe she could handle Michael's clandestine excursions into the night.

And maybe he'd be happier with someone who could accept his life of crime.

I got out of bed. My hands itched to grab the nearest lamp and hurl it at the wall. I wanted to scream. I wanted to smash something—anything—into a million pieces. Preferably my sister's head.

Swiftly, I said, "Thank you for taking care of her. As you say, I've got the kids to look after, plus my computer's on the fritz, so I have to go to the office more often, and the water pipes in the kitchen are making that awful noise again—"

"What's wrong with your computer?"

I couldn't slow my speech. "Nothing that a thousand dollars won't fix, I'm sure. The new plumber quit today, too. So I'm not capable of handling Emma at the moment. Or you. So it's probably for the best, isn't it?"

"Take it easy."

"I'm fine. Don't worry about me." I tried not to hyperventilate, but it was hard. I fought down the urge to slam a few doors, break several dozen windows, scream to the high heavens.

The truth—that they were together now—made my heart begin to pound like a hammer.

Except the pounding wasn't in my chest.

It was coming from downstairs.

Michael sat up straighter. "What the—?"

I caught my balance on the bedpost. "Somebody's knocking."

"Rawlins, maybe?"

"No, I gave him a key."

"So who the hell comes to your house at this time of night?"

"You, for one," I said. Then, "Michael, Lucy's downstairs."

He had already rolled from the bed, quick as a cat. "I'll go."

The pounding on the door redoubled, and then we could hear someone shouting, too.

Michael went out into the hall. Maximus was already standing in his crib, hanging on to the railing with one hand and using the other to rub his sleepy eyes. I grabbed the baby into my arms, afraid to leave him alone. He gave one cry of protest, then nestled against my shoulder. Carrying Max, I followed Michael to the landing, but he was already downstairs. I leaned over the banister. "Be careful!"

Over his shoulder, he said, "Stay there."

I disobeyed. The knocking and shouting were starting to sound like an emergency in progress. The noise echoed through the whole house.

In the living room, Lucy sat up groggily from the sofa. "Uncle Mick? Is that you?"

"Hi, Luce. Yeah, you okay?"

"Aunt Nora?"

As Michael disappeared in the direction of the kitchen, I went into the darkened room and clumsily hugged my niece. "It's okay, honey. We're here."

She blinked. "What's wrong?"

"Just somebody knocking on the door. Probably a person wanting to borrow the telephone. Nothing to worry about."

With a smile, she slid off the sofa. "Mick will beat them up. I want to watch!"

She scampered ahead of me toward the kitchen, and

we arrived just as Michael picked up the plumber's wrench from the counter. He hefted it like a weapon and reached for the doorknob. Whoever pounded on the door was using his fists now, and kicking, too.

I grabbed Lucy from behind and pulled her against me.

Michael yanked the door wide and stood firm, ready to fend off an invasion if necessary.

Lucy shrieked. "Grandpa! And Grandmama, too!"

Like floodwaters from a burst dam, my parents swept past Michael with their luggage and their minions.

Chapter 7

"Muffin!" my father cried. "We thought you'd sold the place! Our keys don't work in the locks!"

"I had them changed," I said to thin air. Because my father swooped down and seized Lucy in his arms. She yelped with joy.

"Grandpa!"

"You remember me?"

"Of course, I do! Do you think I'm dumb or something?"

"Nora, darling!" my mother cried breathlessly as she tottered into the kitchen on the highest of Jimmy Choos. "You won't believe what happened to us!"

All lush blond hair, perfect lipstick and outré fashion statement, my mother was still a beauty. Tonight her bosom was hoisted into a hot pink halter top, over which she'd thrown a Pucci print chiffon fluttery thing that concealed her fondness for desserts. Her snug Capri pants were strategically beribboned to draw attention to her delicate ankles, kept trim by hours of ballroom dancing. Gold bracelets tinkled on her wrists, and several rings decorated her slender fingers. Her sandals were silver and displayed her pink pedicure to perfection. Mama looked ten years younger than her sixty years.

She air-kissed me. "We've had the most extraordinary evening! The Ritz kicked us out! Can you imagine? Some mix-up with our credit card."

"I tried writing them a check," Daddy chimed in, "but they weren't having that, either. Well, I don't have to take any guff from a hotel manager, do I? So I told your mother we'd just come home, that's all."

"But—"

"We knew you'd be overjoyed to see us," Mama said. "It's been years and years!"

"Twenty-three months and twelve days," I corrected, quelling the urge to run screaming into the night.

"And we've missed you every minute, darling!" Mama patted my cheek.

"Muffin, can you pay the cab?" Daddy indicated the sour-faced man in the doorway. "I'm a little strapped for small bills."

· I grabbed my handbag from the chair, but Michael was already digging cash from his pocket. The cab-driver's eyes widened at the size of the wad, and he made a beeline to Michael's side. They had a muttered conversation.

"Time for a celebration!" Mama said. "Do you have any champagne in the icebox, darling? We'll have a lovely reunion, just the family, snug in the house together!"

"Not just family," I said, observing another gentle-man who'd come thumping through the door laden with suitcases. He actually wore a sarong beneath a flowered Hawaiian shirt. Around his neck gleamed a row of Poly-nesian puka shells, but his haircut looked like the one Rawlins just got—courtesy of the nearest military bar-ber. I asked, "Who's this?"

"Oh, our wonderful Oscar!" Mama waved her hand like a magician conjuring up a rabbit.

"Good evening." Oscar's accent sounded heavily in-fluenced by south Jersey, not an exotic island.

"We'd be lost without Oscar." Mama spoke sotto voce, as if everybody in the room couldn't hear her confession. "He's practically family now."

"He's your mother's new spiritual adviser," Daddy said.

To me, Oscar looked decidedly uncomfortable in his island garb. In fact, he seemed downright embarrassed and shifted in his sandals. His otherwise bare feet were glaringly white.

"And he's learning to be your father's valet. He can bartend, too. He's a genius with gin. Karma brought us together!" Mama raised her voice as if he were deaf. "Oscar, dear, can you take the suitcases upstairs? Through that door and—good heavens, Nora, what have you done to our home?"

Mama gave a spin to get a better impression of her surroundings, and she came to an unsteady stop, as if stunned by the massive changes.

"I keep the place dusted," I said.

"Where's my English sideboard? The table that was your great-great-grandmother's? And the chairs from Jackie Kennedy's estate?"

"You gave all the good furniture to Libby when you left the country, remember? I brought my own things from the condo so I could live here."

"The house is practically empty!"

"I'll admit there isn't nearly enough to fill all the rooms. In fact, the second floor is—"

"I think it's charming," Daddy announced, slipping one arm around me and planting a fatherly kiss on my cheek. "I like the clean, uncluttered look of the old place. Very sophisticated. We'd expect nothing less of you, Muffin."

My mother wasn't quite convinced. "You didn't give away our bedroom furniture, Nora? Not the dresser from Ben Franklin—the one Teddy Roosevelt carved his initials on? They were family heirlooms! Worth a fortune!"

The cabdriver harrumphed and went stomping out into the night.

"Mama, you gave—oh, never mind. There wasn't a way to get the bed out of the house without cutting it into pieces, so it's still up here. But that's all. Libby has the rest of the furniture in storage."

"But the bed's still there? Perfect!" Daddy cried. "Very romantic!"

My mother smiled at last. "It'll be like camping, won't it? We'll have a cleansing experience, darling. Oscar loves nothing more than a good cleanse. He's got a few nagging health problems we're trying to address—digestive and performance issues, nothing serious. He'll be perfectly comfortable in any little corner."

"Yes," I said, "but—"

"Wonderful! And with all those tiresome household matters out of the way, we can focus on what's truly important—a party celebrating the reconnection with our family!"

"It's awfully late," I began.

"Nonsense, darling. I feel like dancing! Can't we have some music? Surely you didn't do away with the old piano? Oscar, do you play? I'd love some Cole Porter!"

She began to hum "Too Darn Hot" and do her Ann Miller impersonation, which was really pretty good. She floated around the kitchen table, high kicking and waving her Pucci like wings. Lucy followed, pirouetting and flapping her arms.

"Whee!" Lucy cried. "A party! Can we have cake?"

Daddy beamed with pride and wrapped his arm around me. "A party breaks out wherever your mother goes."

"It's a gift!" Mama broke off singing. "Lucy, we had so many adventures while we were traveling. I can't wait to tell you all about the anaconda that slithered into our tepee one night!"

"Mama," I began, determined to avoid spending the next eight hours soothing the nightmares out of my niece.

"And the twins!" Mama gushed. "I bet they've grown! Are they still interested in ancient death practices? Because I brought them each a Sri Lankan exorcism stick, and I'm dying to try them out. And this must be Maximus! Oh, what a strapping, darling boy you are!"

She snatched little Max from my arms and cooed, nose to nose with the startled baby. "What beautiful curls you have. I only wish I'd met your father!"

Max responded by flinging out one chubby hand and exclaiming, "Da!"

Everyone followed the direction of Max's gesture, and our collective stare landed on Michael.

He stood frozen by the door, the wrench forgotten in his hand as he absorbed the return of my eccentric family. He'd been invisible until that moment. His face was blank, but a certain sort of fear glimmered in the back of his eyes.

In a rush, I said, "Uh, Mama and Daddy, this is—this is—he's—"

"I'm the plumber," Michael said.

A few seconds of doubt ticked by before Daddy cleared his throat and said, "Muffin, why do you have a plumber here at this hour? Don't you know home improvements cost extra at night?"

Mama had placed her hand on her throat as if she needed help catching her breath. She gave Michael's tall frame a thorough examination and obviously couldn't decide whether she should be intimidated or impressed. With a frown, she said, "I know all the plumbers in this neighborhood. Heaven knows, they've all been here and caused more problems than they fix. But I don't know this one."

Her gaze narrowed on him.

"I'm new," Michael said when he found his voice.

"You have beautiful eyes," Mama said. "I might call them choirboy blue. Is that your assistant waiting outside?"

"Assistant?" I asked. "Outside?"

"Yes, waiting in the car out there. A very large man."

"Delmar," Michael said. "Yeah, my assistant."

Delmar, I knew, was Michael's new bodyguard. A man the size of a dinosaur and possessing almost as much intelligence as a prehistoric beast. Why he was waiting outside for Michael, I didn't want to imagine.

Before my mother could continue her cross-examination, I quickly said, "The plumber came to get his—uh—wrench, see? And now he's leaving."

"Right," Michael said. "I'm leaving."

Lucy said, "But he's not a—ow! Aunt Nora, you're pinching me!"

"Sorry, Luce. My mistake. The plumber is going home now, that's all. Say good night."

Smarter than the average six-year-old, Lucy said, "Oh, okay. Good night, Mr. Plumber. Come back soon!"

Michael disappeared.

And if I hadn't been so furious with him, I might have followed.

Growing up with my parents had been a lot like living in Tornado Alley. They were constantly in motion, tearing up any obstacles that got in their way, and leaving chaos in their wake.

As a young child, I'd loved the excitement. Every minute, they were either throwing a party or cooking up an idea for one. We played games of their own invention, painted pictures, produced pageants and plays, ate exotic meals delivered by caterers and drank watered-down wine on birthdays and special occasions. We missed more days of elementary school than we attended, and the truant officer had been a frequent guest at teatime. I played the cello at an early age and learned enough Chinese to make conversation with the woman who washed my mother's delicate laundry. Libby taught herself to draw and paint with extraordinary talent. Emma had been a gifted horsewoman before she'd learned her multiplication tables.

I never remember feeling unsafe or unloved as a child. Just happy.

But as soon as puberty arrived, my sisters and I were quickly dispatched to boarding schools. My parents had been wonderful when we were children, but teenagers were beyond their ability to cope.

As an adult, I found them irresponsible and infuriating.

That night, they snatched a bottle of wine from the

fridge and roared up the stairs with their bartending, spiritual-advising valet. The three of them disappeared into their bedroom. The sound of their laughter floated down the hall to my room, where I lay in bed with Lucy, grinding my teeth and wondering if it was too late to run away and join a circus. At least it would have only three rings.

I slept badly.

The next day dawned with Maximus howling for his breakfast like he was being starved by prison guards. While Lucy slept through his noise, I threw on my shorts and a T-shirt and carried the baby downstairs. The other bedroom doors remained firmly closed.

While I warmed cereal for him, Maximus entertained himself with a banana, and we both enjoyed some fresh air from the open kitchen window. I turned on the television and braced myself to hear the news that Lexie might have been arrested.

But the phone rang.

"You won't believe the dream I had," Libby's voice said in my ear. "It was a nightmare, actually."

"Let me guess." I turned off the television and handed Maximus his binky to keep him entertained while I spoke on the phone with his mother. "You dreamed Mama and Daddy got thrown out of the Ritz."

"Nora! You're psychic! I've always wondered if you harbored more inner gifts than you let on!"

"The only thing I'm harboring at the moment is a couple of fugitives. They arrived here last night."

"What are you talking about? Honestly, darling, sometimes I worry—"

"They're back," I said. "Mama and Daddy have returned. For some strange reason, the Ritz doesn't trust their credit history, so they came here. Beautifully suntanned, I might add, and dragging a new spiritual adviser who's a cross between General MacArthur and Don Ho."

"Are they trying to borrow money? Because I have five children to support."

At the moment, I was supporting her five children, but I decided not to quibble. "They haven't asked yet, but I wouldn't be surprised."

"They will," Libby predicted. "Be careful. They're wily."

"They want to have a party."

"Oh, heavens. Are they going to hire that magician again? Mr. Spectaculation? Because let me tell you, he wasn't the least bit spectacular with me."

"They want to invite all their friends for dinner and dancing. They told me while I put fresh sheets on their bed last night."

"They don't have any friends left!"

"That little detail seems unimportant. You know how Mama gets when she's party planning."

"Don't worry," Libby said. "There's not a caterer in the whole state they haven't stiffed already. Nobody will work for them."

"That's comforting. Except that probably means they'll want me to prepare the buffet. How are you?" I asked. "Feeling better?"

"Marvelous! Er, actually, that's why I'm calling. It seems I may have some residual side effects from my accident."

Max threw his binky onto the floor and I bent to pick it up. "Side effects? Are you okay, Lib?"

"Nothing to worry about. But I might need a couple more days of recuperation."

"Who is he?" I asked. "The man you're staying with?"

"My condition has nothing whatever to do with a—no, really, Nora, I simply need a little more time to refresh—" She laughed and gave up trying to outfox me. "To tell the truth, I haven't felt this rejuvenated in ages, but I'd be a fool to stop now, don't you think? I believe I can be fully charged again, if I just make a little more effort. Considering I just suffered a head injury, isn't that kind of optimism astonishing?"

"Astonishing," I agreed. "But you're still coming home on Friday, right? To take the kids off my hands?"

"Yes, of course. Certainly. No doubt about it. Without fail, I'll be there. Do you think Mama and Daddy will be gone by then?"

Max tossed his binky again and watched me, grinning, as I picked it up. I counted to ten before saying, "I'm under a little pressure here, Lib. I need you to take the kids by Friday."

"Pressure?" she exclaimed. "You think you have pressures? Oh, of course, I read the headline about Hoyt Cavendish's death. At Lexie's office, no less! I was just saying to—well, I knew you'd have insider information! What do you know? Was it suicide? Or did somebody push him off a ledge? The newspaper made it sound as if Lexie had something to do with Hoyt's demise."

"Of course she didn't. Dozens of people were milling around up there."

"Like who?"

"As a matter of fact," I said, "Daddy."

Long silence.

"Oh, my," Libby said at last.

I heard something in her tone that was more than simply surprise. "What does that mean?"

"Just—well, you know, of course, about Daddy and Muriel Cavendish."

"Yes, you were the one who told me about the affair, remember? While we were at summer camp. I thought you were explaining how to braid a lanyard because you were using all those ridiculous euphemisms."

"I wanted to break it to you gently." Libby mused, "What became of that summer camp, I wonder? It might be a delightful getaway for Lucy, don't you think? Anyway, that affair was over years ago."

"Right. And if there were still any hard feelings, it would have been Daddy on the sidewalk, not Hoyt, don't you think?"

"Well," Libby said.

"After all this time, I hardly think either of them would still be . . . Lib?"

"Yes," she said, sounding distant.

"Yes, what?" As usual, she was driving me crazy.

"Well . . . you know about Hoyt, of course."

"What about him?" There was something strange about the man. I couldn't put my finger on it.

Darkly, Libby said, "The wings of a sparrow, you know."

"No, I don't know."

"Consequences. He lived with terrible consequences. And poor Muriel!" Libby gave a wistful sigh. "That's the tragic part that goes with the ecstasy, the fleeting pleasures, darling. No quenched desire goes unpunished. The yin that goes with the yang. Even the text of the Kama Sutra says—"

"Are you talking to me? Or is there someone with you right now?"

Libby went on, "The tiniest sparrow can displace air that spins and whirls and eventually causes a hurricane that can devastate an entire city in one horrible—"

"Libby!"

"Oh, sorry. I was free-associating. Maybe you should talk to Daddy about this."

"About what?"

"The consequences of his affair with Muriel Cavendish. I'm sorry, Nora, but my chocolate-hazelnut crepes are getting cold."

"Lib—"

"I'll be in touch over the weekend, all right?"

"Before Friday," I snapped. "You'll call before Friday."

"Bye!"

I hung up the phone. She hadn't given me time to tell her about Emma's condition. I was willing to bet Libby's reaction to the news was going to be ten times more vocal than mine.

Putting both of my sisters firmly out of my mind, I fed Maximus his cereal.

Then somebody knocked on the back door.

To Max, I said, "This better be a plumber."

It wasn't. The man standing on the back porch was my height and slightly pudgy with a corona of curly hair and wire-rimmed glasses perched crookedly on a cute nose. I guessed he'd slept in his khaki shorts and faded button-down shirt. He wore sturdy hiking sandals and carried a well-used canvas messenger bag with the strap across his chest.

"M-Miss Blackbird?"

"Yes?"

An expression of shy but acute intelligence shone behind his glasses. He stuck out his hand. "M-Mick Abruzzo sent me."

He gave my hand a firm shake, and then we stood there blinking at each other. I had enough experience with various Abruzzo family thugs to know that this one wasn't breaking kneecaps to collect gambling debts for Big Frankie. He looked more like a hitchhiking college student who maybe cataloged butterflies in his spare time. I looked beyond him to see a dusty Jeep parked in my driveway.

He adjusted the glasses, but failed to square them properly. He said, "You're M-Miss Nora Blackbird, right?"

"What? Yes, I'm Nora."

"I'm Henry Fineman. M-Mick sent m-me to fix your computer."

Chapter 8

If he'd announced he'd come to tell me I'd won the lottery, I couldn't have been happier. I pulled the door wide and nearly kissed him. "Please come in, Henry. I'll make coffee. I'll make pancakes. I'll make whatever it takes to keep you here until my computer works again."

He entered the house and looked around my kitchen with the expression of a time-warped wanderer who'd stumbled out of the forest and into a medieval castle. Blackbird Farm had that effect on many people. The crooked chandelier, the ancient slate floor and the antique farm table looked like props from a fairy-tale movie, whereas the Aga stove, the Sub-Zero fridge and the microwave indicated real people actually cooked in the cavernous space.

From his high chair, Maximus waved his binky and greeted Henry Fineman with enthusiasm. "Da!"

I closed the door to make sure the computer repairman couldn't easily escape. "Coffee?"

Henry blinked at Maximus, who had liberally smeared himself with oatmeal and banana. "Herbal tea, if you have it."

"I'll find some." I went into the pantry and found a tin of tea Libby had brought during the throes of one of her dubious health kicks. "How does Green Zest sound?"

"Is it organic?"

I tried to read the fine print and discovered the package was printed in Sanskrit. A naked man in a yoga pose looked ecstatic. "I don't know. But I'm guessing it promotes happy dreams or an active sex life—maybe both. You can't go wrong, can you?"

Henry Fineman was transfixed by the baby and didn't absorb my attempt at humor. "M-Miss Blackbird, I've done a few jobs for M-Mick, and I thought I knew him fairly well. If you don't m-mind m-me asking, is this infant, is he . . . ?"

I interpreted his blush. "No, this one's not Michael's child. This is my sister Libby's youngest. He's Maximus."

"I'm not very familiar with children. How old is this specimen?"

"Eight months. Do you think you could recite the periodic table to him?"

Henry looked startled. "What for?"

I sighed. "He's studying for the SAT exam. The tea is coming right up. There's the computer on the table."

Henry sat down at the table and opened his bag. Judging by his constant fiddling with his eyeglasses, he was uncomfortable being watched, so I got busy at the stove. By the time I filled the kettle and put it on to boil, he had unpacked his own computer and a variety of discs, cables and small tools. Maximus watched his every move, fascinated. Occasionally, Henry gave the baby an uneasy glance.

"So, Henry," I said. "Do you work on computers for Michael?"

"A little, yes."

"I didn't realize he used computers."

Henry peered over his glasses at me. "Everyone uses computers, M-Miss Blackbird. M-Mick simply has different needs than m-most."

"Oh?"

"Databases for the m-muscle car business, accounting programs for Gas N Grub, some inventory software for the fly-fishing store. I'm really not at liberty to say m-more, of course."

"Right. The code of silence, is that it?"

"I'm told I should think of it as professional discretion."

"Especially when it comes to family business?"

Henry studied me for a long moment, perhaps trying to decide if I was giving him a quiz. Slowly, he said, "Correct."

"Makes sense. I mean, it's best if the right hand never knows what the left hand is doing, right?"

Henry looked solemn. "That's one way of putting it, I suppose."

I couldn't help noticing that Henry's social skills—although better than those of most of the characters who hung around Michael's various businesses—weren't exactly going to land him a job in any legitimate company. He frowned intently at the screen of my laptop. His concentration was broken only when Maximus yelled the occasional, "Da!"

Within a few minutes, Henry began swapping discs in and out of the hard drive. He certainly looked as if he knew what he was doing.

When I placed a cup of tea at his elbow, he asked, "Do you have your cell phone handy, M-Miss Blackbird?"

"What does my cell phone have to do with my computer?"

He blinked. "Aren't you fully synced?"

"I don't even know what that means. Do you really need my phone?"

"It would help."

I surrendered my cell phone, hoping I was putting my trust in the right person. His hands were so quick on the keyboard that I couldn't keep up with what he was doing. Was he playing a version of three-card monte? He picked up his mug of tea and sipped it while intently watching the computer screen.

The house phone rang, so I picked it up.

"Nora?" Crewe's voice sounded tense when I answered. "Have you heard from Lexie yet today?"

"I was hoping you had, Crewe."

"She's still with the police, dammit."

"She's not alone. Michael sent his lawyers."

"Well, that's good news. I've tried to see her, but the police have stalled me. I'll try again in an hour or so. I want to be the one to take her home."

I took the phone into the scullery so I wouldn't be overheard. "Crewe," I said, "I've been thinking about who could have killed Hoyt Cavendish."

"Me, too. Especially the gnome."

"Elf," I corrected. "Chad Zanzibar."

"Right, him. Remember how he came barging into the restaurant yesterday? Before we knew Cavendish was dead?"

"He behaved very oddly," I said.

"And I don't think he was acting."

"Behaving suspiciously might be a family trait. I saw his grandmother yesterday, too, after Hoyt died. She was hysterical one minute, then giving me makeup tips the next. She disappeared before the police could question her."

"Interesting."

"And something else is bothering me, Crewe."

"Let me guess. Tierney Cavendish."

"Exactly. He must have gone directly from the restaurant to Lexie's office. But why was he running down the staircase after his father died? I assumed he was rushing to help, but now I wonder if he was trying to escape the police."

"Did the cops even know he was there?"

"Surely someone saw him and said so."

The two of us were silent, considering our own thoughts.

Crewe spoke first. "Nora, did you know Hoyt very well?"

"Not at all, really."

"Me neither. He kept to himself most of his life. Until he started donating to various causes."

"Yes, then suddenly he was everywhere. Giving money away as if he couldn't do it fast enough."

"There was always something . . . strange about him, too. Do you feel that way?"

"He couldn't help the way he looked." Hoyt's small size, his penguinlike gait, his weak voice.

"No, I guess not," Crewe said, sounding as if he wanted to say more, but wasn't sure how to put his thoughts into words.

I said, "I have to come into the city, Crewe. There's a charity event I need to cover this afternoon. Afterwards I was thinking of paying a call on someone who might be able to give me some information about the Cavendish family. Can we get together to talk about this?"

"Unless Lexie needs me, absolutely. I have to be at the Chocolate Festival at six to try catching Jacque Petite for an interview. Why don't you meet me there?"

Having a plan made my spirits rise. "Information about a murder, plus chocolate. My kind of party."

He laughed shortly. "Okay, good. At the convention center, six o'clock."

I hung up the phone just as my father came into the kitchen. He wore a pink and lime green flowered sarong and a pair of beaded moccasins. Bare-chested, he had tied another ascot around his neck.

"Good morning, Muffin!" he sang. "It's a beautiful morning for tai chi on the grass, don't you think? Will you join me? Your mother and Oscar are busy creating a guest list for a little soiree, so I—good heavens, who's this?"

Henry Fineman looked up from the computer and adjusted his eyeglasses. "I'm Henry Fineman, sir."

"Harry!" My father shook his hand with enthusiasm.

"That's Henry, Daddy. This is my father—"

"A pleasure to meet you!" Daddy cried. "Are you a tai chi man, I wonder?"

"No, sir, I'm not. I have a bad back."

"Never mind, I'm delighted to meet you anyway! Nora hasn't breathed a word about you yet, but I was sure it was only a matter of time before she landed a responsible man to support her."

"Daddy—"

"Her mother and I are very pleased to welcome you in the family, young man. And I'm sure we'd love to toss a small celebration in your honor."

"Uh—"

"Oh, don't worry about legal details. We Blackbirds are very open-minded. If you choose not to formalize your relationship, that's all right by me. As long as you both communicate your expectations honestly."

"Actually, sir—"

"I'm sure you make Nora very happy. All our girls can be tempestuous, of course, but it's my experience that if you keep your lady contented happy in her boudoir, if you catch my drift—"

"Daddy, Henry is not my boyfriend."

"No?"

"No," Henry said firmly.

My father frowned. "Why not?"

"I beg your pardon?"

"Isn't my daughter attractive to you?"

"No—I m-mean, yes, she's perfectly attractive, but I—"

"You don't like girls?"

"I—"

"Not that your sexual orientation matters to me," my father said. "In fact, I'd welcome an honest discussion of the homosexual experience. I believe in seeking knowledge, young man."

Henry flushed a startling shade of red. "I am not a homosexual. Not that there's anything wrong with homosexuals. I'm just not one."

"You're sure?"

"Yes," Henry said.

My father looked unconvinced.

"Daddy, would you like some tea?"

"Yes, please. As long as it's organic."

The phone rang again. An interruption was almost a relief. I picked up and took the receiver into the scullery so I couldn't hear my father further embarrass Henry Fineman.

"Hello?"

"Nora?"

I couldn't place the male voice on the other end of the line. "Yes?"

"It's me. Chad Zanzibar. I hope you don't mind me phoning so early. Listen, I've got another call waiting for me—a director—but I need a favor."

"From me?"

"Yeah, I hear you are connected."

"Connected?"

Chad's voice sounded muffled, as if he was cupping one hand against the receiver. "Connected with the mob. I'm doing research for the role I told you about. I'm playing an underworld mook. I'm hoping you can hook me up."

"With a mook? What is that, exactly?"

"I need to shadow a mobster. You know, absorb his mannerisms, get a feel for the character, maybe come up with some stage business. Can you introduce me? To Big Frankie's son. I hear he's the real thing and you're his squeeze."

I resisted the urge to scream. Even Hollywood elves knew about my love life. "I don't think that would be a good idea, Scooter."

"Chad. Hey, I can handle myself. It'll be cool, I swear."

"I'm sure you're always—uhm—cool, but—"

"How about setting up a meet with Abruzzo? Tell him it's me. He'll want to see a movie star."

I remembered Michael's blank look when I'd mentioned Chad Zanzibar. I felt positive he wouldn't take a "meet" with an elf. "Actually, he's not much of a movie patron."

Chad laughed as if I had made a hilarious joke. "Yeah, right. Listen, just give me his number, and I'll call him myself."

In the kitchen, Maximus let out a wail, so I said hastily, "Sorry, Chad, but I've got to run."

"But—"

I hung up the phone and hurried into the kitchen, where my father was determinedly disengaging the binky from the baby's clenched fist. Maximus had a stubborn set to his jaw and murderous rage in his steely gaze.

"Daddy?"

"A child should be allowed to explore his creativity early, Muffin. By providing him with commonplace toys, you will lull his mind into monotony—you limit the many ways he can expand his horizons."

Maximus angrily pounded his tray with both hands, splashing mashed banana in all directions.

Daddy smiled broadly, even as a squishy hunk of banana hit him square in the ascot. "See? Already he's expanding."

Henry shielded my computer screen from flying banana. "I have to agree, M-Miss Blackbird. I've read studies. M-many innovative thinkers have sprung from children raised in primitive circumstances where the necessity to survive triggered very creative thinking."

"Okay, I surrender." I could see Max's temper tantrum losing momentum as he discovered the pleasures of his first food fight. The gleam in his eye grew demonic. "Daddy, would you mind stepping into the garden with me? We can pick some berries for your breakfast."

"Muffin, you know I'm allergic to strawberries."

"A little father-daughter bonding time, then?"

"Do we need to bond?"

Henry said, "Sir, I think she'd like to discuss something with you in private."

"Exactly," I said. "Henry, you don't mind keeping an eye on the baby for a few minutes, do you?"

"Uh—well—"

I grabbed my father by his ascot and dragged him outdoors.

Chapter 9

We went down the porch steps and across the lawn with Toby in hot pursuit, barking. Around us, the garden looked more glorious than it ever had since I had taken possession of Blackbird Farm. Peonies bowed their thick heads of fragrant flowers, and a blue jay swooped around the bird feeder that Michael had helped me put into place in the spring. My bachelor's buttons were blooming, and the bank of white loosestrife looked ready to burst into flower any minute.

But I wanted to knock my exasperating father down into the flower bed and pack his ears with potting soil.

Dragging Daddy, I shoved through the newly repaired garden gate to the strawberry patch, which I had lovingly spread with straw a few weeks back. A flock of blackbirds flapped up from between the strawberry plants as we approached. But even after their thievery, there were still plenty of berries to pick.

Daddy recoiled from the plants. "You don't expect me to work, do you?"

I spun around and cocked my fists on my hips. "I expect you to tell me the truth, that's all."

"Truth?"

"Yes, about why you're here and what happened yesterday at Lexie's office."

"Muffin, I already told you, didn't I? The government has promised to release your mother and me from our tax problems if we cooperate in the investigation of Hoyt Cavendish."

"What investigation?"

As if I hadn't been paying attention all along, he said patiently, "Into his misconduct with client investments, of course."

"You mean Hoyt mismanaged *your* money?"

"Muffin, why do you imagine your mother and I went broke so fast? We certainly wouldn't have run through all the Blackbird money without a little help, could we?"

"You mean—?" An absurd bubble of hope rose in my chest. "Hoyt stole from us?"

"Yes, Muffin, he did." Daddy took my hand and patted it. "I'm sorry if that shocks you, but it's the God's honest truth. And I'm doing my level best to restore some of our lost fortune."

"You—? You think you might be able to get your money back?"

"I'm doing my level best, Muffin, yes."

"How? If he's dead—"

"We're exploring all the possibilities."

Far from being shocked, I found myself suddenly, enormously, gloriously elated. After two years of struggling to make ends meet, could there be the merest flicker of light at the end of my very dark tunnel? All I needed was a measly two million dollars to pay off the back taxes and maybe a few extra hundred thousand to prevent the house from falling into a heap of rubble.

But immediately, I tried to squelch the relief dawning inside me.

I said, "Can you prove it? That Hoyt embezzled your money?"

Daddy's face glowed. "Are you kidding? I have documents out the wazoo! Statements that show all the detail anyone needs to put Cavendish behind bars. If he were alive, that is."

I withdrew my hand from my father's earnest grip. "Now that he's dead, though?"

"Well, yes, there's that complication," Daddy admitted. "Not to mention I might have misspoken when I was in the presence of some law enforcement officials."

"What do you mean? What did you say? To whom?"

"It was an emotional moment." He turned to admire the flower garden. "I might have been feeling a tad melodramatic at the Treasury Department. Surely nobody took me seriously. What lovely perennials! What variety is that flower?"

"It's called bleeding heart. See? The flowers are shaped like hearts and they—wait a minute. Don't try to distract me. What exactly did you say to the Treasury Department?"

He tugged uneasily at the knot on his sarong. "I might have mentioned that I—well, that your mother and I were upset that Hoyt mishandled our investments."

"How upset?"

My father looked pained. "I might have been annoyed enough to—well, to wish him harm."

"You threatened Hoyt? In front of federal officials?"

He blew a deep, regretful breath. "Oh, all right, I might have said I'd like to kill him for putting your dear mother through so much unnecessary misery."

"You threatened to kill him. And now he's dead. And you've run away from the police during his murder investigation."

"It seemed prudent. You don't think they'll come looking for us here, do you? I hate spoiling your mother's pleasure at being in the loving arms of her adoring family again."

For an instant, I wondered if my head might explode. "I don't know, Daddy. They might."

As a child, I had adored my father and his ability to generate excitement wherever he went. He had a gift for conjuring fun out of nothing. At home, we played endless pretend games, trying on new identities and playacting for hours. He was our director, our incorrigible playmate, the captain of our pirate ship. His flights of fancy sparked our imaginations. At the beach, he presided over midnight treasure hunts that culminated in bonfires. We roasted marshmallows and gobbled them while he regaled us with stories of adventure and romance.

One warm afternoon at Blackbird Farm, we lay on our backs in the grass and named passing clouds after Greek gods and Hanna-Barbera cartoon characters. For years, I watched the skies for the return of Poseidon and Fred Flintstone, clouds my father declared were my very own possessions. I still scanned the skies for familiar shapes—perhaps to remind myself of those carefree afternoons with my imaginative and loving father.

But there was no denying he'd also drained our trust funds and run out on the family, leaving my sisters and me to live, not only broke, but also with the universal disapproval of all the friends he'd bilked, too.

Daddy must have guessed where my thoughts went. He put his arm around me. "Don't look so forlorn, Muffin. This isn't the end of the world. Your mother and I have a plan!"

With a twinge of new worry, I asked, "What kind of plan?"

He chucked me under the chin. "No worries. Once all this Cavendish stuff blows over, everything will fall into place. Your mother has learned so much on our travels that she wants to open a kind of spiritual retreat. With spa facilities and workshops that celebrate the soul, and plenty of private spaces for reflection, personal growth and, of course, wedding receptions! We hear wedding receptions can be a gold mine, and you know how much your mother enjoys a party. Just think—she could have one every weekend—on somebody else's dime!"

"Uh-huh," I said. "And where does she have in mind these wedding receptions might take place?"

Glowing with pleasure, Daddy said, "Why, right here at Blackbird Farm, Muffin! It will be a family venture. Think of it! I could be leading the morning tai chi class in this glorious sunlight! Your mother will be counseling young lovers in the joyous festival of life and—"

"And me?" I asked. "What would I be doing?"

"Well, we'll need somebody to look after the guests and their most basic needs, of course. Clean rooms. Healthy foods. Flower arrangements in all the rooms, naturally. You're incredibly talented with flowers. It only takes a glance at this delightful garden to see that you're gifted in that department."

"I have a job," I said. "I'm working for the *Intelligencer*."

"And we're so proud of you! Of course, your mother and I always knew you were headed for big things. You're so clever and dependable and gracious. You must be the best employee that awful newspaper has ever hired."

"I do my best, but—"

"Your best is light-years better than the average person's effort." Daddy beamed. "You'll be running the paper in no time."

"Hardly."

"Well, maybe something better will come along." He squeezed my shoulders, "In the meantime, don't bring down your spirit with a bad attitude, Nora. Think positively! Envision your own success! If you choose to turn your back on your newspaper career, your mother and I want you to be a part of our venture. How exciting would that be? A family—working together!"

I had a very clear vision of how our family venture would turn out—me doing all the manual labor while Mama tossed rose petals and Daddy smoked weed and conned people into handing over their wallets.

Daddy caught my expression at the thought of spending my days cooking and doing laundry. He pinched my cheek playfully. "An open mind, Muffin. That's all we're asking of you right now."

The most open mind in the world would not accept a lifetime of working for my parents.

Time to go into the city, I decided. I needed to get away before I found myself in indentured servitude.

Chapter 10

Upstairs, I found one of my grandmother's Diane von Furstenberg wrap dresses—lemon and white with cap sleeves. The flirty skirt was cool, and the low, crossed neckline flattered my figure. I grabbed my Chinese umbrella and a straw handbag, and then I dragged Rawlins out of bed to drive me to the Yardley train station.

"Sorry to spoil your beauty sleep, Rawlins."

He yawned behind the wheel of his mother's red minivan. "No problem. I have to work later this afternoon anyway."

"All the hot weather makes people hungry for ice cream."

"Yeah, today I'm making blueberry cheesecake swirl."

First thing in the morning, blueberry cheesecake sounded pretty great to me.

His cell phone rang and he pulled it from his pocket without taking his eyes from the road. "Yo?"

I could hear only the squawk of a high-pitched female voice talking very fast. Rawlins winced as he listened to her. At last he cut across her yammering. "Don't get so bent out of shape, Regan. I just woke up. Yeah, I'm driving my aunt to the train, that's all. Listen, I'll call you back."

He shut the phone and sighed.

"Regan?" I asked. "Your new girlfriend?"

"Jeez, she wants to know where I am every minute!"

"She obviously cares about you."

"I think she wants to make sure I'm not hooking up with any other girls."

"She's the jealous type?"

"Insanely jealous. I'm not even allowed to talk to the customers or she goes ballistic. Hey, it's my *job* to talk to the customers!"

"Do you like her?"

"Yeah, I guess."

"More than Shawna?"

"Shawna's a pain in the ass," he said sharply. "She wants to argue all the time about stuff."

I heard frustration in his voice, but also longing. "What stuff?"

"Stuff in books. You know, like philosophy and poems." He said the words in a derisive tone. "A conversation shouldn't be so hard, you know? With Regan, I can just be myself. The most complicated thing she reads is *People* magazine."

"I see."

His phone started to ring again, and Rawlins took his eyes off the road long enough to stare at the small screen. "I just wish she'd leave me alone for five— Hello? Yeah, Regan, believe it or not, I'm still in the car with my aunt."

I sent him a don't-be-rude glance, and he said, "Sorry, Regan. Whassup?"

Thinking I should call my editor and warn him of my arrival, I rummaged in my purse for my own phone and discovered the silver compact I'd picked up in Lexie's office bathroom. I turned it over in my hand and saw the Tiffany stamp on the bottom. I'd have to remember to return it to Lexie as soon as possible.

I phoned the office, but my editor must have been out because his voice mail picked up. Hearing Stan's harried recorded voice, I decided against leaving a message. Better to talk to him in person without giving him time to formulate all his complaints about my work.

Rawlins dropped me at the train station in the nick of

time, so I kissed him good-bye and jumped on the train just as it was departing. I found myself in an empty car. Traveling after rush hour had its advantages.

I used the time to sort through my party invitations and start making my RSVP phone calls for the day. I received dozens of invitations each time the mail was delivered, so it was easy to get behind. Once the invitations started piling up, it was very hard to clean out the backlog.

I got lucky and was able to interview a chairwoman of one of the events. I asked her about the upcoming dance-athon for a teen center she cared passionately about. She seemed glad I had chosen her event to highlight in my column and chatted eagerly about the dance. I scribbled notes on my pad, then drafted a few punchy paragraphs.

On impulse, I said, "The newspaper's Web site posted photos of various school proms in May. It was a big hit with our readers. Would you mind if I brought a photographer with me?"

"I'd be delighted, Nora!"

I arrived in the city in less than an hour. A thermometer on a bank said the temperature had already hit ninety degrees and was rapidly climbing.

I hiked to the Pendergast Building and nearly wept with relief when the office air-conditioning cooled my face.

"You here for the meeting, Nora?" Skip Malone asked me. The seasoned sports reporter pinned his notebook under one arm and juggled a cup of coffee, a bagel and a plastic pen as he passed my desk.

"Meeting?"

"Yeah, the managing editor's here. Rumor has it, there's a big shake-up coming now that Stan's out of commission."

I gasped. "Stan's out of commission?"

"Yeah, the colonoscopy didn't go well. He's had some surgery and needs a few weeks to recover."

Stan Rosenstatz had ongoing gastric issues, no doubt caused by a long career in journalism. Budget cuts further threatened all newspapers these days, which didn't make Stan's life any easier. Plus supervising untrained writers like myself didn't do his nervous stomach any favors, either. I liked my editor, and often felt sorry to cause him exasperation. But his leave of absence was very bad news.

I was already on my feet, following Skip to the conference room. "Is Stan going to be okay?"

"I think so. Unless the Pendergast family decides to fire him."

"But Stan holds this place together!"

Skip held open the conference room door for me. "Yeah, but with circulation down, they can't afford to keep all of us employed, can they?"

"They can't fire Stan!"

Skip shrugged.

With Stan on my side, I'd always felt relatively confident I wasn't going to lose my job. Filled with dread, I slid into a chair at the back of the room and listened to the managing editor give a speech that started out with a lot of platitudes and quickly got to the bad news.

He said, "We're going to cut back in all departments. For the next couple of weeks, we'll study everyone's contribution to the financial well-being of the paper. And we'll make our decisions accordingly."

The roomful of journalists was eerily silent.

He spread his hands as if asking for our indulgence. "I wish we could promise to release people according to seniority, but that's just not economically viable. We'll be as fair as we know how. But we're shifting our focus to the online edition. A video-based traffic report starts next week. Any other ideas you can contribute will be appreciated. And rewarded."

The mood was gloomy after that, with a few of my colleagues taking long lunches to commiserate. I grabbed a salad in the company cafeteria and ate it at my desk—

half in an effort to stay out of the heat, but also to avoid listening to all the speculation about who would keep their jobs and who would be out on the street.

The thought of losing my meager salary frightened me even more than my parents moving back home. I wasn't trained to do anything, really. Attending parties for a living was the one thing I could do well. My long career as a Junior Leaguer had given me organizational skills that made me useful in social situations, but hardly prepared me for any kind of real corporate employment. Except maybe changing beds in the horrible bed-and-breakfast my parents were proposing. Laundry and cooking—two of my least favorite activities. What kind of life could be worse?

Midafternoon, I packed my handbag and took the elevator to the street.

Nearly melting into the sidewalk, I staggered over to Rittenhouse Square. I tried to put the summer heat out of my mind. But the leaves on the trees hung limp in the searing rays of the afternoon sun, and my own energy level hovered near zero. The asphalt felt soft under my shoes as I crossed to the park.

The Music Academy had scheduled a midafternoon performance under a canopy. White folding chairs stood ready for an audience, but the thin crowd—mostly parents of the summer-program students—waited listlessly in the shade of the trees. One pale and sweaty Academy employee stood behind a table pouring lukewarm lemonade into pink paper cups as fast as she could. I saw a big drop of perspiration slide off the end of her nose and splash into someone's lemonade.

Reaching for a cup was Brandi Schmidt. A white skirt floated around her shapely, tanned legs, and she wore a vivid red blouse suitable for the TV camera. She accepted the cup without noticing what had landed in the lemonade.

"Oh, Nora." She tried to turn her chair and balance her lemonade at the same time, so I reached to help by taking her cup. "Thank you. Thank you for coming. After yesterday's horrible tragedy, I was afraid nobody would attend today's concertina."

I didn't point out that a small concert wasn't really a concertina. "Are you on the committee, Brandi?"

"I'm on the board of the Music Academy, so I'm here to lend my supportiveness."

"Good for you."

Board members of prestigious organizations were usually called upon to attend events and contribute generously to the coffers. I wondered if Brandi's television station donated her share to the Music Academy—not uncommon—or if she had given her own money.

"I'm new on the board. Hoyt asked me to serve. How could I refuse? He was so kind to me." Tears started in her dark eyes. Overcome, she propelled her chair to the far end of the table.

I asked the volunteer for another cup of lemonade and carried the fresh cup to the spot Brandi had clearly chosen for a private conversation. She held out her hand, and I gave her the drink.

I said, "Hoyt's death must affect nearly every music organization in the city."

Brandi's lower lip trembled, but she smiled bravely. "Yes. No matter how he died, we can't deny he was a wonderful man."

"You must feel a great personal loss, too, Brandi."

She nodded. "Hoyt was the one who brought me to Philadelphia, did you know?"

"Oh, really?"

"Yes, I was working in cable TV in California at the time. He told me he had a friend who owned a television station here. He even suggested ways to make a video to show the full speculum of my work. His friend saw the tape, interviewed me, and the rest is historical. I owe Hoyt my career. A person with my kind of disability needs a helping hand to succeed in broadcasting."

If Hoyt had asked a friend to hire her as a personal

favor to him, that explained why she hadn't been fired for incompetence yet. She had a certain dewy innocence on camera, but trying to hold a serious conversation without bursting out laughing at her contorted English was a challenge.

She went on, "We became confidences, Hoyt and me. Eventually I realized I could help him, too. We both got something meaningful out of it." She sighed, then lifted her chin. "Nobody will ever know how important we were to each other."

"I'm so sorry for your loss."

"Thank you, Nora. You've always been very kind. Other people will—oh, I don't expect much sympathy. I'm not very well liked, you know. In my job as a newscaster, I have to be tough sometimes. I can't be everyone's best friend. People are always on guard and jealous, too. Surely you feel the same enviousness, being a reporter."

"Well—"

"If I speak up about my relationship with Hoyt, I'll simply look more foolish, so I guess I should just keep it to myself. But it's hard to grieve alone."

Uncertainly, I said, "Nobody thinks you're foolish, Brandi."

"But they don't like me," she said. "Do they?"

"I think you're very much liked."

At least, she wasn't disliked. Despite her good looks, Brandi Schmidt wasn't a very warm person, though. People weren't drawn to her, I supposed. I was surprised—and somewhat abashed—to realize her feelings were so easily hurt.

She shook her head. "Journalism is work that's very alienationing, don't you think? I assume people are only pretending to be my friends so I'll put them on camera. Then, of course, there's my disability. People notice my wheelchair and try to avoid me. I see it all the time."

I suddenly thought to myself that it wasn't her wheelchair that alienated people as much as her passive-aggressive, pity-party behavior. In just a few minutes, she had me squirming with guilt. I knew other people with disabilities—my friend Tom Nelson, for one—whose personalities were so forceful that I quickly forgot the wheelchair when we were together.

But I said, "People are starting to look past each other's handicaps, I think. The world is becoming more open-minded."

"I hope so," she said, although clearly she doubted it was true.

The wounded-deer look in her eyes made me uncomfortable. I itched to get away.

I said, "I'm sorry I won't be able to stay for the whole concert this afternoon. But I have other events to cover today."

She grimaced. "That's what everybody says. I wish we could have moved the musicians indoors, but—well, sometimes we really suffer for art, don't we?"

Two parents pushed past us for lemonade, and I moved aside to give them access to the refreshments. I used the interruption to end my conversation with Brandi.

She waved good-bye sadly.

I hastily walked the length of the sidewalk to exchange greetings with several parents and Margery Hind-Cross, a frail and elderly dowager who had given a sizable donation to the Academy to fund the summer program. I chatted with Margery, but despite her friendly manner, I could see she didn't have the strength to make much small talk. She clutched a parasol in one arthritic hand and used a lace handkerchief to fan her face, too.

Her stoic chauffeur—in full uniform and with sweat pouring off his forehead in a steady stream—lurked nearby, ready to take her home as soon as the heat became unbearable for her.

I thought of asking Margery what she knew about the circumstances of Brandi's appointment to the board of directors, but it was clear the elderly patroness of the arts was silently suffering in the heat.

Within moments, the conductor came out of the Academy's building at the head of a long line of young musicians. The children's faces were all pinched to hold back giggles, as if they had just received a lecture about concert decorum.

The conductor organized the kids, made a short speech and raised his baton at last. The young musicians put their bows to their instruments, and the still air was filled with enthusiastic Mozart.

I found myself tapping my toes, too, but eventually the heat was so oppressive that my mind began to wander. I made a few more scratches in my notebook, but finally, I edged away from the concert. Hoping to avoid Brandi—and the guilt she'd undoubtedly make me feel for leaving early—I slipped away as quickly as I could.

Just two short blocks from Rittenhouse Square stood a small town house with a marble stoop and a lush window box full of flowers. It was one of my favorite houses in the whole city—three floors of solid, classic architecture on the outside, but cozy and welcoming inside.

In the window above the flowers hung the frame of a cello, advertising the shop on the first floor. I rang the bell and waited at the black lacquered door.

The intercom crackled. "Yes?"

"Daniel?" I said. "It's Nora Blackbird. May I come up?"

"Nora! Sure. I'll buzz you in." His melodic voice sounded pleased to hear me. "Come right up the stairs."

A bell clanged, so I pushed the door wide and stepped into the cool darkness of the vestibule. To the left was the door leading to Daniel Schansky's instrument repair and resale shop. Straight ahead, the staircase rose to the second-floor living quarters. Sunlight shining through the beveled facets of the fan-shaped window over the door cast thousands of sparkles on the stairs, giving the impression that heaven awaited above.

Daniel's mail lay on the floor, having been pushed through the slot by the postman. I bent and gathered the envelopes into my hands and headed up the heavenly stairs.

I arrived on the landing in time to catch Daniel buttoning a white shirt around his incredibly toned upper body.

"Sorry," he said with a grin when I gave him a kiss. "Eric and I are going out for an early dinner. I just got out of the shower."

For a forty-something, Daniel looked more like twenty-something. His long brown hair was pulled into a wet ponytail that accentuated the sensual planes of his dramatic face. His jeans were neat as they encased his long, long legs. His gnarled bare feet were thrust into flip-flops. A former ballet dancer, he still had the tall, lean grace of his previous profession.

On the worktable at the large front window lay the pieces of a viola. The instrument's delicate neck had been broken, and I saw long-term, major surgery was in progress. The tools of Daniel's meticulous work were neatly lined up on a folded cloth. An assortment of varnishes sat in a straight row along the windowsill.

The living room was airy and spacious, yet cozy with personal touches. Beside the worktable hung a sepia portrait of Daniel's grandfather, a Russian immigrant who had been a first-class violin maker. An old, framed poster dominated another wall, depicting Daniel himself lifting a ballerina into the spotlight. Around the poster, someone with more humor had dragged a pink feather boa and some Mardi Gras beads.

In front of the white marble fireplace, a pair of creamy sofas faced each other, separated by a glass coffee table artfully cluttered with books, seashells and casual photographs in silver frames. The wooden floor gleamed warmly. The walls glowed with a pale blue green, the color of sea glass.

Through an archway, I could see the long dining room, with a massive table situated on a tasteful Turkish rug, an ideal spot for dinner parties. Beyond that room lay the gourmet kitchen, where a collection of pricey copper pots hung in descending order of size from a ceiling rack.

"This is a nice surprise, Nora." Daniel finished buttoning his shirt and accepted his mail. "I haven't seen you in ages."

"Not since I gave you my old cello to sell. Thanks again, by the way. I really needed the money."

He smiled shyly. "Sorry I couldn't get more for it. But I found it a good home—a student at the Academy, in fact."

"It wasn't worth much. And it was hardly the kind of instrument you usually deal in."

"But well loved, and that counts sometimes. Please sit down."

"I shouldn't stay if you're on your way out."

"Nonsense. It's a pleasure to see you."

I perched on the arm of one of the sofas. Daniel leaned against the worktable.

Head bent, he glanced through the envelopes in his hand and winced at some of the return addresses.

I pretended not to notice by lifting a small, framed photo from the collection on the coffee table. An attractive man with a gray crew cut smiled mischievously at me from the picture, his arm thrown across Daniel's broader shoulder and the pink boa curling around his neck. I said, "Is Eric around?"

"He just left to go back to the shop. Last-minute flower delivery to a longtime customer, and he had to show his replacement exactly where the flowers needed to go."

"His replacement?"

Daniel smiled at me over the envelopes. "Eric's taking a leave of absence in a couple of weeks. Training the new manager has been very trying." Daniel dropped his bills onto the worktable and tried to forget about them. "Shall I call his cell phone and tell him you're here?"

"Oh, no, I just wondered if he was at home. You know he's one of my favorite people."

Daniel smiled again. "And mine."

"I don't mean to keep you from your dinner date," I said. "But I have an odd question I was hoping you might answer."

"I can try. What's up?"

I'd thought of Daniel on the train. But now—sitting in his lovely home—I felt awkward. I decided there was no use beating around the bush, however. "You know Hoyt Cavendish died yesterday."

Daniel's mouth tightened. "Yes, I heard that."

"You—look, Daniel, I know I could be prying. But I'm trying to help a friend who's mixed up in Hoyt's death, and I—"

"The morning paper said his death was suspicious. I understood that to mean he might have killed himself. Or was he murdered?"

"I think it must have been murder." I observed Daniel's expression. "You don't seem to be surprised."

The former dancer crossed one leg over the other, still leaning against his worktable. "No, I'm not surprised. Curious, perhaps, about who else might have been angry with Cavendish. Mind you, I have an alibi." His smile was fleeting. "I was with a client all afternoon, tuning a temperamental viola."

"I'm sure you don't need an alibi." Cautiously, I asked, "But—were you angry with him?"

"Frustrated," Daniel corrected. Out of habit, he picked up one of the curved pieces of a broken instrument from his table. "And getting more angry with every passing day."

"Every passing day? I'm sorry, I don't want you to reveal more than you're comfortable saying, but—"

"I had nothing to do with his death," Daniel said with a shrug. "So I can speak as freely as I choose. In fact, I expect the police will show up here eventually. Hoyt owed me money. Quite a lot, in fact."

"For the violin he gave away?" I guessed.

Daniel's eyes widened. "Yes. How did you know?"

"I didn't really. But I wondered if you might have been involved in acquiring that particular instrument for him. You're the foremost broker in the city now that Armand Gruyet is gone, so I assumed you helped Hoyt."

He brushed off the compliment with a gesture. "Cavendish came to me in the winter. Brandi Schmidt introduced us, saying he wanted to make some kind of splashy gift in the arts community. I knew the orchestra was trying to help Kiki Ling locate a really good instrument, and I had heard from a contact in Vienna that a violin was available."

"So you brokered the deal?"

"Yes, and did some refinements on the violin. Nothing major. Frankly, I'm not in that league yet, to go fooling around with a priceless instrument."

"But Hoyt didn't pay for the violin?"

Grimly, Daniel sighed. "He paid the owner in Vienna half of the purchase price, in two installments. But he had been dodging the rest of the bill for weeks. It's a considerable amount—nearly a million dollars. I'm embarrassed, because my reputation is at stake, you see, and I certainly can't afford to pay it for him. Hoyt never made good on his promise to pay my fee, either. Which is a pain, because Eric and I were counting on that money."

"On a violin of such caliber, your fee must be enormous."

Daniel shook his head. "I wasn't going to make a killing on a charitable act. But I figured I should at least be reimbursed for my expenses. I traveled to Vienna to pick up the instrument myself. And my time is worth something, too. Eric and I are going to Spain for a few months, and we owe quite a large deposit on a house there. But Cavendish never got around to paying me."

"Maybe his estate will settle all his accounts," I suggested.

"Soon, I hope. I hear he also owes the opera a significant chunk of the money he pledged to them last year. He's been making sizable donations all over town."

I thought about what I'd learned and asked, "You said Brandi Schmidt brought Hoyt to you?"

"Yes, they're both on the board of the Music Academy. I was asked to talk to donors about making mutually beneficial contributions. Instead of giving money, some donors find it more advantageous to give cars or property that can be sold for cash, or investments that can be liquidated at a better time. I spoke about giving instruments instead. Win-win for everyone. Hoyt was interested in giving a violin, and I thought he wanted a fat tax deduction."

The Byzantine rules of tax breaks for charitable donations had long since confounded me. But I wondered about Brandi Schmidt. She probably knew a lot of Philadelphia's extensive community of philanthropists, considering how often television personalities were asked to be honorary chairs for events and to emcee everything from charity galas to fashion shows. What did it mean?

For a moment, I stewed about how I could learn more about Brandi's relationship with Hoyt.

"Nora?"

I realized I had been allowing my thoughts to ramble. "Sorry. Do you know Brandi well?"

"Only a little." Daniel composed his face into a suspiciously neutral expression. "But not just through the Music Academy. When she first came to town, she joined the Gay, Lesbian and Transgender Coalition. Eric and I were active before the politics got so crazy and the organization imploded. She left before we did. We assumed her bosses told her to cool it."

I hadn't known of Brandi's sexual orientation. But, then, it was hardly a subject I went around asking people.

"Do you know anything about Brandi's personal relationship with Hoyt Cavendish?"

"Personal relationship?" Daniel frowned. "Did they have one?"

"To hear her tell it, yes."

"How can you be sure? Her vocabulary is so tangled up sometimes—well, that's unkind, isn't it? I didn't see any signs of affection between them, if that's what you mean. In fact, my observation was that Hoyt disliked her intensely."

"What makes you say that?"

"They were cold with each other, that's all. Hoyt was an icicle."

I had another question on the tip of my tongue, but just then Daniel's partner, Eric, came through the downstairs door and sang a greeting. I heard the jingle of a dog leash, and their brindled greyhound came bounding up the stairs, happy to be home.

The dog poked his snout under my skirt. Apologizing, Daniel seized his collar and hauled him away.

Eric arrived wearing a tank shirt and shorts that showed off his toned body and various tattoos. He carried the rhinestone dog leash and a sheaf of lilac branches.

"What a wonderful fragrance!" I hugged Eric. "Congratulations. I hear you're off to Spain very soon."

"It's a dream come true, sweetie pie." Eric was much more animated than his subdued partner, and he bounded across the living room to drop the dog leash in a box marked *Butch*. Over his shoulder he said, "Did Daniel tell you why we're going?"

"No," Daniel said. "Not yet."

Eric laughed. "We're staying in a house next door to my cousin. She's having a baby next month."

He sent a merry glance at Daniel, who sighed with feigned weariness and said, "Tell Nora the rest. You're dying to."

"We're adopting the baby! We're going to be dads!"

"I'm terrified," Daniel confided. "But Eric's totally gung ho."

Exuberantly, Eric led the way to the cheery kitchen, where he filled a glass vase with water from the tap. "Oh, don't be silly. Daniel will be a brilliant father. He's the conscientious one. We'll stay in Spain for a few months until we think we're ready to fly solo as parents. Can we invite you to the adoption party?"

"Of course." I helped unwrap the lilacs from the paper. "I'd love to come."

"Bring a present," Eric commanded as he tucked the flowers into the vase. "Maybe something in the heir-loom category, like a random silver spoon. Or something you've used yourself and swear by. Don't you have experience with poppets?"

"Babies? Not much."

I chatted with the two of them for a few more minutes, but keeping in mind their dinner plans, I soon bade them good-bye.

As I went down the stairs, I couldn't help thinking about Emma and her unborn child. When had the whole concept of family turned so topsy-turvy? All I wanted was a baby of my own, and it seemed I was the only person with empty arms.

On the sidewalk outside, I briskly pulled myself together. No wallowing. I checked my watch. I had plenty of time to meet Crewe at the convention center as long as I didn't keel over during the hot walk. The tall buildings around me blocked out the sun as it dropped lower in the sky, but the heat still radiated intensely from the broiling pavement.

I managed to keep up a steady amble, but once I ducked into a Talbots store to cool off a little while pretending to check the sale rack. Plenty of other over-heated women were doing the same thing.

Sufficiently refreshed, I went outside, and under the red awning I called home.

"Hey, Aunt Nora," Rawlins said when I identified myself. "Whassup?"

"I thought you had to work."

"I'm at work right now."

"Oh, sorry. I didn't mean to—"

"Hey, I'll take any phone call that isn't Regan. The busy signal will drive her nuts."

I laughed. "Okay. Was everybody alive and well at the farm when you left?"

"Def Con Zero—perfectly quiet. Grandma was still upstairs with the weird guy. I don't want to know what they're doing, but I think I heard a cocktail shaker. Anyway, Grandpa's cool with it. He's with the twins right now. They're digging a fire pit."

"A—? It's not too close to the house, is it?"

"No, it's out in the field. They want to set off fireworks from it on the Fourth of July. Grandma's planning a big party."

"Of course she is. And she'll use the national holiday as an excuse to make it more extravagant than ever."

"Sounds bitchin' to me. Think Mick could get us some fireworks? The real stuff?"

"Don't count on it, Rawlins." Michael seemed hell-bent on the road to self-destruction already, and buying illegal fireworks for minors seemed like an unnecessarily risky side detour. I began to wonder if I could get my hands on some tranquilizers instead of pyrotechnics. "How was Lucy?"

"She and her imaginary friend were tormenting Henry."

"Henry's still there?"

"Yeah, he's cool. We're all cool, Aunt Nora. You're as bad as Regan. Stop with the worrying."

"Okay, Rawlins. Thanks for the update."

"Anytime."

I closed my cell phone. Ready to make the final assault on the convention center, I took one of the narrow side streets, walking hurriedly past alleys that were crowded with overflowing Dumpsters. Certainly a less tourist-friendly glimpse of the City of Brotherly Love. A rear exit for one of the city's parking garages had been blockaded by union workers protesting the use of scabs during the parking strike. But the heat had chased away picketers. Instead of human protesters, a giant, inflatable rat stood in protest, its humming motor keeping it full of hot air.

I passed the rat and crossed Broad Street, then cut up some side streets.

At the stroke of six, I found Crewe waiting for me in the shade of the overhead walkway. A throng of people streamed past him into the convention center. In the traffic jam on the street, we heard a squeal of tires and a crash. I turned around to see a TV truck up on the curb, having barely missed hitting a busload of tourists. Immediately, four taxis pulled every which way and blocked the street. Typical convention center gridlock.

Crewe's first words were, "Have you heard from Lexie?"

"Good heavens, she's not still with the police?"

He looked grim. "She must be. I've tried her cell phone a dozen times, and there's no answer."

"She hasn't been arrested, has she?"

Crewe shook his head. "If she had, somebody would have called me from the paper."

"Should we skip the Chocolate Festival, Crewe? Go over to the Roundhouse to check on her instead?"

"The police won't let us see her. I already tried." Crewe took my arm and guided me into the busy convention center. "Maybe we can be more useful to Lexie here. I should find Jacque Petite, but I understand he's been skipping all the Chocolate Festival events, for some reason. The organizers are going nuts."

He pointed at an immense poster that showed the famously cherubic face of Jacque Petite, a Food Channel chef who had become world famous for his almost sensual use of chocolate in various kinds of cooking. His cookbook had lingered on best-seller lists for months, and his packaged chocolates were selling nationwide. It was impossible to look up at his broad smile and warmly knowing, chocolaty eyes without smiling.

Only Crewe was immune. He said, "There's somebody else I think we should talk to here."

"Who?"

"Elena Zanzibar. She's launching some chocolate spa-treatment products at the festival. If we get lucky, we might get a shot at questioning her about what happened yesterday."

Along with an enthusiastic crowd, we went up the escalator to the entrance of the convention center's large exposition space. The intoxicating scent of chocolate wafted over us as we arrived in the doorway of a chocolate lover's paradise. Crewe and I were swept under a huge Zanzibar banner that stretched over the doorway. Two smiling hostesses in golden aprons offered us trays of Zanzibar spa samples. I dodged a spritz of a chocolate-scented perfume.

Dozens of other exhibitors were lined up in long, crowded rows, displaying every imaginable form of chocolate. Flags advertising famous chocolatiers hung from the rafters. Small purveyors of artisan chocolates gave away samples. People rushed inside, eager to start tasting the goodies. I saw one dazed and happy woman leaving the building, her arms weighed down with huge shopping bags full of chocolate.

"Crewe," I said, "I think I might faint with ecstasy."

"Steady," he advised. "The key to doing a foodie show is to pace yourself. Don't sample everything right away, because you'll be too full to enjoy the pièce de résistance."

"Easier said than done."

"Let's head to the stage. I think Elena should be finishing up her presentation about now."

We took a right turn past a bower of trees and flowers decorated to look like a chocolate lover's Garden of Eden. A miniature mountain was decorated with flickering candles and strewn rose petals, with a path of candy bars leading upward to a giant claw-foot bathtub filled with warm chocolate. A fountain of creamy chocolate flowed into the tub from a statue of a naked man pouring from a ewer.

The tub had been painted with the Zanzibar logo.

And reclining in the tub—with the cascade of chocolate running over her bare toes—was none other than my sister Emma.

"Good Lord," I said to her. "Are you completely naked?"

Chapter 11

From her prone position in the bathtub, Emma lifted a mug in a toast. It was supposed to look like a cup of hot chocolate, but I was willing to bet she was drinking vodka.

With a woozy grin, she said, "If you want to see a riot break out, I'll stand up."

Crewe stared into the tub. "That doesn't look very sanitary."

"You're not supposed to drink it." She splashed her chocolate bath. "You're supposed to fantasize. It's some kind of Zanzibar spa potion."

I said, "I should have known you weren't giving candy bars to kiddies."

"Hell, no. This is an R-rated chocolate show. There's a woman around the corner who makes lollipops in very interesting shapes, Sis. You ought to buy a few dozen to give your stuffy friends next Christmas."

Emma didn't seem to mind the throng of people who stared at her as they moved toward the other exhibits. In fact, she seemed to enjoy her role. She smiled broadly and waved to everyone.

Suddenly furious with her, I snatched the cup out of her hand. "What the hell do you think you're doing?"

"Hey! Give that back!"

"Can't you think about someone else for once?"

"Who?" she demanded.

"Your baby! You've been given a miracle, Emma. A blessing! And you can't see that?"

"Dammit, Nora, give me my drink."

"No."

"This is none of your business."

"Maybe not," I said. "But you can spend one hour not drinking, and after that, another hour. And maybe a few more hours until you sober up and think straight about the child you're bringing into the world."

"Why the hell do you care?"

"You know damn well why," I said.

"Screw you."

"He already did," I shot back just as crudely. "But apparently he prefers you. The least you can do is take care of his baby."

Emma let out a string of curses that turned heads, but I was unmoved. I walked away with her drink in hand.

Crewe caught up with me. "Wow, Nora, I've never seen you so . . . so . . ."

"Pissed off?" I said. "Well, stick around. If she comes after me, there's going to be a fistfight."

Even though I was only half-kidding, Crewe looked horrified.

A passing waitress offered us dark-chocolate-dipped strawberries from a boutique patisserie in the suburbs. Crewe turned her down. I grabbed one. I needed to self-medicate, and chocolate was the nearest sedative.

"I'll talk while you eat," Crewe said as we inched into the crowd. "This morning I spoke with some of the reporters who are covering Hoyt Cavendish's death."

"Mmph?" I swallowed. "What did you learn?"

"First of all, there's some kind of news blackout going on. The police are controlling all information about the investigation—and I mean serious control. The DA has promised somebody will get fired if there's a leak. I thought the radio silence was because Hoyt was a powerful and influential man. But the reporters say this feels different—like the police are holding back something really big."

I wished I'd thought to get an extra napkin. I licked

chocolate from my thumb. "Any theories about what the big information might be?"

"That maybe somebody important is a suspect."

"Crewe, the building was crawling with Philadelphia fat cats. The important suspect could be half a dozen people, even Lexie."

"The police can pinpoint nearly all of the big names at the time Hoyt went off the balcony. Only a few were alone or can't explain exactly where they were in the building."

"Not just the building," I said. "Scooter Zanzibar—remember?"

"Yeah, he looked guilty as sin when he arrived at the restaurant."

"He called me this morning."

Crewe stopped dead. "Chad Zanzibar called you?" He couldn't control the astonishment in his voice. "No offense, Nora, but what for?"

"He wants to follow Michael around. To research his next acting role."

Crewe laughed. "I can see Mick giving acting tips! What did you tell the kid?"

"That I have no contact with anyone in organized crime."

In my handbag, my phone rang. When I picked up, Michael's voice said in my ear, "Hey. Where are you?"

"At the convention center."

"I'll be there in half an hour."

"What's wrong?"

"It's all good," he said, soothing.

But he hung up without explanation.

Crewe guessed the identity of my caller by the expression on my face. "So much for no contact with anyone in organized crime."

The serendipitous timing amused Crewe, but I tucked my phone back into my bag and frowned. "That was strange. Michael's coming here in half an hour."

I didn't want to see him. Not with my sister around.

Crewe didn't notice and gathered my arm in his hand. "That gives us enough time to talk to Elena Zanzibar. There she is." He pointed.

A mob of chocolate lovers had come to a standstill in front of a small stage where beautiful models in slinky spa bathrobes held containers of various products. Elena Zanzibar herself stood with a microphone in her hand. She wore a gold lamé formal gown that sparkled in the bright lights. A luxurious chocolate-colored wrap encased her shoulders. Her hair was precariously tall, and her makeup more colorful than ever.

In the audience sat a dozen similarly coiffed ladies— Elena's fan club. One carried a hand-lettered sign: *We'll do anything for you!*

Elena was giving a rambling speech. Before edging closer to listen, I decided I'd better ditch Emma's drink, so I headed over to a strategically placed trash can. As I prepared to toss the cup, I took a quick sniff of the contents. To be certain, I took a small sip.

And discovered it wasn't booze after all, but plain ginger ale.

Emma had been drinking nothing more potent than soda pop, I realized with a pang of guilt. Maybe she'd been sober all along.

"Oh, dear," I said.

Crewe looked around at me. "Something wrong?"

"Something right," I said. "For once."

There wasn't time to go apologize to my sister. Elena's presentation came to a conclusion, and the crowd broke into polite applause. The fan club jumped to their feet, clapping with enthusiasm. Elena cast them a strained smile. Two television crews had been filming her remarks, but they shut off their lights as the applause died down.

A tall man wearing stage makeup took the microphone from Elena. "Don't forget to come back Friday night when we feature the great Jacque Petite—star of the Chocolate Festival!"

More applause, but most of the crowd dispersed. Given the choice of free chocolate or the autograph of an elderly cosmetics executive, everyone seemed eager to move off in search of the free samples. The man with the microphone gently helped Elena off the stage.

Crewe and I worked our way close to the autograph table and soon found ourselves in front of Elena as she signed head shots of herself. The photo, I noticed, had been taken at least twenty years ago.

"My dear Nora!" She pushed the remaining head shots aside with hands that were encased in opera gloves. "Surely you understand what a sacrifice I've made to come here. I wanted to stay at home, but my VP of PR insisted I honor my commitment to the new spa line."

"I'm sorry you're unwell," I said. "You're very brave to come tonight."

I introduced Crewe, and Elena tugged her gloves higher before extending her hand to Crewe. "Hello. I knew your father."

"It's a pleasure to meet you, Mrs. Zanzibar."

Crewe's father had been a notorious philanderer, a subject that Crewe found painful, so he switched subjects with the ease of a man who often steered conversation away from unpleasant memories. He said, "I was very sorry to hear of yesterday's tragedy."

She nodded, forlorn. All the energy she had shown the previous day had been sapped away. This evening Elena looked haggard beneath her makeup. Her eyeliner was smeared, and she had chewed off half of her usually perfect lipstick. In a shaken voice, she said, "Would you be so kind as to escort me to my car?"

"Of course. Would you prefer we call a doctor?"

As best she could, Elena tried to collect herself. "A doctor can't fix a broken heart."

"I'm so sorry," I said. "Hoyt's death is a terrible loss."

"Terrible loss?" she cried, losing the last shreds of self-control. "I'll tell you about terrible loss! The bastard stole nearly fifty million dollars from me."

I gasped. "He stole from you?"

"I thought he was my friend! I thought I was helping him by giving him my affairs to manage. But he was stealing me blind. I'm broke!"

"Surely not completely—" Crewe began.

Elena's chin trembled. "My grandson brought me all the facts and figures last night. For years Hoyt steadily drained all my accounts."

"I'm shocked," I said.

"You and me both." She tried to look haughty, but managed only to look frightened. "How can I possibly help my grandson's movie now? He's so angry with me." She tugged at her gloves again. "Nora, didn't your grandmother sell off her jewelry to keep your family going when things went to pot?"

"Yes, she did."

"You must give me a contact—the name of someone who can help me."

"You're upset," I soothed. "Everyone's upset. It's too soon to make important decisions."

"I must raise cash immediately!" Her gloves slipped lower, and I saw bruises on the fleshy part of her arm. But she was too distressed to notice. "My grandson doesn't deserve to have his future ruined this way. I was devastated by Hoyt's death, but now this! A violation of trust!"

"I spoke with Brandi Schmidt this afternoon, and she—"

"Brandi Schmidt! That hussy!"

Crewe cleared his throat, and with an inclination of his head indicated that the television news crew still loitered nearby.

Elena got the message. But instead of shutting up, she pulled the two of us to the edge of the stage to continue our discussion. There, she said, "I know I can trust the both of you when I reveal that Hoyt and I had an understanding. We were going to marry later this year."

"I had no idea, Mrs. Zanzibar."

"We wanted to keep it quiet." She summoned her dignity. "I'm very glad of that. Especially now that things have turned out to be so ugly."

Crewe murmured, "I'm very sorry for your—uh—loss."

"My point is," she said, "that nasty Brandi Schmidt was probably milking Hoyt for all he was worth. And he was milking *me*! For once, she's not the victim here. I am!"

Elena's handlers finally noticed her distress and swooped over to take charge of her. She introduced me to her assistant, a tall, chic woman wearing a corporate suit and a capable expression. A pin shaped as the Zanzibar logo flashed on her lapel.

Elena tried to calm down. "This is Cherry. She's going to spend the night with me. Isn't she a saint?"

Cherry shook my hand with a crushing grip, then Crewe's. "You shouldn't be alone, Mrs. Z."

I was glad to see Cherry help Elena into a golf cart and whisk her off the exposition floor. Elena needed someone she could trust close by.

"Well, well," said Crewe. "Elena was going to marry Hoyt Cavendish?"

"Question is," I said, "when did Chad discover Hoyt was stealing from his cash cow? Before or after the murder?"

"And did Chad blame his own grandmother for losing the money to Hoyt?"

"You saw her bruises?"

"Hard to miss," Crewe said. "Even with the gloves. Do you think that little shit beat his grandmother?"

We looked at each other, thinking over what we'd just seen and heard.

"I'd better go after her," I said. "If she's in danger, she needs our help."

"I think she's safe for the moment." Crewe flexed his hand, as if remembering Cherry's strong handshake. "Her assistant looks as if she could rip Scooter's head off."

"I suppose you're right."

"I'm starting to see why Lexie was so upset last weekend."

"You think she discovered Hoyt embezzled money from Elena's accounts?"

We exchanged speculative looks, and Crewe said, "There were a lot of clients who attended that meeting in Lexie's office."

"Dollars to doughnuts, I bet Hoyt stole money from all of them. No wonder Lexie went ballistic."

"Come on." Crewe edged away. "If I can't find Jacque Petite, I've got one more chocolate purveyor I want to see tonight."

We wound our way along the crowded aisles until we arrived at a double display with the Amazon Chocolate Company sign hanging from some faux jungle trees. The company mascot, a stuffed black panther, peered down at us from the fake foliage. On a large screen, a video showed the spectacular scenery of a South American cocoa plantation.

Various Amazon employees stood behind the tables dressed in safari-style khakis and chatting up passersby. Although the company provided the raw ingredients for making chocolate, they were distributing small squares of designer chocolate wrapped in foil and stamped with the panther image.

Nowhere among the Amazon people did I see Tierney Cavendish.

"I figured Tierney would be here." Crewe sounded disappointed. "It's his big night. The first public appearance of his company."

On the video screen, handsome Tierney appeared, chatting with local farmers. He frowned and nodded with sympathy while one child pointed at bulldozers flattening a swath of trees.

"Tierney's got a great idea," Crewe said in my ear. "Most of the world's chocolate comes from West Africa, where children and slave labor are often used to harvest the cocoa beans. But Tierney's working near the Amazon River where the cocoa is grown under the jungle canopy by indigenous farmers who don't want to grow drug crops. He's saving the jungle, fighting the war on drugs and making a profit for everyone all at the same time."

"He really looks like a hero."

The video screen changed to footage of sacks of cocoa beans clearly marked with the panther illustration. Smiling workers loaded them onto cargo ships.

"But he needs capital to get the company stabilized," Crewe said. "I talked to one of the business-page reporters today. Tierney's looking for investors to keep Amazon Chocolate going until the next season's crop is produced."

I remembered the scene in the restaurant where it appeared local bankers hadn't liked Tierney's business proposition.

"But his father's death gives Tierney a reason to stay away tonight. Surely nobody truly expects him to appear."

"Or," Crewe said, lowering his voice, "is he guilty of killing his father? Why didn't Hoyt finance Tierney's company? Especially if he was stealing millions from Elena and probably other clients, too?"

Keeping an eye out for Tierney Cavendish, we made a quick circle of the Chocolate Festival. Crewe made cursory notes for his piece on artisan chocolates. He was recognized by a few vendors, who pressed samples on him. By the time we were ready to leave, I was half-nauseated from all the chocolate I'd nibbled—either that, or the confusion of my thoughts concerning Hoyt's death.

As we were descending the escalator, my phone rang again, and Michael said, "I'm outside. Look for Lexie's car."

Crewe and I hurried out into the warm evening air, and we saw Michael standing at the corner alongside Lexie's black BMW. Dusk had arrived, and the streetlight over his shoulder came on just at that moment.

Michael wore a dark business suit with a white shirt underneath—his go-to-court clothes.

He caught sight of us, and I saw a flash of concern cross his face when he realized I was with Crewe. He walked toward us and met us halfway down the block.

I said, "What's going on?"

"It's Lexie," he said shortly, without greeting. "She asked me to pick up her car and head over to the Roundhouse to take her home."

Without a word, Crewe started toward the BMW.

Michael caught Crewe's arm and stopped him. "Wait. She's—not in great shape."

"Is she hurt?"

"No, no, nothing like that. She's on the edge, though. And she wants to go home, but reporters have staked out her house, so I can't take her there."

No, Lexie Paine seen in the company of Big Frankie Abruzzo's son would not be good publicity.

"That's not a problem," Crewe said. "I'll take her to my place."

"Sorry, Crewe," Michael said, "but she doesn't want to see you right now. Or anybody else, really. But I don't think she ought to be alone. So, Nora—"

"I'll go with her," I said.

"She's not going to be happy about it," Michael warned.

"That's okay." I took a deep breath. "Thank you, Michael."

He shrugged, taking no credit for doing a good deed. "What about the kids? You want me to go to the farm?"

At the farm, he'd have to meet my parents again.

I smiled grimly. "No, the kids are safe enough. I'll call Rawlins just to be sure, but they seem fine."

"If you decide they need somebody to go out there, call me. Meanwhile, I'll see if I can't get rid of the reporters long enough for you and Lexie to make a quick entrance."

"Can you do that?"

"I can try."

Heaven only knew what ruse he had up his sleeve. Michael had orchestrated more than a few distractions in his lifetime. But he said, "Crewe, what do you say you and me go get a beer?"

Crewe stood on the sidewalk looking shattered. The color had drained from his face, and his hands hung limply at his sides.

I touched his arm. "Give her time, Crewe. This won't last, I promise."

I gave him a kiss on the cheek. Then, without saying good-bye to Michael, I went down the sidewalk and climbed into the passenger seat of Lexie's car.

Behind the wheel, Lexie snapped, "Are you my new au pair?"

"Consider it payback," I replied. "Remember the night Todd died? I didn't want anybody with me then, but you insisted. Look, I brought chocolate."

She glared at the gift bags in my hands and blew a sigh. "Close the door and fasten your seat belt."

I obeyed. She put the powerful car into gear and we pulled away. I had only a fleeting glimpse of Michael turning Crewe by the shoulder and walking in the opposite direction.

Finally, I noticed that the covering around the steering column of Lexie's car had been broken. "What happened to your car?"

"I didn't feel like hiking across town to pick it up with all the reporters badgering me. So I asked your beau to bring it to me. He has many talents."

Including how to hot-wire a BMW.

But Michael's proficiency for boosting cars wasn't the only reason Lexie had asked him to come for her. I'd been to the Roundhouse myself a few times, and the grimy police station was no place for a sensitive man like Crewe. Lexie had wanted Michael because he knew the conditions she'd been subjected to. And he wouldn't make a big deal out of her suffering. Crewe, on the other hand, would have been shocked and sympathetic—exactly the kind of empathy Lexie wouldn't want.

Trying to sound nonchalant, I said, "You okay, Lex?"

For two blocks, she didn't answer. But her hands were tight on the steering wheel, and I noticed she paid the strictest attention to the speed limit. She was forcing herself to focus on the job of driving.

At last, she said, "Michael has the most interesting lawyers. They're all smiles and jokes until some invisible switch is thrown, and suddenly they're wolves."

"Do you trust them?"

"I wouldn't want to be on the other side of the table, that's for sure."

We passed the museum and headed into the curving avenue that led to Boathouse Row, the stretch of picturesque Victorian houses built along the Schuylkill River and owned by various regional colleges for their rowing teams. Lexie had managed to purchase one of the buildings—by way of payoffs and at least one shady deal, I was certain. Her house stood in the middle of the historic row. On either side of her property, racks of rowing shells threw shadows across her well-tended lawn.

By the time we reached her home, half a dozen cars were roaring away from the curb where they had been waiting. I assumed Michael had pulled off whatever diversion he used to lure the reporters away. He worked fast.

Lexie pressed a button, and the automatic gate opened. She drove between the wrought iron posts, and the gate closed behind us.

She said, "Those damn kids next door have a portable john now. It's like living beside a fraternity house. I should call the police. They're public servants. They ought to be serving me a little, too, don't you think?"

"Do you still have your Ambien prescription?"

She shook her head. "I want to stay mad for a while."

She drove into the boathouse and closed the garage door behind us, and we got out of the car. Lexie reset the security system, and we went upstairs to her home.

Inside, Lexie's house was a pristine space with simple furniture and a drop-dead art collection that she rotated according to her whim. Lately, she had hung her tall Warhol portrait of Elvis over her fireplace. A vibrant riverscape by a local artist glowed on the opposite wall. The carpet, walls and furniture were white, so the pictures were almost living creatures against the pure backdrop.

She threw her keys into a Waterford crystal bowl and kicked her shoes off onto the thick white rug. The air-conditioning made the house as cold as a Jersey beach in January.

I dropped my things on her dining room table and went into the kitchen to find a bottle of pinot grigio in the fridge. Lexie followed me. While I opened the bottle, she rummaged through the gift bag and free chocolate samples. She found the artisan truffles someone had pressed on Crewe. She opened the box and inhaled their scent.

Then she put the box on the white counter and left the kitchen without a word. I heard her go into her bedroom and close the door.

I puttered. I tidied up her kitchen, put soap into the dishwasher and started the machine. Then I tapped on Lexie's bedroom door. When she didn't answer, I poked my head into the room to check on her. I heard the shower running in her bathroom and figured she was doing as well as anyone could expect.

I closed the door again and went to the living room, where I phoned Blackbird Farm. No answer. Concerned, I called Rawlins on his cell phone.

"Hey, Aunt Nora," my nephew replied when I identified myself. He sounded just as laid-back as before. "Whassup?"

"Rawlins, I'm held up in town for a while, so I'm calling to check up on you again."

He laughed. "Will you give it a rest with the mother-hen routine? Mom leaves us alone all the time."

"Not at my house, she doesn't. Wait, come to think of it, that's exactly what she does. But look, nobody's answering the phone at the farm."

"They're probably outside saluting the sunset or something." Rawlins yawned. "I get off work pretty soon. I'll go make sure everything's under control."

"Thanks. Rawlins, one more thing. If a guy named Chad calls looking for me or for Michael, don't give him the address of the farm, okay? I don't want him showing up there. "

The discovery of Elena's bruises had made me think Chad wasn't as harmless as we'd first thought.

"Whatever you say, Aunt Nora."

"Okay," I said. "Thanks for the update. I'll call you later."

He was laughing. "Anytime."

"Rawlins? I love you."

But he had disconnected.

I snapped my phone shut. "I'll never be a parent," I said.

Although the shower had stopped, Lexie still hadn't come out of her bedroom, so I collected the mail from the front hallway and put it on her desk. I turned on lamps and went outside to listen to the river and to collect my thoughts. Lexie's kayak sat upside down on the deck. Next door, one of the rowing clubs was having a party. I could hear rap music and someone vomiting in the bushes. Not an atmosphere conducive to my quiet reflection.

I went back inside the house and put on a CD of classical music—loud enough only to drown out the rap next door—and I read yesterday's newspaper.

About half an hour later, Lexie came out wearing a demure white nightgown and a light robe thrown around her shoulders. She had showered and washed her hair. But she looked exhausted.

"I'm ready for wine," she said.

We trooped into the kitchen, and I poured us each a glass. I went looking for some food. As usual, Lexie's refrigerator contained little more than chilled wine, some bottled water and a selection of dried-up condiments. There was a take-out container that might have been sitting in the fridge for a week or six months—I couldn't be sure. A bowl of spoiled pears sat on the countertop.

At last I found peanut butter in the cupboard and a box of cocktail crackers. I opened the package of crackers.

Lexie sat on one of the stools, and as if continuing a bizarre conversation she'd started with herself in the shower, she said, "I love my work. The company was important and successful when my father ran it, but I like to think I've made it something even better. I value the reputation I've built."

Soothingly, to keep her from bursting into the hysterics that seemed to bubble beneath the surface, I said, "You deserve credit for what the Paine Investment Group is today, Lex."

"Not all," she said. "But a lot. And now the whole damn place is going to collapse like a house of cards."

"No, it isn't," I protested.

Lexie's face had looked drawn a moment ago, but now the tendons in her neck tightened. "Yes. The situation is very bad, Nora."

"Can you tell me? Can I help?"

She smiled wryly. "I doubt you can help, sweetie."

"I'm a good listener, you know."

"Yes," she said, and quelled a tremor with effort.

She needed food. Perhaps she hadn't eaten since yesterday. Quickly, I opened the jar of Jif and got a knife out of the drawer. Wine and peanut butter—my comfort foods. I slathered the crackers and lined them up in front of my friend.

As I hurried to feed her, Lexie said, "About a week ago, one of our midlevel accountants didn't show up for work. We were worried, of course, and called his home, contacted his family. We discovered he had left the country. That's a hell of a red flag in my business."

"What happened?"

"He disappeared. His departure triggered an immediate internal audit. And the auditors came to me with the news that some of our accounts had been tampered with. He'd been helping to move client money without the proper authorizations."

"How does that happen?"

"It shouldn't happen at all, of course." Calmer, Lexie explained, "When we move large amounts of cash, we require two officers to sign off on the transaction, not to mention other safety controls. Which Hoyt Cavendish helped set up. He knew how to beat them, Nora. Turns out, this accountant had been juggling accounts at Hoyt's request, then hightailed it to a lovely hacienda by the sea."

"You mean they stole the money from the firm?"

"Technically, Hoyt stole the money. He'd been pilfering accounts for a couple of years, and the accountant helped cover his tracks. Last week they must have realized they couldn't make the books appear to balance anymore, so Hoyt paid off his accomplice with a final lump sum. A couple of million dollars."

"Hoyt's been giving the money away, Lex."

My conversation with Daniel about Hoyt's inability to pay the rest of his debt for the Stradivarius made sense. If Hoyt had made charitable donations all over the city—cash he'd stolen from Paine Investment Group clients—he might have made "withdrawals" from client accounts periodically, not just one big theft.

Lexie said, "Yes, I realize now Hoyt has been throwing donations at every charity and orchestra that will sit still long enough to catch his largesse. The little prig loved the spotlight. I assumed he was flashing around his own dough. But, of course, it wasn't his."

"How much cash is missing?"

She massaged her temples. "At least a hundred million."

The sum rocked me back on my heels.

Acknowledging my shock with a nod, Lexie said, "We reported the losses to the Securities and Exchange Commission on Friday. Over the weekend, the IRS got involved. They found a secret witness—someone who had evidence that would prove when Hoyt's wrongdoing got started—someone who obviously had something to gain by playing along. On that person's evidence, I believe, the Treasury Department intended to arrest Hoyt in our offices yesterday."

"They called the meeting of all Hoyt's clients, so they'd be there for the arrest?"

She shook her head. "It was dumb luck the two meetings happened on the same day. As soon as I learned about Hoyt's stealing, I had to break the news to our clients that their money was gone. I wanted to assure them that I intend to repay them, of course. And I had a repayment plan ready."

"So soon?"

"We worked all night on it. If I didn't have a plan, I'd have been out of business within ten minutes of the world discovering Hoyt's scheme. Who would leave their life's savings with a company that loses their money like socks in a dryer?"

"My God, Lex, can you come up with a hundred million?"

"It's going to take time and," she added grimly, "quite a bit of personal sacrifice. But I'll do it. Otherwise, I might as well close the firm and start knitting."

My heart went out to my friend. Not because she stood to lose an incredibly huge amount of money. It was her reputation that mattered most to Lexie. Just looking into her eyes, I could see she was devastated at the thought of losing her most precious possession.

I said, "How did your clients take the bad news?"

"The meeting went as well as could be expected. At

first, almost everybody took it calmly. Then Hoyt showed up—uninvited—and all hell broke loose."

"What happened?"

"The Treasury Department people burst in and announced they were going to arrest Hoyt on the spot. Scooter Zanzibar started shrieking about needing money for a movie. His grandmother, Elena, said something about the marriage being off. Did you know Hoyt was going to marry Elena Zanzibar, of all people?"

"I just learned it myself. Chad Zanzibar was at the meeting?"

"Yes, the little troll."

So he could have run down the street after killing Hoyt, I thought, and shown up at the restaurant fast enough to almost have an alibi. "What about Tierney Cavendish? Was he there?"

"You know Tierney? No, he wasn't at the meeting. But he had visited the office earlier in the day, looking for his father. Heavens, I forgot all about that." Lexie frowned, as if trying to recall details.

Perhaps Lexie hadn't been aware of Tierney's return to the Paine Building. But Crewe and I had seen him in the stairwell, so he had certainly gone back to see his father. I wondered why.

"The Paine Group situation must have been embarrassing for Tierney, too," I murmured.

"His father stealing from friends? Yes, that would be pretty awful."

Lexie caught herself. "Sorry, sweetie. I didn't mean to rub salt in your wound."

"I know. Forget it." My situation paled by comparison with hers. "I can imagine how Tierney felt the moment he realized his father was a crook, that's all." I pushed a cracker into Lexie's hand.

She accepted the cracker, but didn't eat it. "If I'd known the Treasury Department intended to ambush Hoyt in front of everybody, I'd never have called the meeting. And I certainly didn't know they had a secret witness in the wings for added drama."

I took a breath to tell her who the secret witness was.

But Lexie kept talking. She said, "It was such bedlam, let me tell you. Scooter threw a temper tantrum. Elena was so furious I thought she'd have a stroke. And Brandi Schmidt went into hysterics on the spot. Others were angry, too, of course. And Hoyt looked like he was going to collapse. It was a real melodrama. I immediately called a halt to the meeting. I'd been blindsided, too, but I knew shouting wasn't going to help. I insisted everyone clear the room so I could get Hoyt's story straight."

"That's when you argued with him."

"Yes." One-handed, she continued to rub her forehead. "I'm so ashamed, Nora. I was furious. He stole money from people who trusted me, but I—I shouldn't have lost control the way I did."

"What did he say? Did he defend himself?"

She laughed shortly. "Believe it or not, that's when he punched my painting."

I winced. "What did you do?"

She shook her head, unable to say more. I saw her quiver with emotion—fear or revulsion or anger, I couldn't be sure.

I reached to cover her hand with mine. "Lexie, we'll help you beat this. The police must realize they're wrong about you. The pressure's off you now."

"Nora—"

"Crewe and I have been asking around."

"Don't." She pulled away from me and shook her head. "I don't want either of you dragged into this."

"But—"

"I'm serious, sweetie. It's my problem. Let me figure it out." Her eyes were wild again. Then she clasped her hands until the knuckles turned white while she fought for control. I wanted her to cry, to let out the tension that clearly thrummed inside her. But she didn't.

Coldly, she said, "For one thing, I want to know who this damn secret witness is."

"Oh."

"Whoever it is may have triggered the whole thing. Of course, I know it all starts with Hoyt. But this goddamn secret witness has some explaining to do, too."

"Oh, Lex, I sincerely hope not," I said on a sigh.

"Why?"

"Because the secret witness," I said, "is my father."

Lexie stared at me. Then she said, "Oh, hell."

Chapter 12

My phone rang on the counter and I picked it up. I didn't recognize the number displayed on the screen, so I answered warily.

"It's me," Michael said. "How's the patient?"

"Not bad."

"Would she flip out if a couple of guests dropped in?"

"You mean you? Now?"

"And Crewe. He just got a hot tip that's going to blow the lid off your murder case."

I took a look at Lexie, who was still absorbing my bombshell about Daddy. I said, "I think she can handle it."

"We'll be right over."

I told Lexie that Michael and Crewe were on their way.

Instead of exploding, she went back to her bedroom to get dressed and dry her hair.

I took that as a good sign.

Twenty minutes later, I turned off the security system and opened the door to Michael and Crewe, who were laden down with take-out bags marked with the logo of a restaurant that required ordinary citizens to wait weeks for a reservation.

"What's all this?" I asked.

"We ordered dinner before I got the phone call," Crewe explained. "So we decided to bring it here. There's plenty to share. The chef heard I was in the dining room and sent out extra food. I hope that's okay."

"You're a lifesaver. We were just about to scrape out the bottom of the peanut butter jar. Why don't you take it all to the kitchen, Crewe? You know the way."

He had regained his color and looked positively jaunty as he carried the food to the kitchen.

I held Michael back, and we lingered in the hallway. I said, "Let's give them a minute alone."

"You sure that's a good idea?"

"I'm afraid all I'm doing is helping her stay under control. It might help if she could blow off some steam."

"By yelling at Crewe? Well, it can't hurt." He leaned against the newel post. "What about you? Have you been in touch with . . . the rest of your family?"

I put my back against the opposite wall, creating as much distance between us as possible in the small space. "I called Rawlins a little while ago. He'll make sure everything's under control."

"You sure about that?" He smiled a little.

"No," I said ruefully. "But my parents managed to raise three daughters without endangering our lives, so I think they can manage a few grandchildren for one night."

Michael shook his head in wonder. "I guess everybody has parents, but somehow I never pictured yours so—well—"

"Outlandish?"

"Crazy, I was going to say. You sure you're from the same gene pool? I mean, your sister Libby fell right out of your mother's apple tree, and Emma's the spitting image of your dad. Come to think of it, the twins—"

"Okay, okay, I get the point." I smiled, too, but it faded quickly.

A moment passed while we kept our distance. There was something new between us now. Something painful.

Although I'd never been happier with anyone in my life, I suddenly found it too hard to look into Michael's face. Last night after he'd left the farm, I had struggled to put a name to the feeling I had inside. In the middle of the night, I figured it out.

I couldn't help feeling betrayed.

And humiliated.

Why did he have to choose Emma, of all people? The one woman who could make me feel the most inadequate. And now she was the fertile one, too.

During the most tumultuous time of our relationship, Michael and I had deliberately tried to have a baby together. And we'd failed. Maybe it was for the best, I supposed, because it would have been wrong to bring a child into an unstable home.

But here was Emma, impregnated in a matter of weeks.

So I hugged myself and avoided Michael's gaze. I found my voice and tried to sound neutral. "How's Em?"

"She's been better." He shrugged. "You okay?"

"No, but I—"

I wanted to say I'd get used to the situation. But I doubted it.

So I said, "Lexie just told me the whole story of what happened in her office. It's bad. Very bad, Michael. She could lose the firm. And she—she's never been like this—all emotionally shut down. Not since she was a kid. Not since her cousin raped her. Back then, Lexie was too young to cope. Now she seems just as distraught and unable to voice it."

"Whatever happened to the guy? The cousin?"

"Why?"

"No reason. Just curious."

"Her family decided she shouldn't have to go through an unpleasant trial. They sent him to Arizona, I think. He's a real estate developer or something now."

Michael kept his face impassive. "Interesting."

I shivered suddenly. The house's air-conditioning had finally chilled me.

Michael took off his suit jacket and slung it around my shoulders.

His hands lingered there, and he squeezed me. "Don't worry. You need to hear what Crewe's learned."

He took me by the hand, but I pulled away. I turned and led him to the kitchen, where Crewe had just told Lexie something that sent her plunking into a chair.

I hurried to her side. "What's going on? Lex, are you okay?"

"The police," Crewe said triumphantly, "have just issued a warrant for the arrest of Tierney Cavendish."

"Tierney! Why? How? What did they learn?"

"Somebody must have told them that Tierney was in the Paine Building at the time his father died. But get this—he can't be found. He's disappeared."

"Why would Tierney kill his father?" I asked.

Almost gleeful, Crewe said, "He must have been angry with Hoyt for not giving him the money to stabilize Amazon Chocolate! So he killed him."

"But," I said, "there wasn't enough time, was there? Crewe, we saw Tierney at the restaurant just a few minutes before we ran up the street to see Hoyt's body on the sidewalk. How could Tierney have—"

"He must have moved fast," Crewe acknowledged. "But the important thing is that Lexie's no longer Public Enemy Number One."

I frowned. "I can't believe he'd kill his own father."

"He ran away," Crewe said. "That's incriminating, isn't it?"

"Yes, but—"

"Lexie's in the clear," Crewe insisted. "The police believe Tierney killed Hoyt. Isn't that fantastic?"

"Sure." Michael defused the tension by reaching for the take-out containers. "It's a good development for the moment."

"For the moment?" Crewe's tone was tense.

"Relax," Michael said. "This is good. The heat's off Lexie while the cops hunt for Cavendish's son."

"In other words," Lexie said to Crewe, "down, boy. I'm not off the hook yet."

Crewe flushed.

Michael began opening containers. "That's not what I mean. Maybe he killed his dad, maybe not. You know the family dynamic better than I do. The cops are grabbing at anything because the case is high profile."

"So they're busy chasing down any suspect that looks possible," I said.

"Right. Let them focus on the son for a while. Meanwhile, the rest of you can keep asking questions. With all those people involved, there's bound to be a lot more information floating around. The game isn't over yet. And you guys know the players better than anyone."

Crewe said, "You don't think Tierney did it?"

"It doesn't matter what I think. Only what the cops are thinking."

"But surely you have a theory."

Michael popped a plantain chip into his mouth and spoke around it. "I dunno. It wasn't premeditated. Nobody had enough time to figure out the logistics."

"So it was a crime of passion," Crewe said.

With a grim smile, Michael said, "Sure, call it that if you like. Does the son have that kind of passion in him? Or does he do drugs? Have a violent history? A short fuse?"

"We don't know him well enough," I said.

"So the cops needed to start someplace. They are probably thinking he's got the best motive. He needs money, right? That's always a good one."

"Hoyt doesn't have any money left," I said. "I think he gave it all away."

"Did the son know that? Do the cops know now?"

"Probably not."

"So until they do . . ."

I said, "We try to solve the case."

"How do we do that?" Crewe asked. "Nobody's going to confess."

"You talk to people," Michael said. "Finesse them."

I said, "Hoyt's personal life was obviously more complicated than it appeared. That's a place to start."

Lexie handed her empty wineglass to me for a refill. She had dressed in a pair of skinny jeans and a sleeveless white T-shirt that showed off the muscle in her toned arms. She still looked tired, but more composed than before. And definitely more glamorous. She'd taken time to brush on some makeup. But she kept her distance from Crewe.

She said, "I could look at his day planner. I'd like a few answers myself."

I poured her another glass. "You have his day planner?"

"Sure. It's on the Paine Group computer system. I have the override code."

"Will the police let you back into your office, I wonder?"

"I don't need to be at the office," she replied. "I can do it from here. Come with me."

"Can we eat first?" Michael asked. "I'm starving."

"Bring it along," Lexie said over her shoulder, already on her way to her home office.

Pulling Michael's coat around me more securely, I followed her.

Lexie's desk faced the windows, and we could see the river and shapes of the trees on the opposite shore, thanks to the outdoor lights and the moonlight. She flipped on the Tiffany-style desk lamp and slid into her chair.

Behind her desk hung a triptych by an emerging contemporary Chinese artist. The half-human, half-machine figures on the canvas seemed to twist over a fiery red lake that burned with color. Fleetingly, I wondered why Lexie had chosen to place such a tortured piece over her work space.

The laptop computer blinked awake as soon as Lexie touched the keypad.

She said, "Unless the police have shut down the system, it should only be a matter of moments before I can—ah, yes, still up and running. I knew I could count on Carla. She would keep the system up in the event of nuclear war."

"Lex," I said. "About Crewe."

"Yes?"

"He's only trying to help."

"Of course, sweetie. Okay, here we go." She peered at the computer screen. "Into Hoyt's day planner. Let's see, shall we?"

I leaned over her shoulder and watched the computer screen as Lexie clicked expertly through the calendar. It took me several pages before I caught on enough to follow the information.

Lexie said, "Hoyt only worked two days a week, see? And he saw a few clients—mostly over the lunch hour. Good thing his assistant was so meticulous. She's got every six-minute segment accounted for."

"Every six minutes?"

"So we can calculate how many hours we devote to each client, sweetie. Standard procedure. Oh, and his out-of-the-building appointments are in red, too. Look."

I followed her finger and saw the names clearly typed. "Murusha and Donaldson?"

"Yes, Hoyt had an appointment with them last Wednesday."

"Can't be the Murusha and Donaldson I know. They're OB-GYN oncologists. Todd did a research project with them."

Lexie laughed drily. "Okay, must be a law firm with a similar name. We do a lot of business with trust lawyers, and I'm not familiar with them all. Look, on this day Hoyt had lunch with Elena Zanzibar at the Palm. And a meeting at three with Brandi Schmidt. A four o'clock with someone else. I never took him for a ladies' man. He certainly didn't look the part."

"I don't think Hoyt and Brandi had that kind of relationship."

"Me neither." Lexie scanned the screen quickly. "The rest of these names are clients and coworkers. Ah, here's the crucial meeting with that damned accountant I was telling you about." She planted her forefinger on the screen. "I wonder if this is the day Hoyt paid him off. I'll check the transaction records."

She skipped to another screen, and I gave up trying to follow. I said, "I never realized how easy it would be to steal money from a company like yours, Lex."

"It isn't easy at all. It requires two people who are willing to jeopardize their entire lives for—usually—very little money. Hoyt gave his accomplice just two million. Is that enough to subsist on for the rest of your life? While evading extradition? Not unless you're willing to live in a shack in a Third World country. Life on the run is expensive. Michael, dear, would you run away from your life here on two million bucks?"

Michael preceded Crewe into the office, both of them juggling plates. He said, "Not alone, I wouldn't, no."

Lexie smiled without taking her steely gaze from her computer. "How romantic. Does that mean you'd do it with Nora? An idyllic life in a cottage by the sea for the rest of eternity together?"

"She gets sunburned," he said.

Lexie laughed, then got a whiff of the aroma rising from the take-out containers. "Good heavens, Crewe, what are we eating?"

"Cuban sandwiches."

As far from Lexie's desk as he could manage, Crewe cut the pressed sandwiches in half and put them on plates. He handed one to Michael, and he picked up a sandwich for himself. "They're a delicacy, Lexie. Some pork that's been marinated in garlic and citrus, then roasted for hours, add some cheese, pickles and a dash of mustard. Then you press it in a double-sided grill. It's called a 'midnight sandwich' because Cubans ate them after working all day in the sugar refineries. It doesn't look like much, but—" He kissed his fingers.

She took a careful peek between the halves of the bread on her plate. "It looks messy."

"Life is messy," Crewe said. "Think of this meal as a metaphor."

She got up from her desk chair and carried her meal to the sofa. Sitting down at one end, she crossed one long leg over the other and said, "I do like the literary side of you, Crewe, darling. Better than the protective, alpha-male side, perhaps. It's more authentic somehow."

Crewe smiled at last and sat down cautiously at the other end of the sofa.

I took Lexie's desk chair. Michael slid a plate across to me and leaned on the far edge of the desk. Unconsciously, he glanced up at the abstract Chinese painting behind me. I thought I saw him flinch at Lexie's choice in art. He popped another plantain chip into his mouth. "What have you found?"

"That Hoyt Cavendish was either seeing an obstetrician or a law firm with the same name." I smiled wryly. "Other than that, it's going to take Lexie more time to make sense of Hoyt's appointments."

"What about his phone records? That's usually golden."

"His calls aren't listed here."

"Next screen," Lexie said. "Go up to the top and click on the little telephone icon. It's blue."

I obeyed, and immediately a long list of phone numbers popped up with names and notes in an adjacent column. Every column flashed with a different color to help make the information more readable. To me, it just seemed more confusing. So I concentrated hard on the screen and barely heard what the others were saying as they ate.

I interrupted them once. "You'll have to read through this, Lex. It makes no sense to me. Wait—here's the Murusha and Donaldson name again. And the number."

"Don't worry about that, Nora. Have some dinner. You must be starved."

Michael nudged my plate closer to the computer keyboard, but I sat staring at the screen and trying to think.

"Delicious," Lexie said after a bite of sandwich. "You say you know the chef?"

"Only by phone," Crewe said. "I'm still incognito."

"I don't suppose he'd give you this recipe?"

"It's not hard to make a Cuban sandwich."

"No?"

"No," Crewe said. "It only takes time. We could try it sometime."

"I don't really care for your fancy cuisine," Lexie said. "It's getting ridiculous these days. Piling all the food in the middle of a plate like an edible Eiffel Tower? All those Asian, Latin, French flavors fused into something unrecognizable? It's as if some chefs are trying too damn hard to impress, and we have to swallow the swill they force on us. It's an assault on the palate. An assault . . ."

Her voice wavered on the word, and suddenly her eyes filled with tears.

I stood up to go to her, my heart aching. But Michael sent me a look that stopped me.

Crewe slid across the sofa and gently disengaged the sandwich from Lexie's hands. He put it on the desk and gathered her up into his arms.

Lexie wept then. She put her face into his shoulder and cried. Hoarse sobs wracked her throat and shuddered through her body.

Crewe held her, rocked her, said nothing.

It took all my strength to sit down again. I was relieved to see Lexie finally show some emotion. She would need time to recover from her ordeal with the police and from her partner's terrible death. Maybe Crewe was a better friend for her than I could be right now.

But it was hard to see her suffer.

Michael watched her, too, looking thoughtful.

Fighting down my own tears, I found a fat yellow phone book in the desk drawer. I flipped through the pages until I found the lists of physicians. I compared the number in the book with the number on the screen. The same.

"Huh," I said.

Michael turned to me. "Something interesting?"

"Why would Hoyt see a gynecologist?"

"Maybe one of the doctors was his client."

"That's probably it. Would I be violating twelve different laws if I printed out the information on these screens?"

"Yes. You don't want to become an accessory."

"You think I should use more finesse, right?" I hesitated. "How do I do that?"

"Depends," he said around a mouthful. "Who do you want to learn about?"

I considered the possibilities. "Brandi Schmidt, for one. She lied to me about her relationship with Hoyt. But I can't just ask her why she lied."

"What else do you know about her?"

"She works in television. She's disabled, in a wheelchair. She's on the board of the Music Academy."

Michael shook his head. "I mean a weakness."

I looked up at him uneasily and found his blue eyes looking anything but choirboy.

He said, "Find something. Find it and use it."

"You mean, use information against her? Blackmail."

"Pressure," Michael corrected. "Find a weak spot and poke it. Or if she's got a secret, make her think somebody knows it. Let her worry until she makes a mistake."

"That's . . ."

"Finesse."

"Immoral, I was going to say."

"Murder isn't?"

His gaze was steady and challenging. But Michael's phone buzzed in his pocket then. He glanced at the screen before going outside onto the deck to take the call.

Her storm of tears over, Lexie sat back and dried her eyes with Crewe's proffered handkerchief.

"Don't you wonder," she said, trying to sound normal once the door slid closed behind Michael, "who he talks to? Bookies, do you suppose? Underworld kingpins? Contract killers?"

Crewe said, "Maybe it's just his dry cleaner calling to schedule a pickup."

I doubted Michael did much business with dry cleaners.

"I don't think so," Lexie said. "When I asked him to bring my car to the police station, he broke into it and hot-wired the engine, slick as can be. And you should have seen the way he walked in. Like he owned the place. The police looked at him like he was Tony Soprano. Or maybe the mayor. I couldn't tell which. They dislike him. But there's some strange kind of respect, too."

"Weird," Crewe said.

"I'm afraid I didn't do him any favors," Lexie said. "When he showed up to get me out of there, the cops probably decided he has a connection to me—and to Hoyt's murder."

"Old news." I was surprised to hear my voice sound so hard. "The police assume he's connected to all crime."

"Do you ever ask him about jail, Nora?" Crewe said. "About his prison experience?"

"Oh, God." Lexie shivered.

I stowed the phone book back in the desk drawer and closed it. "No, I don't ask. He doesn't talk about it. I know he doesn't want me to hear about it. But it was awful for him."

Michael came back inside, thoughtfully snapping his phone shut. He looked at me, all business, his dinner forgotten. "You staying here tonight? Or you want to go home?"

"Go." Lexie shooed me away with one hand. "I'm finished bawling. I don't need you here."

I was unwilling to leave, but with the hope that Crewe

might be allowed to remain with Lexie, I said, "Okay. But only if you're sure."

"I'm very sure, sweetie."

"I can take you home," Michael said. "Delmar's bringing me a car. But then there's a thing I need to take care of."

"Well, the good news is that at this time of night," Lexie said cheerfully, "it can't be anything too serious. Or can it?"

The expression on Michael's face said it was serious indeed.

"What's going on, Mick?"

Without answering Crewe, Michael slid his cell phone back into the pocket of his trousers. Almost to himself, he said, "It's going to be common knowledge soon."

"What is?"

The three of us sat still and waited.

Michael sighed and came clean. "My brother stole a truck. It was full of microwave ovens. At least, that's what everybody thought. The cops just found the real cargo hidden inside the boxes. Knockoff goods from China. Sneakers, mostly. And some purses."

"You mean designer handbags? Imitations?"

He shrugged. "Whatever they are, they're worth, like, five thousand bucks apiece. A bunch of celebrities are on a waiting list to get them. Some comedian's wife had a meltdown in Barneys when she heard the purses got impounded. Let me tell you, I don't understand at all. These purses are ugly as hell."

"You've seen them?" I asked.

"Yeah, with buckles and straps and junk hanging off them." He used his hands to vaguely identify the size and shape of a handbag. "Anyway, the worst of it is there's some endangered snake that donated its skin for these purse things. Suddenly, it's an international incident. A bunch of federal agencies got wind of that, so it's . . . more complicated than I first thought."

"Yikes," Lexie said.

"Anyway, I gotta go see some people. And then I need to pick up Emma."

"Emma?" Crewe said. "What for?"

"She's staying with me," Michael replied, not meeting anyone's eyes.

"Really? Isn't that kinda dangerous?"

Lexie poked Crewe, who stopped smiling abruptly.

I said, "Has she given up drinking?"

"She's trying," Michael replied steadily.

"With your help."

"Yes."

So there it was. They'd been driven together by the perfect storm of conditions. He had wanted a family of his own, and now he was going to get it. Emma had been longing for another bad boy to replace her dead husband, Jake, and who could be badder than Michael?

And now he was helping my sister stay sober, too—perhaps the ideal way to solidify a relationship.

My head got light, and a swampy gush of the river started to ooze around my feet.

Michael came over and eased my head between my knees. "Breathe," he said.

I breathed. The ooze eventually receded. His hand felt very warm on the back of my neck.

"You could have told me," I said, not exactly talking to Michael. I wanted Emma to hear me, too.

"Come on," he said quietly, steadying me as I sat up. "I'll take you home."

Lexie stood abruptly and went to Michael. She gave him a fierce hug. "Thank you, sweetie. I'm so sorry I asked you to rescue me tonight. That's the last thing you need, right? To be associated with this Cavendish mess? And me?"

Michael held her at a distance by her arms. "That doesn't matter. The important thing is you're out of there. Take some time to think now. You've got options."

"I will."

Crewe stood up, too. "Mick, thanks."

They shook hands. "No problem."

"We'll ask more questions, see what we can find out about the people around Cavendish."

"Be smart about it," Michael advised. "Make sure you're a few steps ahead before you go cross-examining anybody. And when in doubt, call the cops. Don't try to be a hero."

Crewe nodded. "Yeah. I could end up looking stupid."

"Or worse."

I pushed Michael's coat off my shoulders and got unsteadily to my feet. "I don't need a ride home. I'll just take the train. Rawlins can pick me up at the station. If I could just call a cab—"

"Sweetie," Lexie began.

"It's okay," Michael said to her.

I didn't want to go with him. In fact, I dreaded being alone with Michael. I needed time to think.

He wasn't taking no for an answer, though.

We said good night to Crewe and Lexie, who both hugged me and tried to behave cheerfully. Michael and I went outside into the muggy heat.

Delmar, the hulking Abruzzo bodyguard with the dent in his forehead, waited outside Lexie's house. He leaned against a long car that was parked on the street, and he watched two giggling coeds try to climb the fence of the house next to Lexie's where the party still rocked.

Delmar removed the earphones from his iPod when we approached. I might have been invisible, because he didn't even glance my way. "You want me to sit in the back, boss?"

"Yes." Michael held the door for me while I slipped into the passenger seat. The vehicle was a low sedan shaped like a spaceship. It had white leather seats and an eight-track tape player in the dashboard. The word ROYALE was etched into the glove compartment. Michael closed the door.

The two men muttered outside the car.

Then Delmar climbed into the seat behind me. The springs under his seat groaned. Very faintly, I could almost hear the music from his iPod, too. It sounded like Dean Martin.

When Michael slid behind the wheel and closed his door, I said, "I'd be happier taking a cab."

"I wouldn't." He tipped his head to indicate the muscleman in the backseat. "Delmar's under orders to stay with me. Sorry."

"Whose orders?" I asked, even though I knew it was Big Frankie who cared enough about Michael's safety to provide round-the-clock protection when the situation warranted it.

Michael said, "It's not a big deal."

"Is he carrying a gun?"

"I don't know," Michael said testily. "You want me to ask him?"

"You don't frisk your employees?"

Michael started the car. "He's not my employee. He works for my father. Relax, will you?"

"I don't want to relax." I turned in the seat to face him. "Lexie says you made quite an impression on the police tonight."

"So what else is new?"

"How involved with this truck hijacking are you? Or is there something else going on, and the truck is some kind of decoy story you cooked up? If Delmar's got your back, that means you're in danger."

"I'm not. Delmar doesn't have anything better to do now that my brother's locked up. My father can't stand Delmar hanging around the house all the time. So chill. I'm stuck with him."

"You're making it all sound so plausible," I said. "But if federal agencies are involved, there's serious jail time coming for somebody."

"That's what has you so upset?"

"That, and a few other things." I took a deep breath. "You had to steal Lexie's car tonight, Michael? You had to break into it and—and jump the engine or whatever?"

"What was I supposed to do?"

"Call a taxi. Take a bus. Walk, for crying out loud, like a normal person!"

"She wanted her car. She wanted me to pick her up so she could drive it home without going to her parking garage, where some reporters were looking for her. What's the problem?"

I grabbed the door handle and shoved. A second later, I was out of the car and standing in the street. Michael got out of his side, too, and slammed the door. We glared at each other over the roof of the car.

I said, "You don't even think like a law-abiding citizen. Your first impulse is to commit a crime."

"Jesus Christ," he said. "I did a favor for your friend."

"And what about all that advice you gave us in there? How to pressure people into telling us what we want to hear?"

"You asked! It's not my fault if you didn't like what you heard."

"That's not what's going on here. Eventually, Michael, I worry you're going to find yourself doing more than stealing cars."

"I didn't steal—"

"You broke the rules. Worse yet, you *like* breaking rules. It comes naturally to you."

"What about you? Talk about natural inclinations. How come you can't leave this Cavendish murder alone? Don't you see where it's taking you?"

"I'm trying to help the people I love!"

"Okay, so I boosted Lexie's car tonight because she's somebody you love, too. What's the difference?"

"You can't see it?"

Delmar chose that moment to get out of the backseat. He said, "Boss?"

Michael's voice turned icy. "Get in the car, Delmar."

"I'm just saying, we got to get going." Delmar tapped the enormous sports watch on his wrist.

Michael checked his watch, too. "I know, I know. Get back in the car."

Delmar obeyed.

Trembling with the effort not to scream at him, I said, "What are you and your goon planning to do tonight?"

Michael braced both hands on the roof of the car, put his head down and shook it. "You don't need to know, Nora. I don't want you in this."

"Illegal goods from China, endangered species, crossing state lines? I'm doing the math, Michael. Federal crime means penitentiaries."

He lifted his head and stared hard at me from across the car's roof. "I think you're upset because I'm picking up your sister."

In the dark, I couldn't see the nuances in Michael's face. But the challenge was in his voice. I got back into the car and closed the door.

He walked around the car twice to calm himself down. When he got into the driver's seat and slammed the door at last, he said, "I thought we were on the same side in all of this. It's Emma who needs both of us right now."

The last person I wanted to hear about in that moment was my sister. "Will you take me to the station, please? Or should I hitchhike?"

He drove. Delmar listened to his music. I sat in the passenger seat and tried not to let my emotions overwhelm me. Once we got back into the city, Michael parked at a hydrant and walked me to the train, where he was crazy enough to try to kiss me good night.

"Don't," I said, turning away.

He put his hands in the pockets of his trousers. "I'll call you later."

"No."

"I want to know if you get home safely."

I walked away without looking back. From the train

car, I telephoned Rawlins to ask if he could pick me up at the Yardley station.

"Sure," my nephew said. "I get off work in fifteen minutes."

"Thanks, Rawlins."

I closed my phone and sat in the train, thinking, as it pulled out of the city. I was one of two passengers in the car on this, the last run of the night. The other woman sat with her nose in a Lisa Scottoline novel. I wished I had something equally diverting to take my mind off the mystery of my own life, but I didn't.

I thought about crying, but quickly decided it was better to stay angry. Sometimes Michael seemed so close to becoming a domesticated animal that I had hope for him. At other times, I realized I had been fighting a part of his personality that would probably never change.

The other woman finished her book and left the paperback on an empty seat when she got off. I picked up the book on my way off the train.

I tried to immerse myself in the Scottoline story until Rawlins appeared at the train station. He drove me home, talking animatedly. He was excited about his new girlfriend, I realized. A girl who was easy to talk to, unchallenging and simple. Who wasn't going off to college in a couple of months. Tonight Rawlins seemed happy, all annoyance at her constant pestering gone. Or maybe he'd just eaten too much blueberry cheesecake ice cream and was on a sugar high.

At Blackbird Farm, Rawlins parked the minivan beneath the oaks, and we got out. A shiny black car sat on the gravel driveway near the paddock fence. Emma's herd of ponies were poking their noses through the rails.

Toby trotted across the lawn to us, tail wagging. Rawlins bent down to ruffle his fur, and Toby wriggled happily.

"Whoa," Rawlins said, looking at the house. "Who's having a party?"

Every light in the house was turned on.

I said, "Your grandparents, no doubt. If anyone offers you marijuana—"

"Just say no?"

"'No, thank you.' They're due a little respect."

We headed up the sidewalk together, but Rawlins snapped his fingers. "I forgot my backpack in the car."

While he jogged back to the minivan, I went up the porch steps, sniffing the air for any telltale scent of illegal substances. I pushed open the unlocked back door. Toby shoved ahead of me, and I stepped into the kitchen after him.

And someone put a gun to my head.

He said, "Don't move. Or you're dead."

Chapter 13

My whole family sat very still around the kitchen table, their hands laid flat on the tablecloth. They stared in silent horror as the gunman snaked his arm around me from behind and grabbed my shoulder. He pressed the cold barrel of the gun into my cheek, and my heart stopped.

He said, "Don't say a word."

I said, "My nephew's outside. He's coming right behind me. Don't hurt him."

"Didn't I say not to talk?"

"Sorry. I wasn't—sorry. Just don't hurt my nephew."

He gave me a push, and I stumbled away from him. I caught my balance on the kitchen counter and turned around.

The man with the gun was Tierney Cavendish.

He had sweated through his white shirt, and his grip on the gun didn't look very steady as he pointed it at me. His long dark hair hung in damp strands around his face. He wasn't handsome anymore. He looked desperate.

He said, "Shut up. Don't talk. Let the kid come inside and I won't hurt him."

A second later, Rawlins be-bopped through the door. Tierney caught him with the same maneuver he'd used on me, only Rawlins was smart enough to obey and didn't make a sound. With the gun jammed to his throat, my nephew dropped his backpack on the floor and stared at me with wide, frightened eyes.

I said, "It's okay. Don't panic."

Tierney goaded Rawlins forward. "Sit down at the table, everybody. Keep your hands where I can see them."

Mama and Daddy sat very still beside each other. In the chair at the head of the table perched their valet, Oscar. At the other end was Henry Fineman, the computer repairman. Between them, Lucy glowered.

"Where's Maximus?" I said. "Where's the baby?"

"Sleeping," Mama said. "Finally. He missed his nap and got a little cranky. I put him down half an hour ago."

"He was very bad," Lucy said. "He wouldn't stop crying."

"We couldn't find his binky," Henry volunteered.

Rawlins said, "I left it on the counter by the coffeepot."

Lucy said, "I didn't go near it. I'm not allowed to drink coffee."

Patronizingly, Henry said, "Coffee is bad for little girls."

Lucy stuck her tongue out at him.

Oscar said, "This man is pointing his gun at us again."

"Shut up." Tierney quaked as he waved the gun first at one person, then another. He looked exhausted and angry. "All of you. Be quiet so I can think. Why there's a whole French farce going on, I don't understand. I thought only you lived here."

He had pointed the gun at me again, so I said, "Normally, it's just me. You caught us at a bad time."

"Sit down," he commanded.

"There aren't enough chairs," Rawlins pointed out.

"I'll stand," I said.

I tried to think of all the hostage situations I'd ever seen on television. Unfortunately, the only ones I could recall were those that ended in a shoot-out or with the cavalry charging through the back door. A few psychological tactics swirled vaguely around in my head. I wondered if my father really did have any marijuana.

I cleared my throat. "Would anyone like some lemonade?"

"We've had lemonade," Mama said. "Then everybody had to go to the bathroom, which was a terrible ordeal."

Tierney said, "We're not going through that again."

"Then we ordered pizza for dinner."

"We're not going through *that* again, either," snapped Tierney.

"Nora, dear, you should really have something besides Lean Cuisine in your freezer. What if friends drop by?"

"Hey," Henry objected. "I was the one who paid for the pizza! Somebody owes me forty bucks. And I don't even like mushrooms!"

"Mushrooms are good for you. It's the pepperoni you insisted on that's giving everyone heartburn." Mama gave an indelicate burp. "There. You see?"

I put both hands up to silence the squabbling. "How long has this been going on?"

"Since three o'clock," Henry said.

Sounding victimized, Mama said, "It's been a very long day, Nora. First we missed our afternoon yoga session because Oscar and I got to talking about his diminished libido—"

Oscar muttered, "Dear God."

"It's nothing to be ashamed of," Mama told him. "But you can't expect to perform your best without taking corrective measures. I can prescribe a diet. Which will not include pepperoni, I'm telling you right now."

Lucy said, "Can I go to the bathroom?"

"No," Tierney said.

Daddy said to me, "He finally locked the twins in the powder room. It seemed like a good idea to all of us."

"Those two," Tierney said darkly, "are insane."

Daddy explained, "They tried to poison his lemonade. With some of that plant food you keep on the windowsill."

Good for the twins, I thought.

"But Henry drank it instead."

Henry said, "I didn't drink enough to make me sick."

"You threw up," Lucy said accusingly. "You threw up in the sink. It was gross."

"I did some spitting. There's a difference. And let's not talk about gross, Miss Smarty-pants. You were the one who—"

"All right, all right!" Tierney shouted. "I can't stand it anymore!"

Everyone fell silent. The muscles in Tierney's neck looked ready to tear from strain.

From my handbag on the floor where I'd dropped it, my cell phone began to jingle. Michael was calling, I thought. Making sure I got home safely.

I wanted to scream for his help. But Michael was an hour away, maybe longer. And I hadn't left him in the mood for rescuing me.

Meanwhile, Tierney's anxiety had clearly reached a breaking point. He pointed the gun at my purse.

But he didn't pull the trigger. We all waited while the phone rang six times and finally stopped. But immediately, Rawlins's phone began to play a tune. We waited while it finished, whereupon the house phone shrilled. When the answering machine kicked on, we all heard Michael say tersely, "Call me."

Then he hung up.

Into the silence that followed the answering machine's beep, I said, "I don't think we've actually met, Tierney. I'm Nora."

"I know," he said. "You followed me yesterday."

"Not intentionally." Endeavoring to sound nonthreatening, I said, "Look, I'm very sorry about your father. You have my condolences. Hoyt was a kind man. A generous man."

From the table, my mother made a rude noise.

Tierney pointed the gun at her.

"Sorry," she mumbled, looking only slightly contrite. "But he didn't like to dance. In my experience, small men have small feet and are usually light on them. But not Hoyt. What a wet blanket."

I said, "We're all very sorry for your loss, Tierney. You must be feeling terrible."

"How did you guess?" he asked. "Was it the gun that tipped you off?"

My own temper suddenly sizzled to life. "It's been a long day for all of us. So sarcasm is hardly going to make this situation better. Plus there are impressionable children in the room."

"I know what you're trying to do. You're trying to be reasonable."

"Well, somebody has to try! What exactly do you hope to accomplish here? You've taken a whole family hostage—for what? What do you want?"

"I don't know anymore! It was much clearer before I met all you people."

"Would you like an aspirin?" I asked. "I know I would."

"Yes." With a glimmer of resignation, he said, "I'd like two aspirin, please."

"Then we'll listen to what you have to say," I suggested. "We'll all be quiet, won't we? And you can tell us what you want us to do."

Mama sat up straighter. "If you want to know what I think—"

"We're *all* going to be *quiet*, Mama, while Tierney has his aspirin."

Obediently, she subsided in her chair.

I found a bottle of Excedrin and portioned out tablets for Tierney and myself. When Oscar looked hopeful, I gave him some pills, too. He gulped them gratefully. Mama gave him a disapproving look.

After swallowing the pills, Tierney seemed to get a grip on himself. He said, "Okay, here's the new plan. I want to lock everybody up someplace while I talk to you." He pointed the gun at Daddy. "And you." He pointed it at me.

"Very sensible," I said. "Why don't we ask everyone else to step into the scullery for a few minutes?"

"The—?"

"The little room right over there. It has a lock on the door, if that makes you comfortable. And the windows have been painted shut for years. Nobody will get in or out without your permission."

"I hate the scullery," Lucy said. "Remember when the twins kept that lizard in there?"

I said, "What lizard?"

"It's okay, Aunt Nora. He went away all by himself."

"C'mon, Luce," Rawlins said, seeing my expression. "We'll play a game in the scullery."

"What game?"

"Any game you like. We'll tie up somebody and play Joan of Arc again. Remember that one?"

She pointed at Henry. "I want to tie him up."

"It's a deal."

"Wait a minute," said Henry. "Joan of Arc?"

"Okay, everybody." I raised my voice. "In our most orderly way, let's proceed into the scullery, shall we? I promise it won't be for long."

With his gun, Tierney gestured the family group across the kitchen and into the scullery, where my mother could be heard chiding Oscar about his diet as the door closed. I turned the lock and put the key on the counter.

Then Tierney came back to the kitchen table and sat down.

For the first time I noticed a bandage on the thumb of his left hand.

I said, "What happened to your thumb?"

"Your daughter bit me." He peeled off the bandage cautiously. "At least it's not bleeding anymore."

"When was your last tetanus shot?"

"I live in the jungle. My immunizations are all current."

"Then you should be safe. Lucy's not my daughter, by the way. She's my niece. My sister Libby's child."

Tierney peered at me as if I had suggested a second onslaught was on its way. "There are more of you?"

"Just two more. Libby and my sister Emma."

He shook his head as if trying to clear cobwebs. "I have a vague memory of only one of you. One who beat up Carlton Streetman, the basketball player's son. Broke his nose."

"That would be Emma." Tierney was about Emma's age, I guessed. A couple of years younger than me.

Right now, though, Libby would take one look at him and declare he had an old soul. A certain kind of life experience shone in his gaze—behind the current expression of barely suppressed terror, that is—and I wondered about his life. Like me, he'd been kicked out of the lives of his parents early. Yet, like many of us who grew up in the world of Old Money and long pedigrees, he'd probably absorbed a notion of family tradition. With Amazon Chocolate, he'd clearly tried to create something both profitable and socially responsible.

And I didn't see the usual signs of profligate wealth gone to seed. No ridiculously expensive watch. No foppish haircut or fussy manicure. His white shirt had been expensive once, but someone had laundered it hundreds of times. The Gucci logo on his belt looked worn. His shoes were the kind suitable for hiking, yet fashionable in a hip, urban way.

I wondered about the contradictions, and found myself staring deeply into his eyes.

He stared back at me, and for a strange moment I felt something electric start to buzz in my head.

"Nora." Daddy cleared his throat. "I'd like an aspirin, too."

I forgot about Tierney and his gun and finally took a close look at my father. He was pale, and a faint sheen of sweat shone on his face. Now that Mama and the children were out of the room, he allowed himself to sag in his chair.

"Daddy? What's wrong?"

"It's nothing," he said. "But . . . that aspirin?"

I hustled to the kitchen counter for the Excedrin.

"What's the matter?" Tierney asked.

My father waved his hand. "A little nausea, that's all."

"Nausea?" I said. "Would you rather have a Tums?"

"No, no. Aspirin. Several, please."

I knelt beside his chair with the tablets in my hand. "What's the matter, Daddy? Tell the truth."

"It might be a little angina. Nothing serious."

"Of course angina is serious! Where does it hurt?"

"My arm. My jaw." He put one trembling hand on his chest. "And here."

I pressed two tablets between his lips. As he chewed them, I seized his wrist and tried to find his pulse there. But I had no experience with such things and ended up holding his hand. I cursed myself for overestimating his health. I had mistaken his tan for vibrancy, I realized now.

I'd often thought of my father as Hepplewhite furniture—one of the many things for which he had a collector's appreciation. He was slim and graceful with considerable inner strength, but not enough strength to withstand a crushing weight. And lately, he'd been carrying a very heavy load. I liked to remember him the way he looked in the photograph I kept on a living room shelf. The camera had caught him winking, holding the bridle of a black horse with twelve-year-old Emma on its back—yet somehow my father had dominated the picture, not the animal or the pretty pixie in the saddle. His raffish expression, the elegance of his posture and the classic pullover and threadbare trousers looked more genuinely aristocratic than any Ralph Lauren stylist could dream up.

But now his eyes looked frightened.

I gentled my tone. "When did this start?"

"Two years ago. No, three."

"Have you seen a doctor? Do you have some medication?"

"I left my nitroglycerin tablets on a boat last month." He gave me a sheepish smile. "Your mother and I took a day cruise to see the remains of an island temple on Talikit. The boat was a lovely two-masted—"

"Talikit?" Tierney said. "That's a beautiful island."

"Lovely," Daddy agreed. "The cliffs, the turtles."

Tierney's face darkened. "Who's taking tourists to Talikit? That island has a delicate ecosystem. If people start hiking all over it, they'll destroy the plants and kill off the turtles. Those are very rare turtles."

"Let's focus on the pain," I said. "You've had it before, Daddy? How bad is it now? Compared to the last time?"

He wagged his head back and forth. "So-so."

I shook a handful of pills into my hand. "Here. Chew up a couple more. It should help. And I'll call for an ambulance."

"Wait a minute," Tierney said as I scrambled to my feet. "No ambulance."

"Are you kidding?" I demanded. "We need help! He could be having a heart attack."

"No ambulance," Daddy said just as firmly, around a mouthful of aspirin.

"Don't be crazy! You need medical attention!"

Tierney eyed my father with suspicion. "He's faking."

"How do you fake these symptoms?" I asked. "Look at him!"

Daddy said, "Muffin, I'd rather avoid contact with any kind of officials. It might put your mother and me in an awkward position."

"Me, too," Tierney said. "No ambulance. No police."

"So what do you suggest?" I said to my father. "We should stand around watching while you have a heart attack?"

"No, of course not. The two of you go about your business. I'll just sit here quietly. But—another aspirin, please."

This time he was too weak to chew the pill. I rested my hand on his forehead. His skin felt clammy to me, and I didn't like the gray color of his face. My own heart had begun to hammer in my chest.

"He'll be fine," Tierney said, without sounding convinced.

Daddy nodded. "Sure. Fine. But maybe I could lie down for a minute?"

"That's it," I snapped. "I'm calling 911."

I crossed the kitchen to the phone, but Tierney kept the gun trained on my father. He said, "If you're faking, I could get very angry."

"You don't really look like the angry type," Daddy said.

I pressed 911 on the phone and spoke to the woman who answered my call. I described my father's condition succinctly and gave the address. She must have heard the edge of fear in my voice, because she spoke soothingly to me and asked me to stay on the line.

Behind me, Daddy was saying, "How do you know about those turtles?"

"I have a friend who studies them."

"A friend? Is she pretty? From a nice family?"

"He's a he," Tierney said. "A guy."

Daddy looked surprised, then dismayed. "You're not a homosexual, are you?"

Tierney bristled. "He's just a friend. A grad student I met. We're not—I've had girlfriends, you know. Just not at the moment."

"Nice girls? Anyone we might know?"

"Daddy," I said, "we need to talk about your homophobia."

"Ma'am?" the 911 operator said in my ear.

"Sorry," I said to her. "There's a lot going on here."

But Tierney swung the gun in my direction. "Hang up," he said.

"I'm supposed to keep talking." I pointed at the receiver.

"Ma'am?" the 911 operator said. "Is that the patient you're talking to?"

"No," I said.

"Hang up," Tierney said again.

"Ma'am, who else is there with you?"

Tierney put the gun to my father's head. Daddy's eyes widened.

I hung up the phone.

"They're coming," I said to him. "The paramedics will be here soon. The fire station is just two miles down the road."

"Okay," Tierney said to me. "If help is on the way, then you're coming with me."

"What?"

"What?" Daddy said. "Why?"

He was holding on to the edge of the table with both hands, trying to stay upright.

Even Tierney couldn't help seeing how desperately my father wanted to stay in command of himself. Tierney said, "I'm not going to drag you around. I'll talk to her instead."

"No, don't," my father protested. "She doesn't know anything that can help you."

I said, "Yes. I do. Take me. Don't hurt anyone."

To me, Tierney said, "Help him lie down someplace. Then we're out of here."

I did as he ordered and helped Daddy into the living room. He stretched out on the leather sofa, one hand instinctively resting over his heart. I fussed with a cashmere throw, trying to put it across his legs, but Daddy pushed it aside. Toby put his forepaws up on the sofa and sniffed my father's face.

Tierney grabbed my elbow and pulled me to my feet. "Stop stalling," he said. "Let's go."

"He needs somebody with him. Let me get Rawlins. My nephew can—"

"The ambulance will be here in no time. We're out of here."

Then Tierney pointed his gun at my father one last time. "Don't die, old man."

Daddy tried to smile. "I'll try."

I choked and found I couldn't say good-bye. Tierney wrestled me out of the room. I grabbed my handbag as he pulled me through the kitchen. We went out the back door, down the steps and across the lawn to the black sedan.

Chapter 14

Tierney put the gun in the pocket of the driver's-side door and made sure my seat belt was tightly fastened. He told me to put my handbag on the floor and my hands on my knees.

He started the car and a chipper female voice suddenly said from inside the dashboard, "Turn left."

"What's that?"

Tierney sighed. "It's the damn navigation system on the car. I can't turn it off."

"She sounds a little like Goldie Hawn. Without the giggle."

Helpfully, the voice said, "At the next opportunity, turn left."

"Shut up, Goldie," Tierney said.

"Where's she trying to take you?"

"I don't know. They used my passport when I rented the car. Maybe she's trying to get me back to South America."

He drove down the driveway and turned right onto the highway.

Goldie spoke up again, sounding disappointed. "You've made an error. I'm recalculating your route."

Tierney muttered, "Don't do me any favors."

We'd gone only a few hundred yards before the ambulance came toward us and flashed by.

I sat stiffly in the seat, trying to imagine what was happening at my house. Trying to imagine life without my father. He'd abandoned us more than a few times in our lives, but somehow he'd never truly left us. There was a difference now. I peered into the side mirror, but the red light on the ambulance had disappeared in the darkness behind us.

Tierney glanced at me. "He'll be fine."

"No thanks to you." I felt a flood of anger inside. "If he dies, it will be your fault."

Shaking his head, Tierney said, "If he's stayed alive this long in your daffy family, he's tougher than he looks."

"Turn left," said Goldie.

"What did you want from my father?" I asked. "What's all this about in the first place?"

"I need to know some things."

"About what?"

"Hoyt Cavendish's death."

"I think you know enough already," I said. "Didn't you kill him?"

Tierney sent me a squinting glance. "That's what the police think, isn't it?"

"They're looking for you. Dozens of people must have seen you at the Paine offices before you ran away. And you had a reason to kill your own father, didn't you? Because he wouldn't give you enough money for Amazon Chocolate."

"How the hell do you know about that?"

"It wasn't hard to figure it out," I said tartly. "And the police are way ahead of me."

"What are you? Some kind of private detective?"

"No, just a friend of Lexie Paine. Because of you, she spent last night and today going through hell."

"If you really thought I murdered him," he said, "you'd be more scared than you are."

I contemplated that truth. I wasn't afraid of Tierney. Not really. Now that the gun was out of sight, I was more angry than frightened. "I'm worried about my father," I said finally. "You could have two murders on your hands, buster."

He made a snorting sound.

"And you've put Lexie through a terrible ordeal," I said. "She wouldn't hurt anyone, let alone a partner in her firm, a man she's known all her life—"

"A man who's going to bring down her business? Ruin her reputation? Make it impossible for her to work in her chosen field for the rest of her life? And he punched a hole in her painting, too."

I turned in the seat to look at him. "You were there when that happened?"

"I had just arrived. The woman at the reception desk said he was in a meeting. So I waited."

"For how long?"

"Less than a minute. I didn't even have time to sit down before all hell broke loose. I went to the doorway in time to see Hoyt and Lexie Paine arguing. I saw him hit the painting."

"Then what?"

"Then your friend shut the door, and they started shouting at each other."

"Did either of them see you there?"

"No, but the receptionist knew I was in the office. Several more people were milling around. A woman in a wheelchair, for instance. I guess one of them could have told the police I was there."

Trying to imagine the melee, I asked, "Did you see Chad Zanzibar?"

"Who?"

"An actor. He played an elf in that big movie that came out last Christmas."

"I haven't seen a movie in years. There was a short, rude kid hanging around the reception area, though. I don't know what happened to him when things started popping."

So Chad had been in the Paine Building before Hoyt died.

I asked, "Why did you run away?"

"I didn't run away," he snapped. "Lexie came out of

the office saying Hoyt had fallen or—I forget her exact words. I ran into her office and out onto the balcony. I saw Hoyt on the—I saw him, that's all. I wanted to help. I ran downstairs to see if he—if—look, I wasn't trying to run away."

My first instinct had been right, I realized. While Crewe assumed Tierney had been trying to make his escape, I thought he had run down the stairs to reach his father.

"Why didn't you take the elevator?" I asked.

"A bunch of old ladies blocked my way. I figured I could make it faster on the stairs."

I thought about a frantic son trying to reach his father, unsure if he was alive or dead. Hoping he was okay, despite the odds of surviving such a long fall. Fearing he was gone forever.

Unconsciously, I glanced at my watch. I touched it nervously.

Tierney saw my gesture.

"Call your house," he said finally. "You have a cell phone, right? The paramedics are there by now. Call and find out how your dad's doing."

I grabbed my cell phone and punched my home number. The phone rang and rang before someone finally picked up. I heard Lucy's small voice. Thank heavens someone had found the key and released everyone from the scullery.

"Luce? It's Aunt Nora."

"Oh, hi," she said, sounding as calm as if I had interrupted her watching an episode of *Blue's Clues*.

"Lucy, is Rawlins there? Can you put him on the phone?"

"He's helping Grandpa," she said. "They're all helping Grandpa."

"Is he okay? Is Grandpa awake?"

"Yes," she said. "He wants everybody to stop yelling. But he's yelling, too. He doesn't want to go to a hospital."

I gripped the phone with both hands to stop myself from dropping it from the relief. "But are they taking him to the hospital, Luce?"

"Maybe," she said. "One ambulance man is talking to Grandpa about it, but the other man is talking to the twins. They want to shock somebody with the electric box."

"Did they use the electric box on Grandpa?"

"No, Aunt Nora. But the twins want to see how it works. I think they're going to steal it."

"Don't let them steal the defibrillator, Lucy. The nice ambulance men need it to help other people."

"Okay. Can I have some candy, Aunt Nora? Grandma says she found your secret stash and we can have it if we're good. I've been good, right?"

"Very good, Lucy, thank you."

Tierney said, "Hang up."

"Gotta go, Luce. Bye!"

But she had already disconnected, hot on the trail of my emergency chocolate.

I closed my cell phone. My hands were shaking. To Tierney, I said, "Thank you."

"He's okay?"

"He's being taken care of, that's all I know."

"But he's conscious?"

"Conscious and arguing with the paramedics."

"Good."

"Don't sound so happy. If you hadn't upset him, he'd be fine right now." I put the cell phone back into my bag. "I don't plan on forgiving you for this. What did you want from him, anyway? Why on earth did you take my family hostage?"

"That wasn't the plan. They all ganged up on me."

"What was the plan?"

"To talk. To get some answers."

"With a gun? Those must have been some monstrous questions."

"I wasn't exactly thinking straight. I haven't slept

since—God, I don't even know. Not in a long time." He glared at the road ahead.

"Then you're still not thinking straight. Let me go, and you can—"

"Forget it," he said. "I'm not letting you out of my sight."

"Why not? What can I possibly do to harm you?"

He shook his head stubbornly. "I need to think. I need time to figure out what's going on. You're going to have to help."

"Okay," I said. "I'll help. I give you my word. But you need some sleep. And I want that gun out of this car. Once the gun is gone—"

"No," he said. "I've got a better idea."

In my bag, my cell phone began to ring. I slipped it out and checked the screen. Michael's new numbers gleamed up at me.

Irritated, Tierney said, "Hand over that thing."

I gave him the phone. He rolled down the window. I cried, "Don't throw it away. Please, don't. It has all my numbers from work, and my job's already in jeopardy. Please don't get me fired."

Taking pity on me, he rolled up the window. He shut off the phone and put it in the cup holder between us.

"Turn left," said Goldie, sounding happy again.

For once, he obeyed. Tierney drove over the bridge into New Jersey. He seemed to know where he was going. We went through a series of small towns, and I saw signs for Princeton before we arrived at the entrance of a drive-in theater. I could see the flicker of the movie through the trees.

Tierney surprised me by pulling into the ticket booth. As he rolled down the car window, he said to me, "Keep your mouth shut, or I'll give you a lot of reasons to be scared, got it?"

I said nothing as the woman opened the ticket window and leaned her elbow on the sill. A cloud of cigarette smoke billowed out into the warm evening air. In a voice like a rusty hinge, she said, "Movie started half an hour ago."

"Double feature?" Tierney asked.

"Triple." She burst into a fit of coughing. Unable to speak, she pointed at a sign that read, TEN DOLLERS PER CARLODE.

Tierney pulled his wallet from his hip pocket and passed her a ten-dollar bill. Still coughing, she waved us through the gate, past a sign that said, TURN OFF YOUR HEADLITES.

The drive-in parking lot was full of station wagons and pickup trucks parked backward so families could sit in folding chairs facing the big screen. Tierney drove past a concession stand pumping out smells of fried food and popcorn. On our right, a dozen children played on a swing set in the dark.

Tierney chose the back row, where only a few cars were parked—each one positioned a distance from the next car to provide a certain amount of privacy. I could see no people sitting in the cars. Then I realized they probably weren't sitting.

Tierney shut off the car and unfastened his seat belt. He retrieved the gun from the door pocket and slid it into his belt. Then he released my seat belt and said, "Get out of the car."

"Why? What are we doing?"

"Get out of the car."

He exited his side, came around the car and pulled me out of the passenger seat. He closed my door and opened the door to the backseat. "Get in."

"What do you—"

He grabbed my wrist and pulled. "Just get in."

I obeyed, but my heartbeat had already accelerated. When he climbed into the backseat with me and slammed the door, though, I panicked and scrambled to get out the other side. Tierney seized my arm, preventing my escape.

"Settle down," he snapped. "I'm not going to hurt you."

"I don't want to do this," I said, quaking. "I don't know you, I don't like you, I don't—"

"Shut up," he said.

Suddenly we were wrestling. I didn't have enough room to kick him, but I made a lunge for the gun in his belt. He batted my hand away, but I managed to punch him in the chest, and he recoiled with a grunt. I yelped when he yanked my arm, so he clamped his other hand over my mouth. I bit him, but he hung on. He was stronger than I was, and soon he had spun me around with one arm twisted behind my back. I struggled with all my strength, determined to fight him every inch of the way. I kicked at the door, hoping to break the window.

"Stop it," he said, breathless in my ear. He twisted my arm until I cried out in pain and froze. I could feel the tense power of his body as he pinned me against himself.

"Calm down!" He was panting, but determined. "I just need some sleep, get it? I need a couple of hours, and then I'll be able to think straight. So relax, will you? I'm not going to do anything, for God's sake. Understand?"

He waited until I nodded my head. Then he released my mouth.

"Just relax," he said. "If you move, I'll wake up. And I might do something stupid like shoot you."

I didn't like it, but I let him stretch out on the backseat and pull me against him until we were spooning. I hated that I was forced to lean my head against his chest. I could smell him, and he hadn't taken a shower in a while. He put one arm around me and gripped my forearm against my breast to hold me in place. Already, I could feel the heat of his body against mine.

Shakily, I said, "Please."

"Shut up," he said. "I'm not going to touch you, Nora."

Stiff in his arms, I said with as much threat as I could muster, "Don't even think about it."

"I won't," he said. "After all, you're my sister."

He put the gun on the floor and went to sleep.

Chapter 15

I've been kidnapped, I thought to myself.

Kidnapped by my brother.

Maybe I'd already known who he was. Certainly Libby had hinted, and long ago I'd accepted Daddy's affair, and maybe a tiny part of my brain had also acknowledged the possibility that somewhere I had another sibling. And now here he was.

Tierney Cavendish was not a Cavendish at all, but a Blackbird.

He fell asleep like a desk lamp being snapped off—exactly the way Emma did when she was exhausted or drunk or both.

I lay there thinking about Emma for a while, wondering if she'd truly decided to get an abortion if she was drinking only ginger ale. Perhaps she'd already reconsidered that dreadful choice. No doubt Michael had something to do with that. He'd tangle with a mountain lion to protect a child. And Emma was only slightly more dangerous than a mountain lion.

Eventually I was capable of thinking rationally about Tierney again, and how he must have felt about his father—Hoyt, that is, not Daddy—dying in a terrible fall.

And if Tierney hadn't killed Hoyt, and Lexie hadn't, either, who had?

Stewing over the possibilities, I listened to the sound track of a silly movie in which the same man played different parts—including all the women—but I couldn't see the screen from the backseat, so it made very little sense. Besides, I couldn't follow a story because of the tangled one already looping around in my head.

I listened to Tierney snore softly, and felt his chest rise and fall, and I thought of Michael with an intense longing.

Eventually I fell asleep.

And woke up when the movies were finished. I could hear car engines starting up around us, and the crunch of gravel under tires as people left the drive-in theater. I decided to throw caution to the wind. Stealthily, I reached for the cup holder where Tierney had dropped my cell phone. My hand found it in the semidarkness. Slowly, so as not to wake Tierney, I thumbed it open. I touched the ON button. A second later, the phone rang in my grasp.

Tierney woke.

Still holding me, he rolled my wrist over and looked at my watch. His voice was rumbly. "Jesus, it's three in the morning. Who calls you at this hour?"

"Let's find out," I said. "May I sit up?"

He gave me a shove, and I straightened in the seat. Praying I'd hear Michael's voice, I answered the phone.

"Aunt Nora?" It was Rawlins. "That you?"

"Yes, honey, it's me."

"You okay?"

"Moderately so. How's your grandfather?"

"Pretty good, I guess. We just got back from the hospital. They're going to keep him overnight. Well—until morning. I don't know. What time is it?"

"It's the middle of the night, darling. Thank you for taking care of everybody. You're my hero. He's really going to be okay?"

"I think so. Where are you?" he asked. "Mick's going nuts."

"I'm fine. We're at the movies."

"Huh?"

Tierney yawned and hauled himself to a sitting position. "Hang up."

"Who's that?" Rawlins said. "You still with that guy with the gun?"

"Yes, but—"

"Hang up," Tierney said.

"I've got to go, Rawlins, but everything's—"

Tierney took the phone and punched the off button to terminate the call. He dropped it on the seat between us, and we sat looking at each other in the darkness.

He had Daddy's expressive brows and the same divot in his cheek that Libby had—not quite a dimple, but almost. And my eyes.

I hugged myself, trying not to be spooked by our similarities.

He shrugged, accepting.

"How long have you known?" I asked.

He shrugged again. "A while. I was a teenager when my mother told me."

"Did she—I don't know—did she tell you gently?"

Tierney's cold smile flickered briefly. "Are we going to talk about our mothers now?"

"Shouldn't we?"

"My mother was a complicated person," he said. "She didn't have it easy."

"Like my mother, you mean."

"Your mother is a natural disaster."

"Welcome to the family," I replied, giving him a shaky smile.

Which seemed to surprise him. He reached for the door handle and got out of the car. I climbed out of the other side, stretching my stiff limbs tentatively. The drive-in was deserted, except for the small mounds of trash everywhere. On the ground beside the car, I saw a used condom in a heap of spilled popcorn.

Tierney walked over to the trees, turned his back to me and relieved himself in the bushes.

I leaned against the car for a while, glad to be breathing fresh air. It was blessedly cool. I put my head back and looked up at the fading stars. A few clouds floated in front of the moon. I looked for Fred Flintstone.

Tierney returned. "I could use some breakfast. And I know a place that'll be open."

When he started the car, Goldie Hawn sounded delighted we were back. "Turn left."

I reached for the control panel and shut off the navigation system. I'd spent at least an hour staring at it from the backseat to guess how to turn it off.

Tierney said, "Maybe I'll like having sisters."

He drove into Princeton and found a diner that probably catered to students with the munchies and truckers who needed strong coffee. A huge neon sign depicted a buxom girl on roller skates. She winked as we pulled into the parking lot. Tierney locked the gun in the glove compartment and put my cell phone in his pocket.

Together, we walked across the parking lot under a sputtering streetlight and went inside. The diner was empty at that hour of the morning, except for a ponytailed waitress who sat at the counter reading a tabloid newspaper and drinking an iced tea. She waved us into a booth with red vinyl seat cushions, and we looked at the menu, printed on the place mats.

I ordered a white omelet with mushrooms and whole wheat toast, then excused myself. In the bathroom, I washed as best I could and reapplied some moisturizer and lip gloss. My Furstenberg dress hadn't wrinkled, despite half a night spent curled up in the backseat of a car.

The perfect dress for a kidnapping.

When I returned to the table, Tierney looked surprised. "You didn't climb out a window and call the cops."

"Not without breakfast." I slid into the seat opposite him. Two cups of coffee had already arrived, and I reached eagerly for mine.

As I swallowed the first scalding sip, a wan streak of

pink daylight glowed across the parking lot. Pink sky in the morning, sailor take warning.

I said, "You must have gone to college at Princeton."

Tierney nodded and stirred sweetener into his cup.

"What was your major?"

"Girls. You can tell your father for me."

Our father, I almost said. Sitting there, looking across the table at Tierney, I could see a certain Indiana Jones quality that must have made the coeds hot.

He said, "I've been thinking about what happened at the Paine office. Trying to remember everything I saw."

I sipped a little more hot coffee and lifted my eyebrows.

He said, "You mentioned there was a kid—an actor, right?"

"He's not a kid, exactly. Not very tall, but with big shoulders, long arms. He was wearing a baseball cap. Chad Zanzibar."

"Wearing shorts? The kind that are falling off his butt? Does he dye his hair, maybe?"

I nodded. "Highlights. Did you see him?"

"Yeah. He was on his cell phone in the reception area when I arrived. I heard him talking to someone—really reading the riot act. About needing money for a production."

"Yes, I think he and his grandmother are producers of a new movie."

"He needed sixteen million dollars. He said so, very loudly, several times."

"He thought he could get that kind of money from his grandmother. But now she's broke. Last night, she asked me about selling her jewelry. Which, in case your college studies skipped this chapter, is something women don't do unless they're desperate."

"Does that give the kid a motive to kill Hoyt?"

I set down my cup. "You don't call him your father, I notice. Not 'Dad' or 'Pop' or anything but his first name.

Has that been a lifelong thing? Or just since learning he wasn't really the man who—"

"I always called him Hoyt. It was easier that way." Tierney drank more coffee. "I don't remember exactly when the Zanzibar kid left the Paine Building. But it was definitely after Hoyt went off the balcony."

Our breakfasts arrived on platters as big as bicycle tires. Tierney's plate overflowed with eggs, peppers, fried potatoes and four slices of rye toast.

As he looked at his breakfast, he pulled my cell phone out of his pocket and pushed it across the table to me.

We ate, and I thought about the ordinariness of meals with my sisters. How strange it was to be sitting here having breakfast with my brother. My new brother. It was a new day, all right.

But Tierney soon lost interest in his breakfast. He sat back, staring at his plate and toying with his fork.

I said, "Why did you come to Blackbird Farm yesterday? Surely not for the purpose of kidnapping me."

Silent, he shook his head. But I could see him wrestling with his thoughts.

"Then, what? To meet Daddy? Your real father?"

"No." He set aside his fork and looked at me squarely. "Because I thought he killed Hoyt."

"You thought Daddy might have pushed Hoyt off the balcony? No, that's not possible."

He lifted his shoulders. "It's what I assumed. I overheard one of the Treasury agents say he was in the office. And once I knew that, I figured he was the one with a real reason to kill Hoyt."

"What reason? Daddy had no—"

"Because of me," Tierney said.

"But wouldn't it be the other way around? That Hoyt resented my father for having the affair with your mother?"

Tierney shook his head. "That wasn't how it happened, Nora. At least, that's not what I have been led to understand most of my life. Hoyt made an agreement with your father."

"An agreement?"

"To help my mother conceive."

I tried to comprehend what he was saying. "You mean, Hoyt wasn't . . . capable?"

Tierney gave a short, bitter laugh. "No, Hoyt wasn't capable of making babies. But he agreed that my mother should be allowed to have a child, so he approached your father—his friend—to help. It started out very civilized."

I considered the kind of favor my father had given his friend, and wondered fleetingly—unfairly, perhaps—if he'd had an ulterior motive. I banished that thought as quickly as it came, trying hard to give him the benefit of my doubt. "But . . . how does that give Daddy a reason to kill Hoyt now? If they all agreed to—"

"The original agreement was drawn up and signed by all three of them. To guarantee your father would say nothing and make no effort to contact me, Hoyt and my mother put five hundred thousand dollars into an investment account. Your father was supposed to stay out of my life until I turned thirty. At that time, he was allowed to collect his reward. Actually, we were supposed to split it."

My stomach began to roil as I thought of previous occasions when Daddy had access to large sums of money. "How old are you now?"

"Twenty-nine. Unfortunately, over the weekend I learned that Hoyt had raided that account some years ago. There's nothing left."

"I'm sorry."

Grimly, he said, "Me, too. Amazon Chocolate could really use some cash right now. I came to Philadelphia hoping to get my hands on that money early. I have a lot of people depending on me. I hate disappointing them. And, to tell the truth, I've got a little problem to fix with some nasty guys back in South America."

"How nasty?"

"Are you familiar with the term crime lord?"

"Intimately." I sighed. "You owe them money?"

"Yes. It's a natural part of the system there. A little bribery goes a long way. But if I miss a payment . . ."

"I understand. How does all this make Daddy a murder suspect?"

Tierney looked directly into my eyes. "Maybe I'm being presumptuous, but I'd like to think he was angry at Hoyt for stealing my inheritance."

"I—well, that would be very noble." I shook my head. "But I'm sorry to say, it's hardly in character for my father. I have to be truthful with you. If anything, Daddy's probably wishing he could have gotten his hands on the money himself."

In a nutshell, I told Tierney about my parents and their flight into financial freedom at the expense of my sisters and me, not to mention many of their good friends who were suckered into lending money they'd never see again. I tried to make my voice sound light, to make a joke of it all, but by watching his face—full of curiosity, but pained compassion, too—I knew I failed to make my parents sound like anything more than what they truly were.

"So you see," I said, "a gallant act on your behalf isn't likely. I'm afraid Daddy is the kind of man who'd swindle a dime from a nun, if he thought he could get away with it."

Tierney said, "I guess nobody's who we'd like to think they are."

He curled his fingers around the handle of his cup and looked into his coffee. A cloud of melancholy engulfed him as clearly as if a fog had rolled off a river.

"Tierney? Is there more I should know?"

He sighed and turned away from me to stare out the window. "There's a lot more. And soon enough, the whole world's going to hear it. I guess I knew it would happen someday, but it doesn't make it any easier. I don't understand why the police haven't told the press yet."

"About what?"

"About Hoyt. He wasn't at all what everybody thought."

"Yes. We assumed he was a generous philanthropist. But because he's been embezzling from clients, I'm afraid his generosity won't—"

"That's not it." Suddenly Tierney's eyes looked glassy, and I realized he was fighting back tears. He covered his face with one hand to hide his emotion.

I reached across the table to touch his arm. "What is it? Can I help?"

He shook his head. Choking, he said, "Hoyt wasn't a man."

My heart went out to Tierney. "Just because he couldn't father a child doesn't make him less of a—"

"No, no, I mean he wasn't a man. He was my father—at least he pretended to be. But he wasn't."

"I don't understand."

"Can I say it any plainer?" Tierney looked at me again. "Hoyt was a woman."

Baffled, I sat back in the vinyl seat cushion. "He what?"

"He pretended his whole life. Surely you noticed his small size? His voice?"

"But—"

"He was a woman. He dressed as a man, acted like a man, chose to live his life as a man. But he wasn't. I don't understand the relationship he had with my mother—that was way too screwed up for me to ask about. All I know is that I discovered it when I was a teenager." Words tumbling together, Tierney said, "I walked in on him—it was an accident. And I saw. He wasn't a man at all. He had breasts, and he was wrapping them tightly with—look, it doesn't matter. I ran out of the bathroom. Out of the house."

My head spun with the truth of what he was telling me. If Hoyt wasn't a man at all, what did that do to the investigation of his murder? Suddenly a whole applecart had been upended.

Tierney went on, his voice rough. "Funny thing is, I think I knew long before I saw it for myself. How did I sense it? I don't know."

I knew what he meant. I'd felt something was off about Hoyt, too, but hadn't been able to put a name to my feeling.

"Finding out the truth," he said, "really messed me up for a while. They tried talking to me about it, but I was hysterical, completely out of control. They took me to a doctor—a psychiatrist—but I clammed up. I wouldn't speak to anybody. Then they sent me away to boarding school, and it was better there. I didn't go home for a couple of years. I went with friends on vacations and holidays, just so I wouldn't have to face my parents. That's when I started traveling in South America. It was a place nobody knew me, and I really love the people there. Nobody has any pretenses. When my mother died, I came back for a few weeks, but I—I didn't talk to Hoyt. I couldn't."

I tried to imagine how a young boy dealt with such a bizarre family story. "You never reconciled with your parents?"

"No. How could I? A month ago, Hoyt contacted me through my business. He wanted me to come home. He said he had something important to discuss. It took me three weeks to agree, but I—even now I'm not ready to forgive him."

"What did he want to discuss?"

"I don't know. But I didn't want to hear anything he had to say. Not only had my parents fed me a gigantic lie all my life, but he—Hoyt—was the only father I knew. The man I imprinted on, the man who taught me how to take a piss standing up, for crying out loud—I trusted him to—to be a man. A real man."

"Have you been able to talk about this with anyone?" A therapist, I wanted to add.

His face had taken on a hard red flush. "Until today, I've never told another person."

I winced. "And soon the whole world is going to know."

Tierney nodded miserably. "I don't know why the police haven't revealed it yet. Surely the medical examiner took one look and knew the whole story."

"The police probably wouldn't reveal his sex until they pieced together more of the truth."

"Which is one reason they're looking for me now."

"And you've given them another reason," I said.

"Right. Waving a gun at your family. Kidnapping you."

"I'm sorry you felt you had to go to such extremes."

Unhappily, he ran his hand through his hair. "Things were better for me in South America. I can be myself there. I'm my own man, have a business I'm passionate about. But here—I'm some kind of freak."

"That's not true. It's not your fault."

My words didn't comfort him in the least. Tierney tried to sip from his cup of coffee, but he couldn't manage to swallow. We sat together, letting the truth sink in.

I could hardly accept it. Hoyt Cavendish—a woman in disguise? Did that mean he was transgender? A crossdresser? I wasn't sure of the label. That time I'd seen him onstage, giving the violin to the young musician—I tried to envision the scene again, knowing what I knew now. It seemed impossible.

And yet. His diminutive size. His strangely weak voice. His hands.

Murusha and Donaldson, I remembered. The gynecologists who specialized in female cancers.

I had an inkling now why Hoyt had summoned Tierney home.

Suddenly my cell phone rang, skittering on the tabletop between us.

Without asking Tierney's permission to answer, I opened the phone.

In my ear, Michael's voice was an urgent growl. "Does he still have the gun?"

"What? No."

Michael hung up. A bubble of tension popped in my chest.

Tierney looked at me, no doubt puzzled by my expression. "Who was that?"

I glanced out into the parking lot, and leaning against Tierney's black car was a familiar figure. Delmar, with his arms folded across his enormous chest. I recognized him as the sunrise glinted off the dent in his bald head.

I said, "Oh, dear."

Like a tiger, Michael pounced into the booth beside Tierney, crowding him against the window and upsetting his cup of coffee. Instinctively, Tierney reached to dam the flow of hot coffee, but Michael pinned Tierney's right wrist against the red vinyl. He put his own arm across the back of the seat cushion behind Tierney's head. To the watching waitress, it probably looked like a friendly greeting. To me, it looked as if Michael was going to snap Tierney's vertebrae with one hand.

Every iota of color drained out of Tierney's face.

To me, Michael snapped, "You okay?"

"Yes, of course—"

Unnerved by the stealth attack, Tierney tried to bluff. "Who the hell are you?"

And I said, "How in heaven's name did you find us?"

By that time, Tierney fully comprehended how big and frightening Michael could be when he was angry. Weakly, he said, "Take it easy, man."

"Shut up," Michael said. "Before I break your pencil neck."

"Michael, please. There's no need to get physical."

"Oh, no? This idiot kidnaps you at gunpoint? And now you're best friends?"

"I'm fine. See? Perfectly healthy."

"You sure?" He glared at me, his grip still unbreakable on Tierney.

"Yes, I'm sure." I felt a surge of sympathy. "You've been through an awful night, haven't you? I'm sorry. I'm truly—wait, how did you find us?"

Plausibly enough, he said, "I talked to Rawlins."

But I saw a shift in his eyes. "Rawlins had no idea where I was until an hour ago. And now I'm here. And so are you. Do you have a bloodhound? Or—good grief, did you put some kind of tracking device in my pocket?"

"Don't get mad," he said.

"You did!"

"It was only a precaution."

"My phone?" I guessed, snatching it up from the table.

"It's a GPS option," Michael admitted.

"My phone tells you where I am?" I stared at the little blue screen as if it were suddenly capable of transmitting a flesh-eating virus.

"Good thing Henry installed it yesterday," he said. "You could be dead in a ditch if we hadn't tracked you here."

"You could have found me and I'd still be dead," I said. "Is it legal to do this?"

The waitress came over with a rag. She mopped up the coffee and righted Tierney's cup in its saucer. She appeared not to notice Michael's seemingly affectionate grip on the back of Tierney's neck. "Some coffee for you, sir? Breakfast?"

"He'll have mine." I pushed my plate across the table, no longer hungry. "But bring him some decaf. He has the jitters."

"I do not," Michael said amiably, releasing Tierney's neck when the waitress walked away. He slid over to make the requisite twelve inches of space between himself and another man, thereby declaring himself off duty. "Who's the asshole?"

"He's not an— Tierney, this is Michael Abruzzo. Michael, this is Tierney Cavendish. My brother."

Maybe Michael's years in prison made him invulnerable to surprise. He didn't blink. He shook Tierney's hand slowly, though, and studied his face.

Wary, Tierney said, "Man, you scared the hell out of me."

"Good," said Michael. "You hurt her, I'll hurt you harder."

I handed Michael my fork. "Have some breakfast. You'll feel better."

He ate a few bites of my omelet, but stayed half-turned sideways in the seat so he could examine Tierney between swallows. I nibbled the whole wheat toast until the waitress came back, holding the handles of two coffeepots in one hand—one decaf, one regular. She put some packets of jam on the table. Ten or twelve more customers had come into the diner. Someone turned on the television behind the counter. An early newscast came on, predicting more hot weather. The place felt almost homey. Someone called the waitress by name and she went to another table.

Michael picked out a packet of strawberry jam for my toast and skimmed it across the table to me. But when I tried to open the packet, I discovered my hands were trembling. He put down his fork, reached over and took the packet back. He opened it and carefully spread the jam on my toast for me.

As if trying to get his mind around the impossible, Tierney asked, "Are you two married?"

"Not yet," Michael said.

"You act like you're married."

I looked across the table at Michael. My hero. My love. The man with the broken face and the heart of a lion.

But then I thought of what Tierney's idea of a marriage must be and I laughed.

Michael did, too.

"So what's next?" he finally asked me.

"I'm not sure," I said. "Tierney needs to stay out of

sight for a little while. Until we learn more about his—his father's—Hoyt's death."

Michael didn't acknowledge the confusion about which of Tierney's fathers I meant. He said, "Out of sight of the cops, you mean. That's my specialty."

Chapter 16

"One of your specialties," I said. "You have many. Where do you think Tierney could go?"

Michael took no offense at my wry tone and made short work of my omelet. "Not your place," he said between bites. "Rawlins says there was some action there last night. Paramedics and cops."

"The police were there, too?"

"Yeah, they were very interested in your parents until somebody remembered about you getting kidnapped. So they forgot about them and started on you. And there's a BOLO out on him." He hooked his thumb at Tierney. "Cops probably have a license plate now, too, so I wouldn't go driving around in his car today."

"What can we do?"

He gave me a long look. "You mean, outside the limits of the law?"

"Yes," I said steadily. "That's exactly what I mean."

"That sounds like a change of heart."

"Are we going to argue about it now, or do you have some suggestions?"

Michael said to Tierney, "You have a girlfriend?"

Tierney was eyeing his breakfast again, trying to decide if he could stomach it or not. "Not at the moment, no."

"That must make your life easier." To me, Michael said, "I have a couple of extra license plates in my trunk. We'll swap. I'll take the two of you in my car. Delmar can ditch the other one."

Tierney looked up from his plate. "Ditch my car? It's an airport rental. I'm already broke. If I have to pay for a car, I'm sunk."

Michael shrugged. "So we'll return it to the airport, no sweat."

"Where can we go?" I asked.

He wolfed the last of the omelet, thinking. Letting the criminal part of his mind explore the possibilities.

Two minutes later, he sat back. "Hot day like this? You want to blend into a big crowd? You go to the shore." He wiped his mouth with a napkin. "We'll buy some beer, one of those big umbrellas for you to sit under. Build a sand castle, maybe, and take a nice long nap in the sun. Later on, we'll have some clams or something."

"I can't go to the beach. Libby's kids, my job—"

"Call in sick. We'll take the kids with us."

"My father's in the hospital."

Michael shrugged again. "Best place for him."

Tierney said, "If we go back to the house, won't somebody call the police? Or maybe they're watching the house right now. I'll be arrested."

Michael wasn't deterred. "So we leave now, buy some towels and sunscreen along the way. No big deal."

A day at the beach. It sounded heavenly to me. But I shook my head. "I can't go. It's impossible to buy a bathing suit on the spur of the moment."

To Tierney, Michael said, "You should see her at the shore. Cute little pink dress, a picture hat with polka-dot ribbons, a big straw purse full of girl stuff. And it all matches. She makes it into a production, but it's worth it. She's dynamite in a bathing suit, too. And watching her put that lotion stuff on her legs makes me want to howl."

His delight was infectious, and Tierney smiled uncertainly.

I said, "That's my brother you're talking to."

The waitress slapped the check down on the table, and Michael picked it up. He went to the register while I gathered up my phone and tucked it into my handbag, then dug out my sunglasses. I stood up.

Hesitating at the table, Tierney glanced up at me. "Nora, I . . ."

I knew what he wanted to say. He'd confided in me about Hoyt, and it had been a frightening admission that now, somehow, felt cleansing. But he still had doubts. I could see the turmoil in his face.

"It's okay," I soothed.

He smiled warily. "Okay." He glanced at Michael. "I can trust him? He's a scary guy."

"You can trust him." I put on my sunglasses and shouldered my bag. "If you want to avoid the police, he's your man."

In the parking lot, Delmar accepted the keys to Tierney's car.

Michael told him, "Wipe down the interior. Don't forget the buttons on the radio."

Delmar nodded.

I said, "The backseat, too."

Michael sent me a look with a raised eyebrow. Tierney's expression was that of a teenager who'd been caught by an overprotective father.

Delmar said, "What about you, boss?"

Michael clapped him on the shoulder to send him on his way. "I'll be in touch."

Leaving Delmar to the task of erasing all fingerprints from Tierney's rental, the three of us climbed into Michael's muscle car. When he started the engine, the rumble under the hood sounded like a jet plane.

On the road, Michael engaged Tierney in a discussion of sports—the universal language of men. I wondered how Tierney had learned such a skill. From Hoyt?

But then I fell asleep with my head on Michael's shoulder.

I woke when we arrived at Michael's home. It was a secluded, modest A-frame house—a weekend getaway he'd bought from some New Yorkers and made into a bachelor pad for himself—a stone's throw from some of the best fishing on the Delaware River. A pair of faded Adirondack chairs sat on the deck overlooking the quietly rushing water. Someone had left an empty beer bottle on the railing. Morning sunlight glinted off the river like a million diamond facets.

I stayed in the car while Michael took Tierney into the house and presumably gave him directions for a quick escape should the police come knocking.

When Michael came outside again, he was carrying something large and unwieldy in his arms. I focused and realized it was a person.

"Oh, my God!" I scrambled out of the car. "Is she hurt?"

"Just hungover, I think." Michael hefted Emma as easily as if she were a pizza box.

My little sister lolled in his arms—oblivious or unconscious, I couldn't be sure. The white pallor of her face frightened me.

Without benefit of her coating of warm chocolate, Emma's boneless body looked thinner than ever—no longer sexy, but downright skinny. She still wore the faded T-shirt that advertised the Delaware Fly Fishing Company, over a pair of unzipped jeans. She had lost one of her flip-flops. Her toes were dirty.

My heart lurched at the sight of her.

She groaned. "Kill me. Put me out of my misery."

Michael said, "Help me get her into the backseat."

I opened the door and held the seat while Michael managed to thread my little sister into the car. Together we got her stretched out and buckled in.

Smoothing her hair back from her face, I looked at Emma and said, "Oh, Em. You haven't done something terrible, have you?"

She gave a slobbery moan. "Not yet."

Michael said, "If she gets sick in my car, you're cleaning up the mess. She's been sick for a week."

"Two," Emma croaked. "But who's counting?"

"It's time somebody else looked after her. Don't look so worried. Under your roof, you can work your sisterly magic."

Emma squinted up at me. "You told him, I suppose?"

"Told me what?" Michael asked.

Emma groaned and rolled over to mash her face into the upholstery.

Michael looked at me. "What am I supposed to know?"

"You can't be this idiotic."

"What do you mean?"

"Michael," I said, "she's pregnant."

The astonished expression on his face could have been comical under different circumstances.

Then he blinked and said, "No shit. Who's the father?"

"What do you mean, who's the father?"

Michael began laughing. He put his hand on the roof of the car and leaned in. "What did you do, Em? Eat him afterwards like some kind of spider?"

"Leave me alone," she muttered, clutching her stomach.

I said, "You really don't know who the father is?"

Michael swung around to look at me, still amused and surprised. "Why would I?"

I'm not entirely clear about what happened next. I remember a dazzling display of stars in front of my eyes and the earth rushing up to my face. And the next thing, I was sprawled out on the front seat of the car, with the sound of Emma retching behind me.

"Oh, hell," Michael said. "I just had this car cleaned."

In a little while, I was sitting upright, and he climbed into the car behind the wheel. He closed the door, but before starting the engine, he reached across and grabbed my wrist.

"About last night," he said. "Just so you know, I don't think I can ever go through that again."

He pulled me close and kissed me. Long, hard and desperately. My own heart skipped and thudded against his, and the lump in my throat throbbed. He hadn't betrayed me. He'd been helping my sister give up drinking.

When he released me at last and we could breathe again, I touched his face and wished I could smooth away the lines of worry around his eyes. "I'm sorry. It happened very fast."

"I figured you were mad at me. But then Rawlins didn't answer his phone, either."

"And you knew I was in trouble."

"For you, business as usual."

"I'm sorry," I murmured again.

He hugged me close and spoke into my hair. "It took so damn long to get to you."

"I'm okay."

From the backseat, Emma moaned, "If I hadn't puked my guts out already this morning, you two would make me sick."

We ignored her, but smiled at each other. To Michael, I said, "Tierney isn't dangerous."

Michael cocked an eyebrow. "You sure about that? Did he push his father off Lexie's balcony?"

"No. And anyway, Hoyt wasn't his father. Daddy is. And there's more."

I indicated Michael should start the car, and he did. While the noise of the engine kept my voice from reaching Emma, I told him what I knew. Although I hadn't asked Tierney's permission, I spilled the whole story. How Hoyt had been a strange kind of father to Tierney. How he'd fooled the world.

Michael interrupted once, saying, "Wait, wasn't there some famous jazz musician? A guy who turned out to be a woman?"

"I don't know. But Tierney's really weirded out by it."

"No shit." Michael stared out the windshield, thunderstruck. "That's the kind of thing that could really screw with a guy's head."

"If there was ever a person who needed some counseling, it's Tierney." I sighed. "My brother. How strange is it that I have a brother now? And Daddy? Did he know Hoyt was a woman when he agreed to father their child?"

Michael shook his head. "You've got one wild family, Nora Blackbird."

Pondering the new development in my family tree, Michael drove us up the river, across the bridge into Pennsylvania and over to Blackbird Farm. The time on my watch read only a few minutes after nine, but it felt as if I'd been gone for days.

A silver Rolls-Royce sat sparkling in the driveway.

Looking at it, Michael whistled, long and low.

We got out into the dappled sunshine, and Michael wrestled Emma out of the backseat.

As he carried her up the stone sidewalk, she groaned. "I need ginger ale."

To me, Michael said, "It's the only thing that settles her stomach. I bought a case yesterday. It's in the trunk."

I dug the car keys out of his hip pocket and opened the trunk. The cans of ginger ale were warm to the touch, but they would have to do.

Henry Fineman was snoring in the hammock strung between two oak trees. His hands were arranged peacefully on his chest. He wore his hiking clothes, but he had taken off his sandals, and they were neatly placed on the grass under the hammock.

Toby burst out from under my peonies and ran over to Michael, leaping up to sniff his burden. Emma was the spaniel's favorite person, and he whined and yelped to see her. I hadn't seen the dog so energized since the moment my sister left the farm.

Michael put Emma into one of the Adirondack chairs by the hammock and tucked a pillow under her head. She gave another groan when Toby scrambled into her lap and licked her face. She tried to push him away, but she was too weak. Eventually the dog laid his head against her chest and sighed.

In her Spider-Man pajamas, Lucy sat on the steps of the back porch, keeping an eagle eye on Henry Fineman and holding a bow and arrow with a rubber tip.

I kissed the top of her uncombed head. "Good morning, Luce. Have you had breakfast yet?"

"I'm working on it." She glared, unwavering, at Henry.

"Is Grandma here?"

"Nope. She's at the hospital with Grandpa."

"Rawlins?"

"Sleeping," she reported.

"The twins?"

"Making fireworks in the barn."

Michael and I exchanged a look.

"I'll go check," he said, and went back down the steps. "If I don't come back, send a SWAT team."

I put my hand on the door handle, and Lucy said, "Be careful. My mom's in there."

I pushed inside and discovered my sister Libby wearing a frilly apron and making coffee. She had cleaned the kitchen, mopped the floor and rearranged my canisters. Her revived domesticity could mean only one thing.

I said, "Did you marry someone?"

"Nora!" Libby cried musically. "How delightful to see—good heavens, you look like you've been hit by a bus!"

"Thanks." I was fully aware that my wrinkle-free Furstenberg dress had been challenged to the max. My hair felt like a curly mess under my hand, and I knew I didn't have a shred of makeup left. I suspected I still had the imprint of Tierney's car upholstery on my cheek.

Libby, on the other hand, wore silver sandals and a lavender skort with a T-shirt printed with the words EVE WAS FRAMED, written in letters made of cartoon serpents. She had tied the lacy strings of the apron fetchingly over her bottom. On her hip, Maximus drooled happily, delighted to be in his mother's arm again.

He pulled his binky out of his mouth and announced his mother's return triumphantly. "Da!"

I said, "You didn't answer me. What happened during your sojourn at the Ritz-Carlton? Or did you go directly to the honeymoon phase?"

Libby continued to putter around my kitchen, whipping up a batch of pancakes, if I was any judge of batter. She had also picked more strawberries, and the first crop of blueberries had clearly come in, because a small bowl sat beside the sink.

My sister's face lit up as if I'd plugged her into a light socket. "Oh, Nora, I can't wait to tell you everything! Jacque is adorable! So giving! So in touch with his feelings!"

"Jacque?"

"Jacque Petite!"

Stunned, I said, "That's who ran over you with his car? Jacque Petite, the chocolate guy? The star of the Chocolate Festival?"

I had seen his picture at the festival, and of course I knew him from his show on the Food Channel. But imagining my sister with the happy chocolate man was beyond me.

For a moment.

Then it made perfect sense.

Libby dimpled. "He can't very well be the star of the festival if he hasn't left the Ritz-Carlton for days."

"Is that his Rolls outside?"

"Yes. He let me borrow it!"

"What's the catch?"

"Catch? Whatever do you mean?"

I grabbed a coffee cup from the cupboard. The last thing I wanted to discuss this morning was the quadratic equation that was my sister's love life. "You always find a man who's in touch with his feelings, but he turns out to be even more in touch with scamming you or stealing from you or—"

"How can you say such a thing? He's Jacque Petite!"

"Remember Sam?" I asked. "The fireman?"

Libby flushed as she snatched the coffee cup from my hands. "The coffee's not ready yet. Sam was delightful except for the candle obsession. I can't concentrate on sexual satisfaction if I'm constantly worried the curtains might catch fire. But Jacque is totally different! He adores me. He says we're on the same astral plane. Why are you so cranky this morning?"

"Nobody told you? While you were exploring astral planes with the chocolate king, I was kidnapped last night."

"Oh, that!" Libby waved off my ordeal with the cup. "I knew that was only a misunderstanding. I explained it all to the police."

"The police were here?"

"Yes, of course the police were here. Thank heaven Rawlins had the presence of mind to telephone them last night. And then me. I've been here for hours, by the way. I rushed out of the city the instant Rawlins phoned. Otherwise it would have been complete chaos at this house. I hardly think I can trust you to look after my children anymore, Nora. Next time, I'll think twice about asking you."

"You won't need to ask. I'll be busy."

She looked wounded. "Even if you were slightly kidnapped, you don't have to be rude. Not when I'm so deliriously happy."

She bit her lip. With exactly the same expression in his big eyes, Maximus gazed reproachfully at me, too.

I had to admit, Libby looked beautifully rested and much happier than I'd seen her in months. She exhibited no aftereffects of her accident, and in fact seemed to exude an annoying good health. In truth, she appeared to be completely rejuvenated. The pink spots of color on her cheekbones were adorable.

I sighed. "I'm sorry. What did the police say when you got here?"

"That you should give them a phone call when you returned. And they want to talk to Tierney Cavendish. Did you know it's illegal to wave a gun around in the presence of children? It's corruption of minors."

"Before you have Tierney arrested, I have some information that might influence your decision."

As if she hadn't heard me, she bounced the baby on her hip and said breezily, "But I could hardly press charges against my own brother, could I?"

I stared at my sister. "How long have you known he's our brother?"

"Good grief, Nora, it's been years! Daddy let it slip ages ago."

"And you never mentioned that tidbit of information to the rest of us?"

"I've been busy! Anyway, I told the police Tierney was under duress, which should be taken into consideration. After all, the man he assumed was his father just died, and he was trying to make a connection with his natural father. I think I was convincing, but the police still want to talk to him. How did it go, by the way? Was Daddy gracious?"

"You mean, before he had his heart attack?"

"It wasn't a heart attack. Just a little fibrillation. He'll be released from the hospital by noon."

"Great," I said, hopes dashed that my parents might be out of my hair for a while. "Emma's outside, by the way. And she's got big news."

"What kind of news?"

I gave up the idea of breaking the latest family bombshell gently. "She had a contraceptive malfunction, and now there's a little Blackbird on the way. She's pregnant."

Libby's mouth opened, but no sound came out.

"That was my first reaction, too."

"Nora," she breathed.

"Hard to imagine Emma being a mother, huh?"

I expected Libby to go into a tirade about karma and

the spinning of stars and whatever hogwash she was currently obsessed with. But Libby put Maximus into his high chair and came over to me with compassion on her face.

Gently, she put her arms around me. "Darling, I'm so sorry. After your miscarriage, too. You must be crushed. Trust Emma to get lucky at the worst possible time."

My voice nearly failed. "She doesn't think of it as lucky. She wants to make an appointment at the clinic."

Swiftly, Libby hugged me. "What nonsense. Don't even think about that. It must feel like a knife in your heart. I'll talk to her. We'll figure out something. Are you going to be okay?"

"Yes. Of course. Don't worry about me."

"You don't get to decide when your family is allowed to worry about you." She patted my cheek. "We love you, Nora. And sometimes you need to accept that love. Okay, I know we can be exasperating, but the bottom line is that we want you to be happy. And you're certainly due. Why don't you take a shower and relax upstairs? Take a nap for a couple of hours."

"I have to go to work."

"Now?"

I checked my watch, but found my vision too blurry to read the numbers. "I guess I could take a nap."

Another hug. "Go ahead. I'll handle things down here."

The coffeemaker gave a final burp, and Libby poured a cup and pressed it into my hands. I couldn't prevent the suspicious expression that undoubtedly crossed my face. Her solicitous behavior triggered a red alert in my brain.

"What?" she demanded. "I can't be counted on in a crisis?"

"Okay, okay," I said, and drank a slug.

Resisting the urge to bust out bawling, I went out through the butler's pantry and up the staircase with the coffee cup in my hand. With every step, I grew more and more tired. A long night of tense melodrama began to ache in all my muscles.

I peeked into the bedroom across the hall from my own. Rawlins lay sprawled on the coverlet, his face squished into an eyelet pillow and both large feet dangling off the edge of the bed. He'd had a long night, too. And when, I wondered, had he grown so tall? He still wore his jeans and ice-cream-shop T-shirt. His cell phone lay on the coverlet near his hand. I could see a red light blinking frantically on it. His chatty new girlfriend, I thought. I closed the door gently and let him sleep.

When I turned around, I let out a squeak of fright.

Oscar stood in the hallway. He had a gun in one hand and a leather identification wallet in the other. He said, "Sorry. I thought you were another intruder. Oscar Bland, U.S. Treasury."

Chapter 17

The sight of the second gun in twelve hours blew a fuse in my brain. Furious, I said, "Put that damn thing away! Do you people think this house is some kind of shooting gallery?"

"Sorry," he said again, stashing the gun in a fold of his sarong. "I heard you come up the stairs, and thought—well, after what happened here yesterday, I don't want any more surprises."

I sagged against the doorjamb. "You and me both." His true identity finally sank into my brain, and I squinted at Oscar with new eyes. "You're a Treasury agent? For real?"

"As real as it gets. I've been assigned to keep an eye on your parents during the investigation of the Paine Investment Group. And let me tell you, this is the worst assignment I've ever had. I spent fifteen years in the Marine Corps, but even that didn't prepare me. Your parents are slippery characters."

"You're not a spiritual adviser?"

"I'm an Episcopalian."

I had a hard time imagining Oscar as an Episcopalian. Maybe it was the sarong. "My parents are at the hospital, you know."

"Affirmative. Another operative is at the hospital. I only came back to change my clothes. I had no idea island people had so much trouble with chafing."

"I see. Os—Mr. Bland, I don't mean to tell you how to do your job, but I wonder if you could stick around here for a few hours. I'm worried we might have another incident like yesterday."

His bushy eyebrows rose. "Cavendish is still on the loose?"

"Actually, I'm concerned about someone else. Chad Zanzibar. Would you recognize him? He's an actor—"

"Short kid? Wasn't he some kind of gremlin in a movie?"

"He was an elf. But don't let that fool you. He's actually capable of violence. I think he physically abused his own grandmother. And I'm concerned he might try to come here." I figured I didn't need to explain that Chad was looking to meet a real live mobster.

Oscar's posture seemed to stiffen with renewed Marine Corps vigor. "It would be a pleasure. In fact, after all this nutty yoga and diet stuff, I'm ready for some honest, hand-to-hand combat."

"If you see him, be my guest."

He nodded smartly. "Don't worry about a thing. I've got you covered."

Fending off exhaustion for just a little longer, I headed for my own bathroom. I put the coffee on the edge of the sink, turned on the shower and stripped off my clothes while the water heated up. One look in the mirror told me I hadn't gotten nearly enough sleep in the backseat of Tierney's car. I winced at my reflection and stepped under the warm water.

A minute later Michael came into the bathroom and shut the door. I heard him kick off his shoes and unfasten his belt.

Over the shower curtain, he said, "If anybody asks, I'm fixing your toilet."

I poured shampoo into the palm of my hand and lathered my hair while he undressed and drank the rest of my coffee. I asked, "Did you try the plumber story on Libby?"

"No, but the guy in the sarong believed me. Is there something wrong with your sister? She was actually polite to me downstairs."

"Scary, isn't it?" I rinsed my hair. "It always surprises me when she comes through in a crisis. But she does."

Michael climbed into the shower with me. As naked men go, he was magnificent.

He grabbed me and pulled me under the cascading water. "I don't want to talk about your sister."

His hands skimmed my body as if relearning the curves. I couldn't help doing the same thing and found all my favorite spots while he nuzzled my neck and planted kisses on my throat.

I asked, "Do you mind talking about my other sister?"

"I don't want to talk about anything," he murmured, pulling me close enough to feel every inch of him against me.

Around his kisses, I said, "I need to know about Emma."

"When I came up here, she was drinking ginger ale and talking to Henry. Why?" He wiped the water from his eyes. "You thought I slept with her, didn't you?"

"I couldn't quite let myself believe it. Not really. But you said some things—"

"Jesus, Nora."

"What was I supposed to think?" I demanded. "The night you came over here, you kept apologizing for—"

"Not for sleeping with your sister!"

"Well, you told me she was with you! And she's always had a thing for you, Michael. Admit it. Did she climb into your bed?"

"Every night," he said, sliding my wet hair off my shoulder. "But, fortunately, I was on the couch, so my virtue was safe."

"She tried, though, didn't she? To seduce you?"

"When she was drunk," he admitted. "But even then, she knew it was wrong, and she stopped it herself. Nora, you can't hold that against her. She hit rock bottom, and I said I'd help her only if she'd quit drinking and go to meetings. She was in bad shape. And now—well, maybe she's even worse off than before."

I found I was trembling again, but this time with relief. Perhaps I had known Michael couldn't have let himself be wooed into bed with anyone else. But hearing it said aloud was enormously comforting.

I said, "You didn't have to keep it a secret for so long."

"She didn't want anybody to know. In case she slipped up. I'm sorry you were miserable."

"Miserable doesn't cover it. But I'm better now."

"Good. But, wow. Now Emma's going to be a mother? It's hard to imagine that will turn out well." He reached past me for the soap and smelled it, trying to decide if it was too girlie to use. Or maybe he was thinking over something much more complicated. When his gaze dropped to me, his blue eyes were full of love. "What should we do? Ask her if she wants us to take the baby and raise it ourselves? You and me?"

I started shaking all over again. "Oh, Michael."

I didn't care anymore if he was America's Most Wanted. I didn't care about his criminal past. Or even if he continued to be tempted by the dark side. My own father was a crook, but I loved him without question. At least with Michael, I knew he'd never steal from me.

He pulled me into his body again until we melted together, slick with water. And probably some tears. He kissed me—gently this time. We played with the soap for a while and eventually turned off the shower, grabbed some towels and went into the bedroom. With the door locked and the sunshine streaming across the bed, we tumbled into the bedclothes and made up for weeks of being apart.

Afterward, Michael fell soundly asleep with his arms around me.

I dozed for a while, too, but eventually I woke and found myself thinking about Emma.

She was a lot like Tierney, I realized suddenly—a bundle of repressed emotions. Too stubborn, maybe, to ask for help figuring out their lives, yet stumbling forward anyway.

Except Emma didn't buy a gun and try to solve her problems by taking hostages.

That thought got me thinking about Tierney again. How troubled he was. How his parents—in their own way—had probably both loved him and yet dreaded when he learned their secret.

I wondered, too, how Hoyt's secret had factored into his murder.

Because surely it had.

Michael murmured in his sleep. When he shifted, perhaps dreaming, I slipped out of his arms and eased myself out of bed, hoping to let him rest longer. I took another, longer shower, dried my hair and eventually tiptoed back into the bedroom to find some lingerie and do my face in the mirror.

Sitting in my bra and panties in front of a tray of cosmetics, I thought about Elena Zanzibar. She had been devastated by the loss of her fortune at the hands of Hoyt Cavendish. Had learning of his embezzlement and her fear of Chad's rage driven the makeup maven to murder? Or had she promised to marry him only to discover his true gender at an inopportune time? And did she have the strength to push diminutive Hoyt off the balcony?

Or—if Michael was correct that Hoyt's murder couldn't have been premeditated—was it Chad who was most capable of the rage it must take to kill another human being?

I flicked on some mascara and sat back to check my reflection. In the mirror, I saw Michael sit up on one elbow.

He said, "You're frowning."

"Not at you." I said, "It's nice to see you back here."

"You mean it?"

"I love you," I said.

He leaned back against the headboard, cradling the back of his head. "I dare you to come over here and say that."

"I do have a job. At least for the moment. And I have places to go today." I turned around, but stayed seated on the slipper chair at my vanity. I crossed one leg over the other and put my hands in my lap. "Tell me what you plan to do about your brother. And don't skip the details. If last night taught you anything, it's how horrible it feels to be in the dark."

He didn't move, but my direct question prompted an answer. "As of last night, it's in the hands of the lawyers. It's time for Cannoli and Sons to earn their retainer fees."

"I want to know what happened."

"I don't think—"

"Michael. Tell me everything. I want the truth so I can understand and not be afraid."

"Okay." He thought it over and finally said, "I maneuvered a thing, and my father and my brother are going down. The whole family, in fact. It's tricky, and there's a lot at stake, not to mention a few loose ends to tie up. But I've thought it through, and this is the only way it's going to end without somebody getting whacked."

"You mean, you?"

"No, I'm not gonna die, Nora. But I don't want anybody else to end up dead, either. So it's taken time to get all the dominoes in order, you know? But now they're starting to fall. I didn't want you to be a part of it, didn't want you to know anything until it's over. Because it's going to get ugly in the papers. Worse than usual. I don't want your name spread around."

Although he spoke of a much simpler game, sometimes I thought Michael could be a chess champion. "Were there really microwave ovens in that stolen truck?"

He smiled, proud of me for figuring it out. "At first, yes."

"And you—? What?" The truth dawned. "You switched the cargo?"

"Abracadabra," he said.

"And last night?"

"Last night I . . ." He searched for the right word. "I convinced my father it would be smart to give some testimony against my brother."

"He's snitching? And you're sending your brother to jail?"

"Trust me, the world will be safer. Nobody wants that big idiot running around loose. And my father will do some time, too, but he'll be comfortable. Maybe learn to play golf."

"Will you have to testify against them?"

"Hell, no. I'm no rat."

Honor among thieves, I thought. He'd send his family to prison, but wouldn't stand up in court to do it. My bedroom was quiet.

I said, "What about you? Will you be safe?"

"Things will shake out in time."

"What does that mean?"

Michael's gaze darkened, but held mine steadily. "A lot of people want to see me back inside, Nora."

"Yes, I know." When he hesitated again, I said, "Prove that you love me and trust me, Michael. Tell me the truth."

He shrugged. "There's a fifty-fifty chance I'll do some time, too."

The window seemed to suck the air from the room. But I got up from the chair and went to the bed. I climbed on top of him, and he let me press both his hands to the headboard with mine. Looking deeply into his eyes, into his heart, I said, "I'll wait, if I must. I will be your wife and the mother of your children, and I will die in your arms. And I won't abandon you if you have to go to jail."

"Nora," he said, a catch in his throat.

"I love you forever."

"It won't take that long," he murmured. "Six months, tops."

I let him roll me into the bed, and we nuzzled and wept and murmured to each other and finally laughed a little when it became apparent he was ready to do more than talk.

I said, "I have Emma to worry about now, too, you know."

"Yeah." With his thumb, he gently smoothed our mingled tears from my cheek. "To tell the truth, I thought Henry might lend a hand in that department."

"Henry Fineman?" Surprised, I said, "How?"

"I figured they might hit it off."

"You're kidding, right? He's not exactly Emma's type."

"Her type hasn't worked out very well in the past. Maybe it's time for a new model. Besides, Henry has some experience overcoming booze."

I should have known he'd thought things through. Michael had an ulterior motive when he'd sent Henry to fix my computer.

I touched his face. "You think he's tough enough to give Em some help with the Twelve Steps?"

"Don't underestimate Henry. He's got a lot of hidden talents."

"Michael," I said finally, "are you matchmaking?"

He grinned. "Put on some clothes, will you? Or we'll spend the whole day here."

I slid out of his arms. "Okay, okay."

Michael swung out of bed and stretched. "Where are you headed today?"

"There's a luncheon in Gladwyne. If I go early, I might be able to talk to someone who works for the hostess—and was once employed by Hoyt Cavendish's wife."

"A butler, or something?"

"Or something. A closet manager. It's the latest in personal assistants."

"I don't know what you're talking about," he said. "But I have a few hours to spare. I'll take you."

"It's not your kind of crowd." I darted into the closet and flipped through hangers.

"I'll take you anyway," he called after me.

Not willing to be apart either, I said, "You won't exactly blend in."

"I'm going."

Among my grandmother's clothes, I found a floaty Galanos summer dress—sleeveless and in a color that could politely be called tangerine—with a hemline that would have hit the knee of a smaller woman. On me, it was enough of a minidress to look contemporary. I dug out a pair of YSL wedge sandals to tone it down, and added a vintage straw handbag with a bright Marimekko scarf—geraniums in tangerine and shades of pink—tied around the bone handle. Later, I'd swap the straw bag for an evening clutch, and I'd be suitably dressed for the chocolate gala.

I had another thought and went looking for the phone. I dialed the *Intelligencer* and asked to speak to Tremaine Jefferson, the videographer. I told him my plan and asked if he'd meet me at a party.

He said, "Sure. I got nothing better going on. Nobody else had any ideas of how to use me."

I thanked him and finished dressing. With myself adequately attired, I heated up the steam iron and found a white shirt of Michael's that he'd left behind last spring. I heard him shut off the shower as I touched up the collar and placket with the iron. I brought the shirt out into the bedroom just as he emerged from the bathroom in his jeans.

"Put this on," I told him, just as he started to pull a T-shirt over his head.

Amiably, he obeyed, and I rolled the sleeves up over his forearms. While he buttoned up, I went down the hall to the room where my parents were staying and found a braided leather belt of my father's. I brought it back and threaded it through the loops on Michael's jeans. It fit, but barely.

As I combed his still-damp hair back off his forehead and teased one curl alongside his temple, he looked down at me with suspicion. "Am I getting a makeover?"

"Not until we stop at Brooks Brothers or somewhere to buy you a blue sport coat."

He said, "I'm going to try, you know. To make this thing work out."

"I know. Trust me to be on your side no matter what."

He kissed my forehead. I closed my eyes and let the feeling inside me grow warm. It could be like this always, I thought. Having him in my bedroom. In my life. Maybe with a baby to raise. We'd make the kind of family we wanted most.

We lingered there, holding each other.

He said, "I love you. We're going to get it right this time." With a light kiss on my forehead, he released me. "It's going to be a hundred degrees outside today. Do I really need a coat?"

I laughed, shaky and happy. "A blue blazer will get a man into any occasion. And as long as you're coming along with me, you need to look the part."

"Of what? A Main Line gigolo?"

On the landing we encountered Rawlins, whose hair stood up in a classic bedhead. He was yawning and peering at the screen of his cell phone.

"Good morning!" I gave him a kiss on the cheek. "What's new with your girlfriend?"

"Aunt Nora! You're okay! And Mick! What are you doing here?"

When he figured out the obvious answer to his own question, Rawlins blushed and stammered. "I mean—uh—"

Michael said easily, "Good to see you, kid. I hear you were the hero last night."

Rawlins recovered quickly and snapped his phone shut. "I don't know. I felt pretty lame most of the time. What happened, Aunt Nora? How'd you get away from that guy?"

"That guy," I said, "is actually your uncle."

Rawlins gaped at me as I filled him in on the new

family history. I gave him the short version of my night with Tierney.

"So," I said, "I think we ought to stand by him, if that's possible."

"You mean, with the police and stuff?"

I said, "What he did was very wrong, of course. And I think we need to discuss it—as a family. But I hope we won't have to press charges."

Rawlins sighed. "That's going to be one heck of a family meeting."

We went downstairs together and found Libby snoring on the sofa with little Max comfortably molded on her chest and sucking contentedly on his binky.

A surprise awaited us in the kitchen.

While Oscar Bland lounged with deceptive nonchalance against the refrigerator, none other than Chad Zanzibar sat at the table, talking a mile a minute to Delmar.

Rawlins stopped dead in the kitchen doorway. He stared at Chad and stammered. "You—you—you're from *Valley of the Lords*! You're king of the elves!"

"I've got other projects going now," Chad snapped without getting up from the kitchen table. "But, hey— I'm proud of the work I did on *Valley*. Nice to meet you, dude."

Dazed with delight, Rawlins shook Chad's hand. "This is so cool. Like, mind-blowing. You're right here! Man, can you do the song? To summon the dragon?"

"Sorry, dude. I need backup singers for that."

"Right, right, the maidens of the forest. Wow, you got to kiss Christina Aguilera! How fantastic was that?"

"The bitch bit me," Chad replied. "Said I tasted like Tic Tacs."

"What are you doing here?" Rawlins asked, enthralled to find the star of his favorite movie in the kitchen.

Oscar listened attentively, one hand resting alertly on his hip. Michael eyed him while pouring himself a cup of coffee. I made us some cinnamon toast.

Chad said, "I'm doing research. Talking with my man,

Mick Abruzzo, see?" He gestured at Delmar. "We're working on my character for a TV show."

Rawlins looked mystified. But I sent him a meaningful glare, and he caught on. Uncertainly, he said, "Wow. Cool."

Chad went on. "Mick was just talking about stool pigeons, y'know? How a wiseguy would talk to the cops, right, Mick?"

Delmar shrugged. "A wiseguy wouldn't talk."

"You mean, a made man wouldn't say anything? Or just not to the cops?" Chad leaned forward, and his voice slid into an Edward G. Robinson accent—except with a California surfer twist. "Dude, you gotta level with me. I want to get all the details just right. If you hold out on me, I'm gonna be real unhappy."

I poured coffee for Delmar and slipped it in front of him. "Mr. Abruzzo doesn't talk much, Chad. Maybe you'd be better off asking someone else for help."

Delmar said, "Hey, I don't mind."

"See?" Chad looked up at me. Already, he was mimicking Delmar's posture and stolid facial expression. "He doesn't mind. I'm gonna immortalize him."

Rawlins slipped into the chair next to Chad's. "Hey, I can help with your research, Mr. Zanzibar."

"Call me Chad, dude."

"I've been hanging with Mick for a year now."

"Oh, yeah?"

"Sure, I know lots of stuff. I could be a big help."

Michael and I shared a glance, and Michael shrugged. If Rawlins knew anything, it was relatively harmless. We ate our cinnamon toast while they talked.

I dusted my hands on a kitchen towel. Then, in Libby's handbag, I found the keys to Jacque Petite's Rolls-Royce.

While the boys talked at the table, I handed the car keys to Michael. "Let's go, dude."

Chapter 18

Outside, we discovered Emma and Henry in conversation. If shouting at each other could be considered a conversation.

"That's what a sponsor is for!" Henry pushed his glasses up on his nose. "To call when you feel like you can't stop yourself from drinking. A sponsor is somebody you talk to."

"I don't need a sponsor," Emma snapped, adding a few expletives. She sat in the garden chair with her feet propped up, hugging her knees in the classic body language of a woman who didn't want to hear a word of what was said to her.

Henry sat down opposite her. "The first step is admitting you've got a problem."

"Oh, I've got p-p-p-p-problems, all right," she said, mocking his stutter. "Here come two of them right now."

"You two getting acquainted?" I asked.

Emma glowered at me. "How come you've got this geek hanging around?"

"Computer repairs," I said.

She laughed. "That makes perfect sense. What a nerd."

"He does excellent work. Even the jobs I never actually asked him to do."

Guilty of installing the GPS system on my cell phone, Henry had the grace to look embarrassed. "Sorry, M-Miss Blackbird. I was asked to do that, of course."

Michael said, "Don't get me into any more trouble, Henry."

Emma squinted up at Michael. "You've got a belt on. And your shirt is tucked in. What's the occasion? Big date in court?"

"You have a smart mouth for a girl who threw up in my car. Henry, you got a minute?"

Henry obediently got up. "Sure. How'd it go last night?"

"First of all," Michael said, "we need to discuss keeping your mouth shut in front of the ladies. Last night never happened, got it?"

Chagrined, Henry went across the lawn with Michael, where they had a serious conversation with their backs turned to us.

Emma watched them. "So you kissed and made up? The Love Machine is moving in with you again? With Mama and Daddy down the hall?"

"We haven't gotten around to discussing the particulars yet." I plunked onto the arm of Henry's vacated chair. "What about you moving back, too?"

"Here?" She laughed shortly. "Are you kidding? I don't need a ringside seat for the family drama."

"It's not so bad. In fact, it's rather nice getting reacquainted."

Emma cracked up, but her laughter sounded bitter. "You expect me to believe that?"

"Maybe not," I admitted. "But we're family, and we stick by each other. We can help you, too, Em."

Her face stiffened. "I don't need help."

The back door banged on its hinges, and Libby catapulted down the porch steps in a flutter of apron strings. "Yoo-hoo! I have just the thing for you, Emma!"

Emma groaned and covered her face. "You told her, didn't you?"

"Yep. I brought in the heavy artillery."

Balancing a tray with a silver teapot, cups and assorted plates with my best linen napkins on top, Libby picked her way across the grass in her sandals. She cried, "The best thing for morning sickness is tea and crackers! And I should know, considering how many times I've been with child. I wish we could celebrate with champagne, but nowadays people frown on the slightest sip of alcohol. Which I find utterly ridiculous. How are you feeling, dear sister?"

"Lib," Emma said, "I'll give you my entire collection of vibrators if you leave me alone."

"You have vibrators? No, don't tempt me." Libby dropped the laden tray onto the wicker table. "I've come to discuss your future."

Emma put her forehead down on her knees and moaned.

"First things first," Libby said. "Who's the father?"

"Might as well start with that," I agreed. "Well, Em? Do you know?"

Emma sat up indignantly. "Yes, of course, I know. I'm not as much of a skeeze as you think."

"Neither am I," Libby said. "I do like foreplay, though. But I don't often go all the way."

"No?" I asked. "Not even with Jacque Petite?"

"A woman should maintain a few mysteries. Not that you would know, Nora. Oh, don't look so innocent! I can imagine what you were doing upstairs this morning. A woman doesn't come down looking so refreshed after napping for two hours."

I blushed. "I—"

"Don't apologize. A woman needs sex as much as a man—maybe more. We have hormones to quell, urges to satisfy. Or we get wrinkles. I'm convinced there's a correlation. So, Emma?" Libby sat on the grass and arranged herself in a ladylike pose, effectively blocking Emma's escape. "Is it somebody we know?"

We both knew poisoned bamboo slivers shoved under her fingernails would have been more pleasant than the torture Libby could inflict. So Emma caved. "Hart Jones."

"Hartfield Jones?" I asked. "The banker? The guy you punched at the bar the other day?"

"I didn't punch him. I—oh, never mind. Yes, Hart Jones."

"Since when did you start dating men who actually graduated from eighth grade? Your last fling was with a car wash attendant."

"Isn't Hart married?" Libby frowned. "To one of the Haffenpepper girls? The beer heiress? The blond one who looks like a Bavarian princess? Her mother behaved like Eva Braun when she was secretary of the Ladies Auxiliary."

Emma turned a little green and took a steadying sip of ginger ale. "He's not married. Not yet, anyway."

"How in the world did you hook up with him?"

"It was an accident. I was in a hotel with—well, never mind, you wouldn't approve of him, either, even if all we did was eat hot wings and watch the fights on HBO—and I met Hart as he was coming out of the other penthouse suite. It was about two in the morning. We talked in the elevator. And he hit the stop button."

"You had sex in an elevator!" Libby cried. "I'm so jealous!"

"We did not!" Emma squinched her eyes shut as if to block out an embarrassing memory. "Maybe we goofed around a little. And then, okay, I guess we had sex in his car later."

"Ooh, I haven't had an automotive orgasm in years!" Libby loosened the strings of her apron. "Bucket seats are so constraining. I wonder if—"

"Lib," I said, "let's focus on Em for the moment, please?"

"Yes, of course. Just—what kind of car was it, Emma?"

"A Porsche. We drove to the Jersey Shore and when the sun came up, we—" She cut herself off and added gruffly, "Anyway, that's how it happened."

"It sounds romantic! Did he—? I mean, was he an attentive lover? Ladies come first, and all that?"

I said, "Did you see him again? Or was it a one-night thing?"

"Yeah, I saw him the following night and we—it happened again. Next thing I know, he's calling me. And—well, maybe I called him once or twice. It was supposed to be a little fun before his wedding, but it—it snowballed."

"So it's just sex?" Libby looked disappointed.

I knew Emma's pattern. Focusing on the physical shielded her from the kind of emotional investment she'd given—and lost—in her marriage.

"N-no," she said slowly. "We talk. We talk a lot, in fact. He's kinda funny. And," she said, "he listens."

Libby was shocked. "Listens? You mean he hears you, or he actually comprehends what you're saying and makes an appropriate grunt now and then?"

"He really listens," Emma insisted.

"Does he know?" I asked. "That you're pregnant?"

"God, no!" Emma was horrified by the suggestion. "What is he supposed to do? Buy me a ring and a house in Bryn Mawr? Can you see me—a suburban house-wife? PTA meetings and the garden club? Sunday dinners with Eva Braun? I don't want him to know!" She hugged herself fiercely.

"Why not? Maybe he'd actually do the right thing," Libby said.

"The right thing?" Emma laughed. "What would that be, exactly?"

"Child support," Libby said. "Very important. If I had to minister to the emotional and psychological needs of my children and worry about their next meal, too, I'd never be as effective a mother as I am now."

Deciding not to point out that she was an effective mother only because the rest of us frequently pitched in, I asked, "Do you love him, Em?"

Emma snorted. "Let's not get mushy. Maybe you and the Love Machine get all googly-eyed with each other, but that's not my style."

But I thought I saw something in her gaze—fleeting, perhaps, but definitely more than total denial.

I said, "Hart's very successful."

"Good-looking, psychologically stable and tall," Libby said, nodding. "All important qualities in a partner. What's his astrological sign?"

"Gee, I don't know," Emma snapped. "Next time I see him, I'll ask. And get his opinion on national health care, too."

I said, "I saw him at the zoo fund-raiser last year. He had some kids from a group home with him, so he's not a corporate robot. He seemed to actually enjoy children."

"Shut up," Emma said. "He's great in the sack. That's all I needed to know."

"So what's your plan?" Libby asked.

"There is no plan." Emma swirled the remaining contents of her ginger ale can. "As soon as I stop puking long enough, I'm going to take myself down to—"

"Don't say it," I said. "I can't stand to hear what you might do to that child."

Emma caught a glimpse of my face and looked away. She sipped her ginger ale and fell silent.

Libby said, "He has a right to know."

"Yes," I said. "You have to tell him, Em."

Briskly, Libby took charge. "I have an idea."

Emma sighed. "Oh, no."

"I propose we meet here tonight, the three of us. And we'll take a little drive together."

"Where?" I asked with caution.

Libby put up her hands to fend off more questions. "Let me worry about that. Just be here at dusk, okay?"

"Dusk? Does that mean we need cover of darkness?"

Emma said, "Are you going to perform one of your cockamamy magic spells?"

"They're not magic spells! I embrace many spiritual practices, and if you paid attention to the phases of the moon like I do, you wouldn't be in this pickle, young lady. So put on your big-girl panties and get ready for tonight."

"Wait," I said. "I have to make an appearance at the Chocolate Festival. Emma probably has to work this evening."

Our little sister shook her head. "I got fired. Last night, after you took my ginger ale, I yakked in the bathtub. They don't want me back."

Instantly, I felt guilty for getting her fired. "You could have told me you were drinking ginger ale."

"You didn't give me a chance," she shot back. "You were too busy yelling at me."

"You deserved it. Will we be finished by ten, Libby, so I can attend the festival gala?"

"Certainly."

Michael and Henry finished their conference, and Michael took a call on his cell phone. Henry returned to the shade under the oaks with us.

Libby gave Henry a once-over and made a snap decision. "Do you know anything about teaching language skills to infants?"

Henry adjusted his glasses. "M-my m-mother read *The Complete Works of Shakespeare* to m-me before I could walk."

"And look how well that turned out," Emma remarked.

"Henry," I said. "Do you know how to find information about people on the Internet?"

An expression of guilt washed over his face. He said, "I paid the fine. No jail time."

"That's not what she means." Michael strolled over, pocketing his cell phone. "She wants you to do a job."

Henry brightened. "Oh. What kind of information do you need?"

"I'm wondering about a woman named Brandi Schmidt. She's a television personality who—"

"I know who she is," Henry said. "The one who m-mispronounces everything."

"That's her. Can you find out where she lived before she came to Philadelphia?"

"Is that all you want to know?" Henry glanced at Michael for reassurance.

Michael said, "Don't do anything fancy. Hear me? I hate posting bail when I don't know half the words in the indictment."

"Okay." Henry looked at his feet. "Nothing fancy."

I said, "I appreciate your help, Henry."

"You want me to start anywhere in particular?"

"She used to work in cable television." I tried to think of everything I knew about Brandi. "She joined a gay and lesbian group when she moved here. And she uses a wheelchair. Does that help?"

"Lesbian wheelchair users on TV," Emma said. "Now, there's a demographic that's bound to have fans on the Internet."

"Watch out," Michael said. "You can't talk like that with a baby around."

"Bite me."

Libby said, "My babies all bit me when I nursed them." She rubbed one breast. "It hurts like the dickens."

The priceless expression on Emma's face made us all laugh.

Finally I said, "Henry, maybe you could keep an eye on Chad Zanzibar, too. The kid in the kitchen. He could be dangerous."

Henry seemed pleased that I entrusted him to keep the family safe. After last night's ordeal, he must have been feeling inadequate.

Emma recovered from the idea of breast-feeding and squashed his ego all over again. "Just knowing the geek is in charge makes me feel much safer."

Michael said, "I think that situation is under control. Between Delmar and that cop in the funny getup, he'd have to be a genius to get away with something."

"He's no genius." I grabbed Michael's hand. "Let's get out of here."

We left my sisters and Henry and walked across the lawn together. Michael tucked me into the cushy front seat of the Rolls, and off we went with Libby's cries about car theft echoing behind us.

From the road, I telephoned Lexie.

She said, "Sweetie, I want to thank you for last night. You were a pal to come home with me. I'm sorry if I said anything unforgivable."

The evening at Lexie's house felt as if it had happened a month ago. "There's nothing you could do that I wouldn't forgive, Lex. You were amazingly gracious, considering. How are you feeling today?"

"Better, now that Tierney Cavendish is the prime murder suspect. So you can give up your little investigation."

I decided not to spoil her good humor. "And Crewe?"

"What about him?"

"Is he there?"

"Certainly not. I threw him out of here at ten last night. But," she added, "since you're so concerned about him, I will admit he's coming over shortly to make lunch. I don't know why he finds food preparation so therapeutic, but he does."

"Listen, I just wanted to let you know that I have your compact."

"My what?"

"Your compact. I found it on the floor of your private loo at the firm. Silver? From Tiffany? Probably some kind of heirloom?" I looked at the filigreed container in my hand. "Anyway, it's safe in my possession."

"I don't own a compact," Lexie said. "Where did you say you found it?"

"On the floor of your bathroom at the office. I—good heavens." I swallowed hard. "Do you suppose the murderer dropped it on her way out after pushing Hoyt off the balcony?"

My head swam with the possibilities. Brandi? Elena?

Or one of her fan club? Who might have dropped a compact?

"Lex, what can you tell me about Brandi Schmidt? Without violating six different privacy laws?"

"Why?"

"Because she was there at the time of the murder and—"

"Nora, the woman uses a wheelchair."

"I know, I know. I just want to know more about her. Where did she get the money Hoyt was supposed to invest for her?"

"I have no idea. The usual places, I suppose. Inheritance, smart investments. The lottery, for all I know."

"Can you find out for sure?"

"Nora—"

"That information is confidential?"

"Sweetie, things are so—so awful right now. I can hardly concentrate. The press is howling at my door. That bitch from channel eight—she called my private line at five a.m."

"I'm sorry."

"And some insufferable asshole from the SEC actually threatened me this morning. I don't know how much more I can stand."

"Forget I asked about Brandi. Relax, Lex. Take your kayak on the river. Clear your mind."

She was quiet. "Nora?"

"Yes?"

"I—thank you. For believing in me."

"Don't be silly," I said. "You're my dearest friend. You know I'll do anything humanly possible for you."

We ended our call, and I tucked the cell phone into my bag.

Michael said, "You didn't tell Lexie about Cavendish's big secret."

"That he was a woman? No. She sounded—I'm worried about her."

"Nora—" Michael caught himself. Slowly, he said, "This one could break your heart, you know."

"You think Tierney killed Hoyt? Or Daddy?"

He shook his head, eyes on the road. "Everything about this feels wrong. And I'm not talking about the whole transgender thing. That part, I can actually understand."

"You can?"

"Sure. Everybody's a little twisted. And we're all capable of extremes. In the right circumstance, the potential for crazy stuff is in all of us. Me. You. Lexie. Even little Max. Watch that baby, and you can see him thinking. What would feel good right now? Most of us learn to control it, but some people never do. Or they get pushed too far at the wrong moment, and it's all over. Last night, I was ready to do some serious damage. It's lucky you were there to stop me, because I could have—"

"But you didn't. What are you saying?"

"Just—maybe something just as big triggered a crazy response. And you should let the cops figure out what and who it was."

I sat quietly in the car, thinking about what kind of human urge might provoke someone to murder.

Chapter 19

I put my speculations aside when we arrived at the men's clothier that my husband and his friends had patronized. Time for shopping. The salesman who had often helped Todd was assisting a boy and his mother choose a suit for his bar mitzvah. We found another accommodating clerk who seemed unintimidated by Michael. He brought three different navy blue jackets to us, and with subtle signals he gave his opinion on which looked the best.

The Brioni was cut perfectly to fit Michael's shoulders and slim hips. The mother stopped fussing over the bar mitzvah boy to peek sideways at Michael's reflection in the mirror.

Michael paid cash, which was the only thing that made the unflappable salesman blink.

Half an hour later, Michael pulled the Rolls into the long governor's driveway that swept gracefully past four weeping willow trees and up to the imposing veranda of White Heather, the family estate of the Scaithe family. In case we needed to tie up a horse or two, a stone, black-faced jockey stood at the bottom of the wide staircase. A charred iron kettle used for cooking apple butter sat in the grass nearby, planted with a cascade of flowers.

Michael took a long look at the place through the windshield. "These people have seen *Mandingo* too many times."

"The Scaithes are a little eccentric," I admitted.

"No kidding."

"But they might have some useful information to share."

"You going to tell me what kind? Or am I tricked out like one of your society boys for a reason?"

"Nobody would mistake you for a society boy. Except maybe one person. You'll figure it out. Follow my lead."

We got out of the car into the sunshine and went up the stone steps. Except for his broken nose and the lack of golf clubs, Michael could have passed for a suburban Philadelphia stockbroker on his way to lunch at a club with a million-dollar initiation fee.

Sigismund Scaithe himself flung open the massive front door and peered at us. "You're too early!" roared the elderly gentleman.

"It's Nora Blackbird, Sigi. I thought I could get a few details about the party before everyone arrives. For my column in the *Intelligencer*."

"Nora? I didn't recognize you. My stars, you got tall, young lady!"

Sigi was glaring at Michael, so I waved my hand. "I'm over here, Sigi. See?"

He squinted myopically in my direction, still refusing to wear glasses after all these years. "Why, there you are! Yes, of course, prettier than ever."

He took my hand enthusiastically, clasping mine in his two gnarled paws.

Sigi's halo of untrimmed salt-and-pepper hair stood out on his head like the mane of an old lion, which he was, in a sense. Having long ago put aside his dignified gray suits, he now wore a pair of plaid golf pants hitched high above his waist by navy blue suspenders printed with the Harvard seal. His shirt was pea green. His shoes were white patent leather. A former adviser to a president, this morning he looked more like a man who'd been dressed by a circus clown.

Sigi's rheumy eyes were so pouched by wrinkles that he couldn't have seen much even if he could find his glasses.

"I get it," Michael murmured to me when he realized I was about to introduce him to a blind man.

"Sigi, I'd like you to meet Michael Abruzzo."

But Sigi Scaithe's gaze had already traveled past Michael to the vague shape of the Rolls-Royce in the driveway. Sigi suddenly quivered like a bird dog pointing at a covey of fat quail. "Is that a Silver Seraph?"

Michael turned around to look at the car. "Yes, it is."

"That's a quality vehicle."

I said, "I was thinking maybe you two have a common interest in cars. Sigi, here's an enthusiastic audience, if you'd like to show off your Duesenberg."

"A Duesenberg?" Michael's amusement vanished.

Sigi's wrinkles deepened into a proud smile. "Commissioned for the Duke of Windsor, as a matter of fact. I pulled a few strings and had it shipped here in 'sixty-eight. Wouldn't you rather take a walk to my garage instead of eating cucumber sandwiches?"

"Yes, sir, I would."

"Run along," I said when Michael turned to me. "Have fun, you two. I'll find Cici by myself. She's in her closet, I suppose, Sigi?"

Sigi didn't bother to answer me. He put his arm around Michael and swept him off to the garage. I heard him say, "I have beer in a fridge in the garage. Would you like one?"

Glad to be rid of Sigi, who rarely left his wife alone, I let myself in the front door and walked the length of the marble foyer. A sweeping staircase rose over my head, but I knew the Scaithes no longer used any of the rooms on the second floor. Not since they added on a modern suite for themselves at the back of the grand old house.

I heard the usual preparty noise of kitchen staff in the distance. Delilah Fairweather's distinctive laugh roared over the voices of others, so I knew the party was in the good hands of the city's best event planner. With the caterers, she was undoubtedly making frenetic last-minute preparations for the luncheon. I decided not to interrupt.

The scent of flowers permeated all the rooms as I passed through them. Huge sprays of mixed blooms sat on all the tables and consoles. Outside a set of French doors, I could see some of the waitstaff smoking on the terrace.

I found my way through the maze of rooms—one salon after another connected by doors like in Versailles. Gilt mirrors, lavish Oriental rugs and French furniture upholstered in delicate silks all reflected the cultured taste of their mistress.

Portraits of the master's ancestors stared at me from the walls—many of them in uniform. I turned the corner by a tall secretary desk and found myself confronted by the full-length portrait of James Hilson Scaithe, the ancestor who made a fortune in mysterious ways during the Civil War. His shady business acumen set up each succeeding generation of his family in enough money so they could devote themselves to more rewarding work. Sigi, for instance, had spent many years shuttling between Philadelphia and the Reagan White House.

In a hallway, I came upon Eric Foster, giving a bouquet a final fluff in a Venetian glass vase. It was a surprise to see him two days in a row.

"Nora! What are you doing—? Oh, of course. You're on the job, right, sweetie pie?"

"Right." I accepted his air kiss. "Want to give me the lowdown on the flowers for my column?"

Eric wore another skimpy tank top, but with a white silk shirt thrown over it, along with chinos and woven loafers. "Nothing special—just expensive. Cici wanted 'acres and acres' of tulips, but they're out of season, and even I couldn't justify the amount of money she'd have to shell out to import enough. How are you? Yesterday when you visited the town house, you looked—a little peaked."

"It was the heat. And I've been upset about Hoyt Cavendish's death."

"Oh, yeah, I heard a bunch of people are under suspicion. Including Lexie Paine." Eric popped his eyes wide at the idea of such a high-profile suspect. "I mean, she's a ruthless businesswoman, but hardly the homicidal type."

"She's not ruthless," I said, surprised to hear my friend characterized negatively.

"You don't think so? My mistake." He shrugged. "So whodunit, do you think? So many possibilities."

"I don't know."

"Daniel said you asked about Brandi Schmidt. What a mixed-up girl, right? Is she, or ain't she?"

"What do you mean?"

"When she first came to town, she hung out with all the kinky girls. She said she was doing research for a story for television. But nothing ever happened."

"Maybe she was too shy to admit she was gay herself, you think?"

Eric gave his flowers one more critical glance and moved to the next table. "I got the impression she was collecting information for nefarious purposes. Everyone felt very used afterwards."

"What kind of information?"

"You know—who's gay and pretends not to be—the whole bent, blackmailable gamut."

"Cross-dressing?"

"Sure—all the naughty stuff that pays so well if you have a money-grabbing soul."

I wondered. Did Brandi have an inkling about Hoyt's true identity? And if so, what did she do with that information?

Eric said, "Funny you should mention Brandi again. After you left, Daniel and I went out for dinner. We saw her on the street. In fact, we wondered if maybe she was following you."

Startled, I said, "Why?"

"I don't know. We didn't talk to her. She was driving the TV station's van, and kind of trailing you. It looked ridiculous to us, and we laughed a little, but afterwards, Daniel wondered if maybe it wasn't a little suspicious."

"I didn't see her."

"I'm sorry now that we didn't catch up to her and ask some questions."

"That's okay. Thanks for thinking of me, though."

"We've thought a lot about you," Eric said. "Nora, you know we're staying in Spain for a few months, right?"

"Yes, it sounds wonderful."

"Thanks. We're looking forward to it. But we were wondering if you could help us solve a problem. Do you know anybody who'd like to house-sit for us? Free rent in exchange for taking in the mail and watering the plants? Maybe until Christmas? We hate to put the dog in a kennel that long, and it's never a good idea to leave a house empty."

"It shouldn't be hard to find someone to stay in that house. It's beautiful, Eric. And who wouldn't love to live in Rittenhouse Square?"

"But the dog," he warned. "We need somebody who'd walk him and make him feel like we didn't abandon him."

"I'll think about it," I promised. "I'm sure I'll think of a dog lover who'll jump at the chance."

"Thanks, Nora."

"I'd better get to work. Have you seen a guy from the *Intelligencer*?"

"What kind of guy?"

"One with a video camera."

"Not yet, sorry."

"How about Cici?"

He pointed down the hall. "She's in her closet."

I waved good-bye and continued down the corridor, tucking the new information about Brandi into the back of my mind. I wasn't sure how to process it yet.

At the door leading to the bedroom suite, I called, "Cici? It's Nora Blackbird!"

My voice was muffled by the thick leopard-print carpet and the lavish floor-to-ceiling draperies on the windows. In one alcove stood a four-poster bed big enough to sleep a platoon as long as they enjoyed pink bedding. A spray of pink roses lay artfully on the pillow—Eric's handiwork, no doubt.

Somebody else had staged the rest of the room just as photogenically. Beside the bed, a pair of chintz chairs sat before a tall bookcase crammed with leather-bound volumes. An open set of double doors led to the second bedroom—obviously Sigi's, judging by the manly leather furniture and the gray and camel colors of the bedclothes. On the pillows, a creative soul had left a box of cigars.

Wand thin and leggy as a colt, Cici Scaithe stalked into view in a floor-length chiffon robe with matching mules. With a jeweled turban on her head, she looked ready to step into a Gloria Swanson movie.

"Nora! I was afraid you were Sigi coming back to pester me. Men who retire definitely need hobbies. You're just the person to help with these damn place cards. You know exactly how to mix people at a party. Must be your mother's influence. I heard a rumor she's back in town. I hope she still has the Peretti bracelets I loaned her."

Chapter 20

"Cici, how delightful to see you." I crossed the carpet and aimed a kiss past her powdered cheek, hoping to derail her first line of questioning. "I thought you might let me have a few party details for my column."

She carried a clove cigarette that glowed in the long ebony holder poised between her skeletal fingers. Her voice was froggy from years of smoking. "Of course, darling, anything you like. Don't you look chic! I love Galanos!"

Unlike her husband, Cici wore an oversized pair of round, thick-framed black glasses that magnified her eyes and gave her the appearance of a long-limbed insect. A very well-dressed insect, of course. The rhinestones on her glasses matched the clustered diamonds in her earlobes.

"Coming from you," I said, "that's either a great compliment or a bald-faced lie."

"I never lie," she declared. "Did you know Galanos started out here in Philadelphia? I have several dresses he designed. More formal than that one, of course. He worked best in ball gowns, don't you think? Doesn't he do draping like nobody else?" She plucked at the pleats around my waist. "And you wear it so well. Why didn't you marry my nephew, Nora, dear? You'd make such a beautiful couple."

If there was one person in the world I hated more than Jamie Scaithe, I couldn't think who it could be. He'd tortured me by selling drugs to my husband and topped it off by suggesting I should marry him only a few months after Todd's death.

But I liked Cici, and so I lied. "I guess the timing wasn't right."

"Hm." She skewered me with a knowing stare. "Well, it's a damn shame. You'd bring some class into Jamie's life. God knows he's a perfect shit. Will you do the place cards?"

"Of course." I took a quick glance through the vellum cards and saw that most of the guests were Philadelphia grandes dames who'd known one another since trading silver rattles in their cradles. The only trick was keeping separate the ones who'd shared husbands or lovers.

Cici said, "Elena Zanzibar was supposed to come early to help with the seating chart, but she fell down a flight of stairs yesterday."

"She fell?" I remembered seeing Elena's bruises. They hadn't looked like injuries from a fall. Nor did she try to explain them away by concocting a story. But I assumed she didn't want her friends to guess the truth.

"Yes, it sounded awful. Look through those cards while I choose something to wear, will you? And find a way to keep Pootsie Burke and Rondanelle Panoline apart, okay? I heard they wore the same dress to a fundraiser and aren't speaking at the moment."

"Did you speak to Elena yourself?"

"Yes, poor thing. It's hell getting old. At her age, she should install one of those chairlifts so she doesn't go splat some night on her way to the kitchen for a snack. Come into my closet, Nora. Tell me if this is the most outrageous idea for a party you've ever heard."

She tamped out her clove cigarette in a Baccarat ashtray and pulled me through the double doors into the vast space where she kept her wardrobe.

Cici's closet was larger than most living rooms. Twin crystal chandeliers sparkled at the ceiling—the bulbs were soft pink to flatter elderly complexions—and cabbage rose wallpaper glowed on the walls. Racks of clothes ringed the space—organized by color from white to black with the entire spectrum in between. Shelves and drawers for sweaters and sportswear lay beneath a white marble counter that ran twenty feet from end to end.

Today, six round tables had been set up in the center of the room, each laid with eight place settings, bowls of flowers and short candlesticks. Suitable decor for a ladies' luncheon. Each upright gilt chair had been festooned with a rose-colored ribbon to match the wallpaper.

Four slipper chairs stood in a row in front of the clothing, each with a fabulous couture dress artfully displayed on it.

"The party is a brilliant idea, Cici," I said. "Who wouldn't want to see your closet? And raising money for women who need suitable clothes to get started in business—it's simply genius."

"My friends were the first to plunk down a thousand bucks apiece to take a gander at my underguchies. We sold out of tickets in one day. I wish I had room for more tables. We could have raised a fortune."

"It's a good cause," I insisted. "And a terrific opportunity to show off your collection. Next year you should set up a tent in the garden to accommodate more tables. Then you could give tours in here. I bet Dilly Farquar would kill to play the tour guide."

Cici stared at me. "By gum, that's brilliant. You're a wonder, Nora."

"Well, I'm starting to understand fund-raising in a whole new way."

"You have so many talents!" She grinned and waved around the whole closet. "What do you think? Prime stuff, right?"

I couldn't resist taking a short tour. On one rack hung a dozen white shirts—all custom-made. On another—skirts by designers who used the finest fabrics. I noted an unmistakable Roberto Cavalli print, another chiffon that screamed Carolina Herrera. One rack held noth-

ing but black trousers—silk, twill, wool and everything
in between. A lit, glass-fronted case displayed immaculate cashmere sweaters in every imaginable color. And
racks and racks of shoes, of course. There must have been
fifty pairs of slingbacks, not to mention sandals, pumps
and slides of every description. The Chinese red soles of
Christian Louboutin were particularly distinctive.

But her collection of couture gowns—everything from
a Lagerfeld Beaux Arts masterpiece with a dozen layers
of carefully shredded lace, to a series of understated Bill
Blass dresses that had surely been worn to inaugura-
tions as well as society balls—that's what took my breath
away. Every one was perfectly hung on a padded hanger
and stuffed with nonacid paper to maintain its feminine
contours. I held on to the handle of my handbag with
both hands to stop myself from caressing each of them.

It was the work of a lifetime. If you could call it
work.

"It's all so beautiful, Cici." I turned to her. "What
would you think of filming a video tour we could run on
the newspaper's Web site?"

"A video tour?"

"Yes, I have a cameraman coming. You could walk
me through, and we could talk about the clothes—just
five or ten minutes. If we gave people a sense of what
you have here, you could sell hundreds of tickets next
year."

Doubtfully, she said, "And who would watch this
video?"

"People on the Internet."

"You mean pornographers?"

I laughed. "The Internet's not all about sex, Cici. Although it seems that way, doesn't it? No, I think our online readers would love a glimpse of your lifestyle."

"I get e-mail, but I don't understand the Internet
completely." She considered my proposal for a moment,
then peeped a smile at me. "It sounds like fun! And you
know I love to show off. Why else would I have a party

like this one? But you wouldn't play the video before today's party, would you, Nora? I'd hate to spoil things for my guests."

"It won't run until the weekend, I'm sure."

"Let's do it! But I'd better get dressed first. Standing next to you, I'll look like an old frump." Cici examined me from behind those big eyeglasses. "But you wear that little number better than your grandmama could have. Who does your alterations?"

I gave her the name of one of Lexie's finds—a young woman who had studied in Paris and was working on becoming a full-fledged designer on her own. She was a meticulous, yet creative, seamstress.

Cici nodded approvingly. "Yes, she does some work for me now and then, too. I seem to be losing my ass, and no amount of exercise can get it back." She put one hand on one buttock and jiggled. "See? Pretty soon I'll have to jettison half my wardrobe. All the tight pants, at least."

"You look terrific," I said. "So do all the clothes."

"Well, I have Jennifer to thank for that, of course. She organized all of this for me. Last year, I couldn't find half my things—and now it's all beautifully arranged. She's an angel."

At the mention of her closet manager, I perked up. "Where is Jennifer? I thought she'd be here today for sure."

"Yes, she deserves a lot of the credit. I'm always throwing things on the floor, but Jennifer's like a curator. She had some kind of family emergency and had to cancel. A crying shame, right? That she can't take a bow today, of all days."

"I'm so sorry to hear she's not here. You got Jennifer from Muriel Cavendish, didn't you?"

Cici began to flick through hangers to choose something to wear. "I sure did. When Muriel died, I snapped her up. Doubled her salary to make it worth her while. Then we started on this project. Can you believe it took us over a year to build and organize this closet?"

"It's clearly a labor of love. Has Jennifer ever talked about her work for Muriel?"

Cici's eyes narrowed behind her round glasses. "Why do you ask?"

"Hoyt's death has certainly raised a lot of questions about the Cavendishes."

"What's your particular question?"

I blushed. "I know I'm being very rude, Cici. I should keep my mouth shut and ignore what's happened. But I have a—a friend who's been questioned about Hoyt's murder."

"Lexie Paine."

"Yes. The police are totally wrong to suspect Lexie, of course."

"Still waters run deep. With you, that is." Cici continued to study me. "Working for a living seems to have done you a lot of good, Nora. You've developed some drive. As for Lexie, well, she comes from a high-strung family. Her mother—you know all about her temper and her love affairs and whatnot. I wouldn't be surprised if Lexie didn't have a few genes that—"

"Lexie's completely innocent," I said firmly. "I wondered if Jennifer might know something that might help exonerate her."

"You think Jennifer knew something about Muriel?"

"Muriel and Hoyt. And anyone else who was . . . intimate with them."

If Cici knew the truth about Hoyt's true gender, her years of good manners enabled her to keep a completely bland face. She said, "Muriel and Hoyt had their problems. We all knew that. Their boy—such a darling child, but he was troubled. They did everything to help him—good schools and whatnot. I'm sure he was a terrible strain."

"Yes," I murmured.

"Their marriage endured that, and more. You learn to live with your husband's frailties, don't you?"

From the knowing, sidelong glance she sent me, I knew she referred to Todd and his drug addiction as well as my father's assorted misbehaviors. But I resisted her subtle attempt to draw me out on either subject. "Did Hoyt have frailties?"

"All men do." She waved one thin hand to include half the human population. "Most of them, we learn to live with. Mind you, Hoyt never made a pass at me. I'm a foot taller than he was, of course, when I wear my heels. And I wear heels at all times, you know. But Jennifer mentioned . . ." She hesitated. "I suppose I'm gossiping now."

To keep her talking, I prompted, "Hoyt had affairs?"

"I don't know how many. But Muriel confided in Jennifer once that Hoyt was being hassled."

"Hassled?"

"To buy a woman's silence."

"I don't know what you mean, Cici. Was he supporting a mistress? Or paying blackmail?"

Cici sighed. "That's such an ugly word, isn't it? Blackmail? But I got the distinct impression Hoyt needed to pay off a lady to save his marriage. Muriel was crushed, nearly inconsolable. Jennifer stayed with her for a week while Muriel mourned. But she snapped out of it, eventually. Hoyt must have made it up to her. She had beautiful jewelry."

"Who was the woman?" I asked. "Do you know who Hoyt was seeing?"

Cici shook her head. "Someone young, that's all I know."

"Do you really think it was a love affair? Or maybe something else?"

"What else is there?"

From a rack of beautiful daytime outfits, Cici selected a chiffon pants suit in a creamy taupe color. To dress, she stripped down to her matching La Perla bra and panties right in front of me. She had no scars that hinted at cosmetic surgery of any kind. Her body was lithe from years of sports, strict dieting and lots of cigarettes. The suit—a column of chiffon that fell straight from her shoulders—emphasized her elegant height and slender build. To conceal the less-than-youthful skin of her throat, the face-framing collar of the suit fitted up under her chin.

Cici turned a key and slid open a wide drawer full of jewelry. A light automatically came on, and the gold, silver and gems sparkled beneath her fingertips. She selected a long rope of graduated pearls and put them around her neck. They draped to the middle of her sternum.

At last, she stepped into a pair of white mules with four-inch heels, then walked to the three-paneled mirror. As soon as she arrived at the mirrors, a bank of pinkish lights popped on—triggered by the motion of her walk. She studied her reflection critically and made minor adjustments to her sleeves.

The turban on her head looked like a crown.

She tipped her head for another view of herself. "The diamond earrings are too much for daytime, but they'll make a good impression on video, won't they?"

"Yes, indeed," I said.

We spent ten minutes arranging the place cards on her tables. Then the videographer arrived. Tremaine wore a photographer's canvas vest over a T-shirt and rumpled khakis, not to mention dreadlocks that needed attention, but Cici welcomed him as if he were royalty.

Tremaine and I had a short conversation, and I was relieved to see that he understood his craft and trusted me that we had an interesting subject to film. He looked stunned by his surroundings, but he quickly got to work filming shots of the closet, the chandeliers and the automatic lights. He hovered over the jewelry drawer for several minutes while I prepared Cici for the tour.

I needn't have worried about her on-camera skills. Cici was a natural. All I did was stay out of her way and lob questions to her while she walked around her closet, identifying certain dresses and reminiscing about the spectacular events she'd worn this or that to. She surprised me by pulling out a suit she'd worn to Ascot, and even found the matching hat in a box on a high shelf, which she modeled, laughing.

At the end of the tour, she pulled a pashmina from a shelf and wrapped herself in its luxurious folds. With a gay laugh, she looked into the camera and said, "It's a wrap!" as she tossed the pashmina over her shoulder.

Tremaine laughed, too. When he put the camera down, he said, "Great stuff, ladies!"

Cici went off to greet her arriving guests, and I had a short conversation with Tremaine.

He said, "I got some good footage here, and I'll go outside to get a few shots of the house, too. Can you come to the office to help edit?"

"When?"

"As soon as possible. This afternoon? In an hour or so?"

I wasn't accustomed to the fast turnaround time other reporters coped with on a daily basis. But I said, "I'll be there."

"Good. I've been listening to the new managing editor critique the stuff other reporters have brought to the online edition. Just so you know, he'll either love this or hate it."

I gulped, remembering the new editor had worn a frayed oxford shirt and a well-worn pair of trousers to his meeting with the staff. I doubted he appreciated fashion.

As the guests began to arrive for the luncheon, I chatted with a few of the ladies I knew. They all had come wearing their most elegant summer suits and *ooh*ed over all the details of Cici's closet. I enjoyed the chatter about her clothes. But my schedule was getting more crowded, so I slipped away just as the waiters appeared with glasses of champagne.

Outside, I found an accident.

The Duesenberg sat crookedly at the bottom of the driveway, one tire flat. A police cruiser had rolled in behind the big car, red and blue lights flashing. The young men who had been valet-parking all the guests' cars hung around the porch, watching the drama unfold.

Sigi stood at the rear tail fin of his grand car, talking to a serious-faced cop in mirrored sunglasses.

Michael lounged against the hood, arms folded across his chest. Calmly, he waited for me to hurry over.

"What happened?" I was breathless with worry.

Michael jerked his head toward Sigi. "The old guy wanted to take his car for a spin. Ended up bashing at least six mailboxes before he sideswiped a cruiser."

"Is anyone hurt?"

"Only his pride. This is going to escalate, though."

I glanced at the cop, who was already ignoring Sigi's bluster and shooting frowns in Michael's direction.

"Did you drive the car?"

Michael shook his head. "Nope. But this cop called for backup. And he spotted the Rolls."

"Oh, my God." I clapped one hand over my mouth.

A second police cruiser slipped through the gate, and the cop got out into the sunlight and walked around Jacque Petite's silver Rolls-Royce.

Michael behaved with complete calm when the questions started. Even when a third cruiser arrived, and the cops forgot about Sigi's bad driving and figured out who Michael was, he answered their questions without getting ruffled. The second cop, though, had a rude manner.

"What?" I demanded, offended by his behavior and quickly infuriated by their obvious suspicion at finding the son of Big Frankie Abruzzo in their bucolic neighborhood. "Do you keep his photograph on your bulletin board?"

The first officer said, "Take it easy, miss."

"This is entirely my fault," I told him, turning away from the bad cop. "I suggested we borrow Mr. Petite's car. He lent it to my sister, you see, and I took the keys from her when—"

"Who's your sister?" the rude one asked in a tone that implied she walked the streets with her pimp.

"She's Elizabeth Kintswell. At the moment, she's Jacque Petite's—that is, they spent a few days—I mean—they're friends, you could say."

"And he gave her a car? That must have been a great few days."

"No," I snapped, "he allowed her to borrow it. And I assumed it would be okay if we—good heavens, he hasn't reported it stolen, has he?"

"Nora," Michael said, "I don't think you're helping the situation."

"So, Abruzzo," said the rude cop, "what are you doing here, exactly?"

"He came with me," I said. "I take full responsibility for—"

The good cop angled his body in front of me, gesturing to the veranda. "Why don't you stand over there, miss? Let Mr. Abruzzo answer the questions for himself."

"But—"

Within ten minutes after consulting with the radios in their cars, the police put handcuffs on Michael and eased him into the backseat of one of the cruisers.

"This is ridiculous!" I cried. "He didn't steal the car! If anyone did, it's me!"

Even that outburst didn't save Michael from being hauled off.

I hitched a ride into the city with Tremaine Jefferson.

Chapter 21

He'd been through it before, of course. Michael had been detained dozens of times, I supposed, and he knew his lawyer's phone number by heart. I tried to tell myself he'd be out of jail in time for dinner.

But I was still angry on his behalf.

I tried to concentrate on the video footage of Cici's closet. I didn't know much about camera angles, but I quickly got the hang of telling a story with pictures. I wrote a short introduction and recorded it myself. Then I joined Tremaine and the rest of the video team and helped choose the best shots of Cici's home and clothes. It wasn't a tough decision. We decided to use her small talk as a voice-over as the footage rolled. We all smiled at her "That's a wrap!" sign-off. Cici looked elegant, but also witty and relaxed. The charming piece ran eight minutes, and at five o'clock I watched as the experts loaded the video onto the newspaper's Web site.

I slipped out of the video room just as Skip Malone arrived to edit his sports highlights.

"Did you hear about Jim Hooper?" Skip glanced up and down the hallway to make sure we weren't overheard.

"The guy who writes the car column?"

Skip nodded. "The editor told him he has to go part-time. And his budget's been cut in half, too."

"How can he do his job in half the time?"

Skip shrugged. "He says he's going to try freelancing

for automotive magazines to make ends meet. It's not a
bad idea."

I slipped away, thinking if I were a trained writer, I
could try freelancing, too, if I lost my job. But my social
expertise didn't exactly translate to magazines.

In a state of anxiety, I tried Michael's cell phone. No
answer. I rushed over to a nearby hotel to cover a party
called "Shaken and Stirred." A disease-of-the-week organization had decided to serve a variety of martinis
while entertaining their guests with shock poetry and
cutting-edge visual art. They asked a hip gallery to sup-
ply huge paintings for decoration. I spoke to the artist,
who was mostly nervous that his pieces—old family photos arranged like crime-scene pictures and splattered
with paint intended to look like blood spatters—would
survive the evening. I noticed a few tipsy guests leaning
close to the art to see the details in the Polaroids, so I
understood his concern.

On the other hand, I didn't like his work much. I thought
the shock value outweighed the thematic elements.

An *Intelligencer* photographer showed up and
snapped a few pictures of the art, the bar and a cadaver-
ously thin young poet who droned her blank verse into
the microphone with her eyes closed and a pained expression on her face. Not exactly photogenic stuff. The
newspaper used a number of work-for-hire photogra-
phers, and their skills varied considerably. I encouraged
him to take some shots of well-dressed guests sipping
martinis instead.

Notebook in hand, I interviewed the chair of the organ-
izing committee—who told me with pride how much cash
they'd raised for their cause. He was already very drunk.
The caterer, I noticed, had run out of food early, while the
martinis kept coming. A recipe for social disaster.

I met a friend in the ladies' room—Maybelle Collins,
a pert blonde who wore a sequined red, white and blue
cocktail dress in honor of the upcoming holiday.

She was pouring her martini down the drain, and she

rolled her eyes at me in the mirror. "I'm stuck here until ten. Everyone's going to be drunk as lords by then."

I laughed. "Maybe someone should order pizza."

She laughed, too. "Good idea! How've you been, Nora?"

"Busy. But good."

"I heard a rumor your parents might be back."

"Did you?"

She pulled the olive out of her glass on a toothpick and watched me in the mirror. "That's the buzz around the racquet club. I must say, that's a brave move. Your dad's been persona non grata for a long time. And your mother!" Smiling, Maybelle shook her head. "Is it true she borrowed Ashland Freeman's sapphire necklace and never returned it?"

I decided to strike Maybelle off my list of friends.

Without waiting for my answer, Maybelle said, "I can't think of anything worse than having that kind of reputation. Which reminds me. I saw your sister Emma last week. I could swear she was with Hart Jones."

I wiped all expression from my face. "Really?"

"That couldn't be possible, though. Hart is going to marry Penny Haffenpepper. She was my maid of honor, you know. I'm going to be hers."

"How nice."

"Her mother has the wedding all planned."

I put on a smile. "Does Hart know?"

No Rhodes scholar, Maybelle glanced at me, trying to decide if I was having fun at her expense. "A lot of people are going to be upset if anyone tries to interfere with that marriage. They've been unofficially engaged since prep school."

"That's a long time," I observed. "How come they haven't gone through with it?"

Maybelle stopped toying with her olive and tried to gather her brows despite the Botox. "Penny's career is important to her. She's learning the family business. But Hart's madly in love, and they're definitely getting married. Her mother tentatively booked Yo-Yo Ma for the music."

"Sounds lovely."

Wedding by Eva Braun. Poor Yo-Yo.

Maybe some kind soul ought to save Hart from a Nazi marriage.

Maybelle said, "At least your life has calmed down, right? You're not dating that mobster anymore? I hear he's in trouble again."

Maybelle's husband was a newly appointed assistant prosecutor with ambitions for higher political office. It wasn't hard to guess where Maybelle got her insider information.

She popped the olive into her mouth and smiled. "Is he rotting in jail yet?"

"No," I said. "He looked perfectly healthy when he got out of my bed this morning."

I heard her choking on her damn olive as I left.

Outside, the heat was still as unpleasant as ever. I checked my phone to see if Michael had called me, but the screen was blank.

Passing an ambulance that had been summoned to help a homeless man with heatstroke, I hiked over to a leafy street of old city town houses that had been refurbished by some well-to-do do-gooders who made the commitment to raise big families in the heart of the city. I found the private home of some friends who were entertaining a visiting historian, in town to present a program for Independence Day at one of the museums. The party had been billed as a "reception," but I knew better. I heard the music almost a block away. I hoped to make a quick stop since I had a very full dance card.

When I knocked, nearly panting from the heat, the door was opened by the host, Barry Castor, wearing a Statue of Liberty spiked hat on his head. He gave me a kiss on the cheek. "Nora, you look fantastic! Come in where it's cool!"

By day, Barry was an avuncular college professor. He

knew how to mix academia with good times at night, however. Escorting me past a jumble of photos of his six blond, whirling-dervish children in exotic locations, he shouted over the music, "How's your sister Emma?"

"How in the world do you know Emma?"

"My daughter Trish took a couple of riding lessons from her last fall. Loved every minute of it! Well, except for the dislocated shoulder. I was hoping we could get a few more of the kids on ponies this summer, since we're not taking that trip to Cairo after all. That is, if we can afford Emma's services."

Barry's wife was a bank executive who pulled down a sizable salary and had inherited part of a scented-candle fortune, so I assumed the family could afford a few riding lessons, if not a whole horse farm, if they chose.

"I'll tell her to call you."

"Thanks!"

The party included dancing to Motown music on the Castors' postage-stamp-sized patio. I found cold beer and a limbo contest in the kitchen, where the visiting scholar humped his way under a broomstick held by two giggling grad students. I nearly stumbled over the Castor daughters playing poker on the hallway floor with a college dean of admissions. All four of them were gnawing on pretzel sticks dipped in mustard.

At that moment, I found myself wishing more than anything that Michael hadn't been rushed off by the police. This particular party would have been a good one to ease him into meeting some of my friends.

My phone rang, and with my heart lifting, I stepped into a narrow pantry to answer it.

"Nora!" Libby's voice crackled in my ear. "We're coming to pick you up!"

I checked my watch and found it was nearly eight.

"Libby, what are you planning?" I still had to reach the Chocolate Festival Gala.

"Never mind that," she snapped. "Just tell me where you are."

"What's wrong?"

"Just tell me where the hell you are!" she shouted. I heard a horn blare.

I told her where we could meet, and half an hour later her red minivan came to a screeching stop in front of Naked Chocolate, my favorite hangout. I gathered up my purchases—a few choice treats—and went out into the muggy night.

The side door of the minivan slid open.

"Get in!" Libby shouted.

I climbed into the backseat. Up front, Emma had her head in a plastic bag.

In the backseat beside me was Tierney Cavendish, white-faced and firmly buckled with the seat belt.

"What are you doing here?" I asked him.

"Praying," he said. "Your sisters are nuts."

"Close the door," Libby commanded. "We don't have much time!"

"Where are we going? Em? Are you okay? Are we taking you to the hospital?"

"To the morgue," she groaned. "I ran out of ginger ale."

Libby whipped the van into traffic and through a yellow light. "There's a mini-market!" Libby pointed at a corner store. "Nora, run inside and buy her some Canada Dry!"

I did as I was told. I bailed out, ran across the street and shoved my way to the front of the line of people buying lottery tickets and cigarettes. Despite the heat, everybody was in a good mood and let me pay quickly. When I climbed back into the minivan, I twisted open one of the plastic bottles and passed it to Emma. She grabbed it without thanking me.

Libby turned around in her seat. She was wearing a black T-shirt with white lettering. It said, YOU'RE ONLY AS STRONG AS THE TABLE YOU DANCE ON. "All right," I said. "What in the world is going on?"

Libby's face was alight with purpose. "We just found out where Hart Jones is tonight."

"What's a heart jones?" Tierney asked, mystified. He was dressed in one of Michael's shirts—too big by several sizes—and he hung on to the door handle to keep himself from being thrown from his seat by Libby's wild driving.

"He's a person," I said. "Hartfield Jones. The banker you met with for lunch the other day, remember?"

Tierney looked surprised. "Why are we looking for him?"

"We heard a bulletin," Libby reported. "Tonight Hart is going to propose to whatsername Haffenpepper."

"Who?" Tierney asked.

"She's a beer heiress," I said.

From the front seat, Emma added hoarsely, "Her mother's Eva Braun."

None of that information helped Tierney. He looked as confused as before—maybe more so.

"Anyway," Libby said, "tonight he's going to ask her to marry him again."

"Again?" Tierney asked. "Is that bad or good?"

"Bad," I said. "Because he's falling in love with Emma."

Libby said, "Men do that a lot."

"Then why is he proposing to somebody else?"

"Because all men are fools," Libby said. "He's making the safe choice, the boring choice, the choice that will perpetuate a Philadelphia stereotype. His life has no meaning."

Emma stopped gulping ginger ale and sat back in her seat. She tried deep breathing to quell her nausea. "If he marries her, his life will have no sex. She's a dead fish in bed."

I said, "We need to get to Hart before he proposes, so Emma can tell him she's pregnant."

"She's pregnant?" Tierney looked aghast.

"I'm not telling him that!"

"You have to, Em," Libby said sternly. "He has a right to know."

"And besides," I added, "Eva Braun has the wedding all planned."

"My God," Libby said. "This is a mission of mercy!"

"I'm not telling him. I'm not ready."

"You'll never be ready," I said. "But you've got to grow up and take responsibility. For once, Emma, put yourself in someone else's shoes."

"Whose?"

"Hart's!" Libby and I cried together.

Tierney said, "Maybe he really does want to marry the other woman."

"You don't know her," Emma snapped. "She's vacant and selfish. He's only marrying her because her family has skyboxes for hockey *and* the Sixers." She looked surprised at her own outburst.

"Lib," I said, "how do we know he's going to propose tonight?"

"His sister told Ellie Pargenter, who phoned her daughter, who e-mailed Rawlins's girlfriend, who text-messaged him—"

"I get it," I said. "It's amazing the bride-to-be hasn't heard by now. What does the ring look like?"

Libby took me seriously and frowned. "I don't know."

I sighed. "Do we know where he is going to propose?"

"That pretty gazebo in Fairmount Park. On the hill, with the view of the river. You know the one?" Libby refastened her seat belt and put the minivan into gear.

"The gazebo with the rosebushes planted all around it?"

Libby pulled into traffic, but kept talking. "That's it. We're headed there now. The city is setting off some pre–Fourth of July fireworks at ten o'clock. We figure Hart's going to propose just before that."

"And we're going to be there?"

"Yep."

"What are we going to do?" Tierney asked.

"Stop him, of course. He only needs to look at Emma one more time to be convinced he can't marry Eva Braun's daughter."

Emma, who looked sweaty and sick with her hair sticking up and her shirt falling off one shoulder, said, "Slow down. I'm feeling sick all over again."

I said, "Why is Tierney coming along?"

"We kidnapped him," Libby said. "Tit for tat."

He said, "I was minding my own business, hiding out at your boyfriend's house, when they came along and ordered me into the van. I thought they had a gun. Turns out, it was a tube of sunscreen." He showed me a container of Banana Boat, SPF 45.

"Oh, for heaven's sake, Libby!"

"It was in the glove compartment! It was the only thing I had. We need a man along, and Emma thought of Tierney. And, after all, he should be initiated into the family."

Tierney said, "Isn't hazing illegal now?"

I said, "Why do we need a man?"

Libby said, "I have it all figured. I'm going to park down over the hillside, and we'll climb up to the gazebo so they don't see us coming. I might be in superb physical condition for a woman of childbearing age, but how are we going to get Emma up there without somebody strong to boost her over the fence?"

"That's not a fence up there," I said. "It's a wall. Eight feet high, at least."

"I have a ladder in the back."

I peered over the backseat of the minivan and saw my kitchen step stool on the floor. "That's not going to help," I said.

"I know. That's why we need a man along! And since that sweet Henry Fineman is busy—"

"What's he doing?"

"Looking after the children."

"Henry's babysitting?"

"With the help of that charming man in the sarong

who's not allowed to leave the house now that Mama and Daddy are back from the hospital."

Emma took a deep breath and pulled her head out of the bag. "Libby flirted with him."

"Who? You flirted with Oscar? What happened to Jacque Petite?"

"Nothing whatsoever." Libby was huffy. "I have always struggled with the societal pressure to be monogamous. I find both men attractive—each in his own way. Tierney, aren't you drawn to more than one partner at a time?"

Tierney looked at me. "Is that a trick question?"

"Slow down," Emma begged. "Or I'm gonna hurl."

I said, "Daddy's out of the hospital?"

"He was discharged this afternoon. He and Mama are having some quiet time in their bedroom."

"God, I hope she doesn't kill him."

The city flew past the windows as Libby roared up the avenue, heading for Fairmount Park. Streetlights sputtered to life as the sun sank below the river. A knot of teenagers hung around the circle at the foot of the museum. A man selling Italian ice began closing up his truck for the night. But Libby kept her foot firmly on the accelerator, and we plunged into the park. Emma burped.

We passed a parking lot full of cars and people preparing to watch the pre-weekend fireworks.

Libby hauled the steering wheel hard to the right, then barely missed the bumper of an oncoming SUV. We thundered around a hillside and entered a long stretch of road covered by an arch of trees.

"Where's the plastic bag?" Emma cried.

My phone rang in my handbag. I pulled it out hastily. "Michael?"

"Aunt Nora!" Rawlins yelled. "Is my mom with you?"

"Yes, she is. Do you want to speak with her?"

"God, no," my nephew said. "Do you think you could

convince her that I should go to Hollywood with Chad and be part of his entourage? He says I could finish high school at Beverly Hills and meet Rod Stewart's daughter."

"Rawlins, darling, you don't want to be in anybody's entourage but your own."

"But it would be really cool! Even Shawna would think so."

"Wouldn't you rather be the star of your own life?" I asked.

Sounding sulky, he said, "Delmar's going."

"Delmar is going to Hollywood? With Chad Zanzibar?"

"I think so," Rawlins said. "Of course, things might change once Chad figures out Delmar's not Mick."

"That might be a problem," I agreed.

"Anyway, Delmar's probably going to break Chad's face pretty soon."

"Good grief, why?"

"Chad made a rude crack about his grandmother, and Delmar got upset. He says nobody should be disrespectful of grandmothers. It's like grandmothers are sacred or something. So I think he's gonna end up hurting Chad."

"So maybe the Beverly Hills trip isn't going to happen."

"Yeah, maybe not." Rawlins sighed. "Henry says to tell you that Brandi Whoever isn't using her real name, by the way. Her real name is Cadwaller, and she's from someplace in California."

I gripped the phone with both hands, not sure I had heard correctly. "Rawlins, is Henry there? Can I talk to him?"

"No, I'm at work. He was playing Joan of Arc with Lucy when I left. Look, the other thing is that Mr. Cavendish, the dead guy?"

"Yes?"

"His real name was Cadwaller, too."

"What?"

"Henry thinks maybe they were cousins or something."

"You're kidding."

"Does that mean anything?"

"I'm not sure what," I admitted. My mind raced. Brandi related to Hoyt?

"So about me going to Beverly Hills?"

"We'll talk later."

"That usually means no." Rawlins disconnected.

I closed my phone, not sure how to interpret the new information. What did it mean? Brandi and Hoyt were related? He had helped her get a job in the city, helped her join an influential board? And then what? They hardly seemed friendly with each other, let alone family.

Over her shoulder, Libby said, "I don't like Rawlins's new girlfriend. She's very demanding."

"Needy," I said, distracted. "That's different from demanding. Shawna was demanding. She challenged him."

"I never liked Shawna, either. She was very forward."

"Sound familiar?"

From the front seat, Emma suddenly said, "That's Hart's car."

A silver Porsche sat parked under the lee of a rock formation, and Libby blasted past it. "Hunch down, Em, in case they're still inside!"

I took a look at the car as we whipped beyond it. "It's empty."

"They must be on their way up to the gazebo already," Libby said. "Hang on, everybody!"

The minivan bucketed over a pothole and took a curve almost on two wheels. Libby cut the lights as we raced over a flat stretch of road planted with flowering bushes on either side.

"I know all the best hiding places in this park," Libby announced. "One summer I had a boyfriend who worked on the maintenance crew. He took me to every secluded glen and we—oh, he was a wonderful kisser. His name was Ramon. He only had one nipple."

Tierney said, "I was better off an only child."

"Nonsense." I patted his knee. "You'll learn to love us."

Libby slid the minivan between two fragrant pine trees and killed the engine. "Okay. Who's got a plan?"

"We thought you had a plan!"

"It was more of a general concept, really—"

Tierney tried reasoning with her. "Why don't we find a place to have dinner and think this through? I haven't eaten since I found some cold pizza in the refrigerator. And I haven't had a cheesesteak in years."

"Don't mention food!" Emma groaned. "I'm out of ginger ale and throwing up! I'm sick! I'm disgusting! I haven't washed my hair in two days! And this is how I'm supposed to tell somebody I'm pregnant with his stupid baby?"

I handed her the second bottle of ginger ale, which she snatched from my grasp.

"Oh, for heaven's sake!" Libby opened her door. "It's not very hard to plan an ambush, is it?"

Emma glugged half the bottle, then opened her door reluctantly. "I need fresh air anyway."

We all climbed out of the vehicle and found ourselves in a hidden glade where the minivan wouldn't be seen by passing cars. We regrouped in front of it.

"Well?" I glanced around and kept my voice down. "Where's the gazebo from here?"

Libby pointed up the knoll. I could see the only way to reach it was a twisted path through the trees.

I noticed that Libby wore camouflage Capri pants and sneakers in addition to her T-shirt. She looked like a commando who shopped at Lane Bryant.

I said, "I'm not dressed for a hike in the woods."

"I have a pair of gardening boots in the van."

Libby opened the hatch of the minivan and rummaged around until she found a pair of green rubber boots. She handed them to me. Next she wrestled out the step stool and heaved it at Tierney.

Tierney stared at the stool. "What am I supposed to do with this?"

Emma said, "I have to pee."

"Big surprise, after all that ginger ale."

My cell phone rang.

"Shhhh!"

I grabbed the phone and hit the button before it could ring again. "Hello!"

Michael said, "Jeez, are you okay?"

"I'm fine," I said. "Just under a little sisterly stress at the moment. I'm with Lib and Emma. Are you out of custody?"

"Yep. But I've got to take care of something. Are you all right on your own for a while?"

"Of course I am."

He promised to call me later and said, "I love you."

"I love you, too."

I closed my phone and found Tierney staring at me. I smiled. "He's not as scary as he looks."

Emma and Libby emerged from the bushes. They were both zipping up their pants.

Midzip, Emma froze. "Shh! I hear voices."

I stopped in the act of pulling on the boots. We listened, straining in the darkness. Nobody moved. Nobody drew a breath. I began to wonder if I could hear music, sounding tinny in the open air.

At last, Tierney said with disgust, "Oh, my God, it's Celine Dion."

Emma burped. "Hart loves Celine Dion."

"How could you sleep with a man who loves Celine Dion? That's just wrong."

Libby said, "I love Celine Dion, too."

Tierney said, "Then I'm definitely not related to you."

I grabbed Emma's arm. "Don't get distracted. Focus.

You need to tell Hart he's going to be a father before he makes a dreadful mistake. You'll be saving him from a life of Celine Dion, not to mention bad sex. Don't blow this, Em. And hurry up, will you? I still have to make it to the Chocolate Gala."

Grimly, she clutched her ginger ale and nodded. "Okay, okay. Let's do it before I lose my courage."

I threw my shoes and handbag into the back of the minivan. Libby had dug into the glove compartment and come up with a weak flashlight.

"Turn that thing off," Tierney said. "We'll see better in the dark without it. Save the battery for an emergency."

Libby surprised me by obeying without an argument. "Are you getting into this?" she asked.

Tierney sighed. "I'm a sucker for a love story. So sue me."

The four of us eased across the road and onto the path. The rocks and dirt underfoot were very dry.

"If we sneak around this way," Libby said in a hushed voice, "we can get right up to the back of the gazebo and see what's going on. We can pounce whenever things get too—"

"No pouncing," said Emma. "There's not going to be any pouncing."

We edged our way around some exposed sandstone, picking across a rough trail before reaching a small stand of maple trees. Instinctively, we all stayed close to the tree trunks to avoid being seen. Heading cautiously up the slope, Libby suddenly slipped. She gasped as her feet nearly slid out from under her. Tierney caught her arm. Emma, on the path below, reached up and steadied Libby, too.

"Stop pinching," Libby hissed.

"Keep moving, will you?"

"Shut up!" Tierney listened again. "This is the end of the song."

"How do you know it's the end?" Emma demanded. "Do you listen to Celine Dion?"

"I had a girlfriend who had this CD. She played it a thousand times a day."

"Oho," said Emma. "So you know all of Celine's songs?"

"That's not a crime if it was forced on me."

"Right." Emma slugged more ginger ale.

I couldn't help noticing the level of ginger ale was getting very low in her bottle. I realized I should have purchased several.

"This way," Libby hissed. "Don't lag behind or you'll get lost."

In the falling dusk, she hotfooted her way across an open glade and led us through some overgrown bushes and across the bed of impatiens that had been planted by the park service. Tierney lugged the step stool, and behind him Emma staggered unsteadily.

"Em?"

She handed me the empty ginger ale bottle. "Damn!"

"Shh!" Libby hugged a man-made cliff built of rugged stones. She pointed upward. "They're right above us!"

We could hear Celine crooning more clearly. And Hart's voice rumbled along with her, barely keeping the tune.

Tierney said, "Is he *singing*?"

"Shut up." Emma glared. "He likes to sing."

"Come on," Libby said. "Put down the step stool. Here, see? And climb up on it, Tierney."

"Me? Why me?"

"Because you'll have to boost us up there!"

"But—"

"Nora, you go first."

"Why can't it be Emma?"

Because Emma was upchucking in the bushes.

Chapter 22

"Shhh!" Libby said. "Keep it down, can't you?"

Emma tried to muffle her retching.

Tierney climbed onto the step stool and put his hand down to me. "Upsy-daisy."

"This dress is worth thousands," I told him as I grasped his hand.

He pulled me up onto the stool, and the two of us teetered there, clutching the rocks to stay upright. In my ear, he said, "Put your foot in my hand, and I'll boost you up."

I followed his instructions. A second later I stifled a yelp as Tierney heaved me upward. I scrabbled for a handhold and felt my dress catch on something. But then Tierney put his hand squarely on my butt, and the next thing I knew, I was up over the wall and clutching the ground. Silently, I pulled myself to a kneeling position.

There, I had a clear view of the gazebo.

It was a lovely spot for a proposal, I thought at once. The picturesque structure overlooked the lights of the city. The surrounding flower bed overflowed with the fragrance of burgeoning rosebushes. A slight breeze rustled in the trees overhead.

"Ooof!"

Libby landed beside me.

"You okay?"

"Damn, I think I just deflated one bra cup!"

"What are you talking about?"

"I bought one of those new bras with the little inflatable thingies. You know, to balance myself out a bit. After nursing Maximus, I'm a little—uneven." She heaved herself to her knees and began to give her bosom a tentative squeeze when she caught a glimpse of the tableau in the gazebo. "Oh, is that Hart? He's very good-looking these days, isn't he? Do you think he goes to a gym?"

The two of us peered over the roses at the couple about fifteen yards away. Hart wore a crisp dress shirt and the trousers of a suit, no tie—as if he'd come from the office. The woman with him was an ethereal blonde in a yellow sundress.

"She's very pretty," Libby whispered. "She doesn't look like Eva Braun at all."

"She has great legs."

"Not as great as Emma's."

"You're right. Are they holding hands?"

The blonde appeared to be wheedling Hart, swinging his hand in hers flirtatiously. As we watched, Hart slowly took her into his arms and began to dance to Celine's singing.

Libby sighed. "He's so romantic! My first husband proposed to me at a Burger King."

"I thought your first husband was a vegetarian."

"He was. We were protesting their inhumane treatment for slaughtering animals."

A second later, Emma scrambled up beside us, snapping over her shoulder, "I don't care who you are—get your hand off my ass!"

"Shhhh!"

Grumbling, Emma peered over the rosebushes. "What's going on?"

I said, "I think they're kissing."

"I could throw a rock," Libby offered. "I used to be a softball pitcher."

"If anybody throws rocks, it's going to be me." Emma sounded dangerous. "Has he proposed yet?"

We squinted, trying to catch a glimpse of Miss Haffen-pepper's left hand.

"I don't think so," I said.

"Oh, man." Emma crumpled back to the ground. "I'm gonna be sick again."

Libby said, "What happened to the ginger ale?"

"I drank it all!"

"It's all in your head. You're just sick because you're scared."

"Either way, I'm gonna vomit."

"Take it easy," I said. "Libby, don't you have something else to drink in the minivan?"

She frowned. "There might be a Diet Coke under the backseat. Sometimes I mix it with a teensy bit of rum when the twins are in detention at school."

Emma croaked, "Ginger ale's the only thing that works."

"I don't have ginger ale!"

In another instant, she was barfing into the roses.

"Shhh!"

I said, "I'll go look for the Diet Coke. It might help. But don't wait for me. If Hart goes down on one knee, somebody has to do something to distract him."

"Like what?" Libby asked. "Bird calls? Coyote howls?"

"No, something that will stop him from proposing! Emma needs to talk to him first." Although Em hardly looked capable of communicating at that particular moment. "I'll be right back."

Tierney caught me climbing down over the wall. Awkwardly, we wrestled with each other until I found my balance. When he set me on the ground, I said, "I'm going back to the car for a minute. If you hear coyotes start to howl, don't be frightened."

"I couldn't get much more frightened than I am right now. You three are truly terrifying."

From above, we heard Emma making inhuman sounds and Libby trying to shush her.

"Hurry," Tierney advised.

I slithered down the path and headed for the minivan.

Libby had left it unlocked, so I heaved open the rear passenger door and stuck my head down under the seat to look for the Diet Coke. The dome light was too meager to see by, so I groped around until my fingers struck the smooth surface of the can. I dragged it out and stood up.

Just as a large vehicle pulled quietly to a stop behind Libby's minivan.

I froze.

"Nora?" A voice called through an open window.

Cautiously, I edged out from behind the pine trees.

The vehicle turned out to be a large white van decorated with the multicolored logo of a local television station. Taking a step closer, I peered through the windshield to identify the driver.

"It's me. Brandi Schmidt."

I went to the passenger door and looked through the open window. Sure enough, the driver was Brandi. She blew a cloud of cigarette smoke and tossed the still-smoldering butt onto the street.

"Hi," I said. "This is a surprise."

"Would you mind getting into the van?" she asked. "I can't get any closer to you."

She popped the automatic lock on the passenger door, and I opened it. Leaning in, I said, "I'm sorry, Brandi. I really can't chat right now. My sisters—"

"I know," she said. "You're busy. Nobody has time to talk to me. But if you could spare just a minute . . ."

She pushed my guilt button again. I automatically climbed into the van. It was a large, clumsy sort of vehicle. I could see the shapes of equipment in the back, including the bulky mechanism of a lift for the wheelchair.

"If you could close the door," she said, "the air-conditioning won't leak out. My chair gets very uncomfortable in the heat."

The van was equipped to accommodate her wheel-chair so that she could manage the steering wheel and all the other controls that had been fitted out for a handi-capped person.

I closed the door.

Brandi smiled at me. "Thanks."

She rolled up the window and put the van into gear. Her hand fumbled on the control—rather like the throttle of a motorcycle. Suddenly the van gave a neck-snapping jump. "Sorry. I'm still learning how to drive this thing. I'm a little clumsy."

"Brandi," I said. "My sister needs me. She's not feeling well and—"

"This will only take a minute. We need to talk about Hoyt."

Instinct told me to open the door before the van sped up too much for me to jump out. But I discovered the door had locked automatically. I yanked on the handle and rat-tled the lock, too. No use.

"This van is kid-proofed." She laughed unsteadily. "You can't get out without my permission."

The sound of her laugh sent prickles up my neck. I decided to launch an attack. "Brandi, have you been fol-lowing me?"

"No!"

"A friend of mine saw you. He says you were driving down the street after the concert."

"It must have been a pigment of his imagination."

"Figment," I snapped before catching myself. "Sorry. You were seen, Brandi. Following me in broad daylight. Can you explain yourself, please?"

She shot me a nervous glance. "It's not against the law. Yes, I've been surveillancing you. I almost lost you tonight. Your sister is a dangerous driver. She needs to slow down."

"What's on your mind, Brandi?"

She wrestled with the steering wheel to angle us around a loop, but hit a pothole with a bone-jarring thump. Then the van sideswiped some bushes. Her driving was much worse than Libby's.

I clasped the seat belt around myself. "Is something wrong?"

"You know there is. You've been trying to figure out what happened in Lexie's office, haven't you?"

"I want to be sure the police find out who pushed Hoyt off the balcony, yes."

"Don't you know already?"

"Was it you?"

I surprised her with that. "How could I have done it? I can't get out of this chair without help!"

"But you were there, in Lexie's bathroom after the meeting broke up. Just before Hoyt died. I found your compact."

She glanced over at me. "Oh, good. Hoyt gave it to me. He gave me a lot of presents—momentos. I'm glad you found it."

We had left the top of the park and had wound our way down toward the river, where the trees and the hillside created a foreboding darkness. Even scarier was Brandi's erratic driving. She struggled with the throttle and couldn't maintain a steady speed.

I said, "I know that *Schmidt* isn't your real name. And you were related to Hoyt."

Her hand faltered on the controls again. "How did you—? Never mind. What else did you find out?"

I cursed myself for leaving my handbag in Libby's car. Without my cell phone, I felt helpless. All I had was a can of Diet Coke. Talking to Brandi seemed my only choice.

I faced her across the seat. "You just said Hoyt gave you a lot of presents. Did he create your investment accounts, too?"

"He was very generous. If you circumcised the whole world, you wouldn't find anyone more generous than Hoyt."

"So he gave you money," I said.

"It hardly matters now. Since he stole it away from me. He used my life savings to make himself feel like somebody important."

"You must have been angry to discover he'd taken it all back."

"I was furious," Brandi said. "I almost wanted to kill him for it."

She bashed a curb, and the van lurched violently again, throwing me against the door. Any minute, she might drive through a guardrail or into a culvert.

"Why don't you pull over?" I asked, trying to squeeze the rising panic from my voice. "We can talk better if you're not distracted."

"I've only been driving the van for two weeks," she whined. "I can't be expected to be an expert right away."

"I understand. Just—pull over when you see a place to park."

She drove the lumbering van down onto the highway and turned into the first opening she came to. It was a boat launch. The gate was closed, fortunately, because for a split second I thought she might drive the vehicle straight into the river. But at the last second she pinched the brakes hard. Flung forward, I braced my hand against the dash. We stopped with a jerk. In the light from the expressway across the river, we could see the current rushing southward. The water was black and quick.

Brandi left the engine running. The van remained pointed at the river. Only the chain-link fence stood between us and the swift current.

She touched a button, and her window rolled down several inches.

To get her talking again, I said, "Was Hoyt your cousin?"

"Uncle," she answered. "Or aunt, I guess."

She sneaked a look at me to gauge my reaction.

Calmly, I said, "You knew Hoyt's true gender?"

"Sure. I didn't know him when he was a she, but my

mom knew all about it. When I was in college, she let it slip."

"Is that when you decided to extort money from him?"

"It wasn't like that," she said, defensive. "Hoyt was already rich! And I needed help to pay my school fees, and he said he'd help. We had a nice, plutonic relationship for a while."

"But?"

"But after graduation I couldn't get a job. I wanted to work in broadcasting, and nobody wants to hire a woman in a wheelchair. I worked as an intern at a cable station for a while, but I needed a real paycheck."

"So Hoyt intervened on your behalf?"

"Yes. He said he'd try to get me a job at a TV station. But it took too long. I got desperate."

"So you threatened him? You threatened to make his gender public?"

"It didn't happen like that," she said, but there was no vehemence in her voice. Brandi looked at the water.

"All right, out of the goodness of his heart, Hoyt got you a job here in Philadelphia."

"Yes. But I've tried to make my own way ever since. I did my job, and I even tried to be active in the community. Hoyt helped me a little, I guess. He got me on the Music Academy board. But my boss at the TV station keeps saying that I have to improve my on-air performance or he might have to fire me. And they had to buy this expensive van for me, and now he says I need to think about their investment. How can I do a good job under that kind of pressure valve?"

"I know what you mean."

She swept on as if I hadn't spoken. "My salary is pathetic. I have lots of expenses. Do you know how much it costs to keep your hair looking good for television? And all the other women—even the ones younger than me!—are getting face-lifts. So I needed more money from Hoyt."

"He opened an investment account for you?"

"Yes."

She had pressured him with her knowledge of his secret. Over and over, he must have paid for her silence. It must have been infuriating. But surely not a dire drain on his finances—not if he had stolen nearly a hundred million dollars.

Brandi said, "At the meeting at Lexie's office, they told me my account was empty. I couldn't believe he'd do that to me—irregardless of how I got the money in the first place. So I went back into the office to ask him why. But he was very upset. I guess it was the wrong time. He snapped."

"And then what happened?"

"Why do I have to tell you? Lexie already explained, right? That's why you were so upset when you left her house the other night. I saw you. I saw you have the fight with that man outside her house."

Brandi must have witnessed my argument with Michael, I realized. "You were watching?"

She nodded. "Lexie said you were asking questions, trying to figure out what happened."

Surprised, I said, "You've spoken with Lexie?"

"A couple times. She wants me to keep quiet."

"I don't understand."

"She told you, didn't she?" Brandi turned to look at me again, her dark eyes wide.

With dread building in my chest, I said, "How about if you tell me, too?"

Brandi shook her head as if to dispel an ugly memory. "It all happened so fast. Lexie called all of Hoyt's clients to a meeting, so I went. And when she said he'd taken all our money, people got really upset. When Hoyt came into the room, everybody started yelling. I could see he was sorry for what he'd done. He really was. Giving all that money to charity? It was an ego thing, that's all. Who doesn't want to feel famous once in a while? He was doing nice things for people!"

"So everyone shouted at him . . ."

"Yes. That's when Hoyt punched her painting."

"Why did he do that?"

"I don't know, but he did. And Lexie went crazy. She told everybody to get out of the room. But I stayed."

"You stayed with Hoyt?"

She nodded. "And when Lexie came back—"

"Wait, Lexie left the room?"

"Yes, she went to call the police, and when she came back, Hoyt was—okay, he was really mad at me."

"About what? Blackmailing him?"

"No, no, I said he should get some help. That he'd had problems all his life—you know, because of being a girl? Maybe he needed to see a doctor. And he said he was seeing plenty of doctors now. He didn't need any more doctors. Anyway, I kinda got hysterical. So he—he slapped me."

I tried to imagine the scene. Shouting clients in the next room, Lexie leaving to phone the police. Brandi and Hoyt arguing.

Brandi said, "He was very upset. He grabbed my dress and—and pulled me partway out of my chair. He hit me." She touched her face where Hoyt's hand must have struck her.

"Then what?" I asked.

"Lexie came back just as he slapped me."

"Wait a minute—"

"She saw what he did." Brandi dashed a tear from her eye. "It happened really fast. I don't know what she thought, but—"

"You're lying."

"You know I'm not! She told you, didn't she? That's why you're trying to find somebody else to blame." Brandi had begun to cry. Her face was blurred with tears. "But it wasn't me. I didn't do it. And it wasn't really her fault, either. It just happened."

I knew what Lexie thought she'd seen as she reentered her office. A powerful man hurting a young, helpless woman.

"So you have to stop," Brandi was saying. "You can't ask any more questions. It wasn't her fault. It wasn't my fault. You're just making it worse. And now that Hoyt's gone, I need to get money from someplace. So Lexie has to stay out of jail."

"Brandi—"

I think she meant to hit the steering wheel with her fist. But she missed and struck the hand controls of the van. The vehicle jumped forward and crashed against the chain-link fence of the boat launch. Brandi grabbed the accelerator to stop it, but she pushed the throttle the wrong way. The engine roared, pushing the fence to its limit. The river rushed just beyond the hood of the van.

"Brandi, stop!" I unfastened my seat belt and lunged at her.

"I'm trying!"

The fence collapsed with a scream, and the van hurtled sideways down the concrete ramp, throwing me back into the passenger seat. The wheelchair came unmoored and slammed sideways, pinning me to the seat. Brandi thumped against me, too—deadweight as the van plunged down the launch ramp.

We hit the river with no splash, just a tremendous hissing roar. The nose of the van sank fast, and Brandi and I tumbled against the dashboard. Black water began to gush through the open window. Brandi screamed.

In slow motion, the van nose-dived into the darkness. The lighter rear end of the vehicle rose, tumbling both of us in a tangle against the windshield. Around us, the water sloshed as if in a washing machine. I lost all concept of up or down, just thrashed against the weight of Brandi and her heavy chair and the gushing black water. Libby's rubber boots filled with water, sandbags on my legs. I kicked free of them and strained for air.

"Help!" Brandi unsnapped her seat belt just as the water closed over her head.

Then the can of Diet Coke hit me in the head. I grabbed it without thinking.

But the water enveloped us. I took a breath just as it seized me.

I'm not sure how I found the half-rolled-down window. Maybe it was by the tiny red glow of the dashboard lights. But with one hand splayed against the window, I brought the can hard against the glass. I couldn't breathe. Couldn't see.

But I smashed the can with all my strength against the window. Once. Twice.

Again and again. With a slamming blow that took all my strength, it broke. Underwater, there was no sound of breaking glass, only an explosion of glittering chunks like puzzle pieces that swept past me on a surge of water. I smashed the remaining window with the can until it burst in my hand, instantly turning to flimsy aluminum, and the water ripped it from my grasp. Then a concussion—the engine or the water or my own bursting heart—as the van struck the bottom of the river with a terrible, shuddering impact.

My lungs were exploding. Brandi's hand clung to my ankle. But I felt her grip weaken and begin to slide away.

I coiled back and grabbed her arm. I kicked her free of the wheelchair. I dragged myself through the window and tried to yank her with me.

The darkness. The cold. The confusion of water, movement and heavy, heavy weight.

"My first husband proposed to me at a Burger King," Libby said.

Michael's voice. *"I promised him a beer later."*

"Can I go to Beverly Hills?"

"But here," Tierney was saying, *"I'm some kind of freak."*

"Maybe you and the Love Machine get all googly-eyed with each other, but that's not my style."

"Thank you," Lexie said. *"For believing in me."*

Chapter 23

Someone with strong hands pulled me from the water. I heard his voice, but not his words. I sucked in hot air as he dragged me up onto the concrete ramp. I flopped like a fish. The blackness cleared from my mind, but I couldn't quite see yet.

I heard Brandi choking, coughing. She was alive. Someone ripped her from my grasp. I heard her crying, saw her white, helpless legs.

"I called 911!" Another voice, hysterical. "I saw the van go into the water. I couldn't believe it!"

"Take it easy, miss."

A person wrapped a dirty shirt around me. It smelled like sweat. I said, "I left my shoes in Libby's car."

Maybe I fainted. I know my brain stopped functioning for a while. Strangers can be very kind, though. I remember someone petting my hair. Someone else brought me a pair of blue Keds without the laces. They were too big on my feet. I wondered what happened to Libby's rubber boots.

A police car came. And an ambulance. The red lights flashed on the water, but they might as well have been pulsing in my brain. Then huge, colorful explosions burst in the sky—fireworks, I realized. For tomorrow. The Fourth of July. They were louder than thunder. Everyone stopped moving to look up. Just for a moment. And then they were kind again.

I said to someone, "I lost my sister's boots."

The paramedics carefully placed Brandi on a stretcher

and fastened straps around her. They talked to her and asked her name and talked about television news. They were excited to have a celebrity in their care. I heard her voice, not crying anymore.

"Come on, miss." Someone put his hand under my elbow. "Let's go to the hospital and get you checked out."

"No, thank you. I'm fine. My friend lives close by."

The paramedic insisted. It was only because Brandi's hysterics bubbled up again that he left me. And I slipped away.

The Schuylkill River runs down past Fairmount Park to Boathouse Row, where all the houses were lit up with tiny lights. Most nights, it's very picturesque. But the rowing clubs were quiet this evening. No parties. With the fireworks over, the night was strangely silent.

I walked. Along the side of the curving highway, I trudged in a stranger's blue Keds, stumbling on the gravel sometimes, and feeling the whoosh of air as cars went by.

The lights blazed inside Lexie's house.

She answered the door. "Nora!" Surprised to see me. "Is Michael with you?"

She came outside and got a closer look at me, and her voice went up an octave. "Oh, sweetie, what's wrong? What happened?"

"There was an accident. I went in the river."

"Oh dear God, God, God. Are you okay? Is anyone hurt? Come inside." She put her arm around me and pulled me into the house. The air-conditioning hit me like a winter blast. On the floor, my sandy, dirty shoes made a crunch.

Four suitcases stood by the newel post. An umbrella leaned against the tallest one.

"Where are you going?" I asked.

"Oh, sweetie."

I faced her. She was dressed in summer-weight trousers, flat sandals and a black T-shirt. Her airplane clothes,

I recognized. Her hair was combed. Her makeup flaw-less. Her diamond earrings reflected the same dark emp-tiness that shone in her eyes.

I said, "You can't leave."

Her face filled with pain. "Nora, I have to."

"Lex," I said. "You were protecting Brandi. You thought you were doing the right thing. Tell me you did it for Brandi. Not for the firm. Not for the money."

My dearest friend said, "Does it matter?"

"It matters to me," I said. "You're like a sister. I un-derstand you. At least, I always thought so."

"Sweetie." She sounded tired. "You're my sister, too. But this is something I have to do on my own."

"So you killed him."

She put her palms together and rested her hands against her forehead, as if she were praying. Her voice was hollow. "I don't know why, if that's what you're asking. Maybe you can tell me, because I—it's still incomprehensible."

"He hit her. Hoyt struck Brandi. You saw it."

She nodded, unable to look at me. "Yes. He'd just ru-ined my painting, so I was still angry. Funny thing, I real-ize now he did that for the insurance money. He knew my Vermeer was worth a fortune and the insurance company would pay off—probably enough to repay all the money he embezzled. I didn't understand that at the time. But when he slapped that girl, I—something inside me . . . ex-ploded." She lowered her hands and looked dully at me.

"So you pushed him."

"Yes. Away from her. Onto the balcony. And he—he went over the railing." She shook her head to dispel the memory, but she couldn't do it. "I know what I did. I'm not pretending it didn't happen. But part of me has been waiting for you to find someone else to take the blame." She smiled wanly. "That's not going to happen, is it?"

"The police will figure this out. If you touched him, there will be fingerprints."

She laughed shortly. "Oh, yes, there will be fingerprints. Mine will be all over him. And Brandi watched me do it, so there's a witness. She offered to keep it to herself. Did she tell you? For a price, of course."

Someone knocked on the door behind me. Two raps.

"Sweetie," Lexie said to me. "I wish you hadn't come."

She opened the door, and Michael walked in from the darkness, very tall and looming. He was still dressed in his jeans and white shirt, with my father's belt, but he looked like a criminal again. Something in his face. He had his car keys in hand.

At the sight of me, he dropped the keys on the tile floor. "Jesus," he said. "What happened?"

From far away, Lexie said, "She went into the river, she says. An accident."

"Libby and Emma?" he asked, grasping me by the shoulders. "Are they okay?"

I nodded, shivering.

"Get her a blanket," he said to Lexie. "She's in shock."

He eased me down to sit on the step. He buffed my arms to get my blood pumping. But his hands were cold, too.

My teeth began to chatter. "She did it. Lexie pushed him."

"I know, love. I'm sorry."

Lexie returned and slung the bedspread from her bed around my shoulders. I clutched at it, my fingers trembling.

I peered up at her. "You can't leave, Lex."

She stood back, arms folded across her chest, irritated. Or maybe detached. "Sweetie, please."

"The police will figure it out. It's only a matter of time."

"And time is running out."

"There's Brandi, too. Once she asks you for money, it won't stop. Blackmail never does. We can help you."

"Dear Nora." She gave me a grim yet forgiving smile.

"I've ruined my life. There's nothing anyone can do for me now."

"So you're going to run away?"

"Yes."

I looked up at Michael. "And you're going to take her? You're going to help her run from the law?"

Before he could answer, she said, "Don't blame him. This is my decision."

"This is wrong," I said, voice stronger as a white heat started in my chest. "Think it through, Lexie."

"I have. I've lost everything—my reputation and my business. My clients. What's left?"

"Your friends! Your family!" I threw off the bedspread and got unsteadily to my feet. "And there's Crewe and—"

"And what? Jail? I couldn't stand it."

"It wouldn't be forever! You were protecting someone! You need to stay and fight."

Lexie said, "I'm going to leave, Nora. I'm going to run away and save everyone the agony."

"Don't. Please don't," I begged. "That's what my parents did, and look what's become of them. Their friends hate them for being petty crooks. Their children don't trust them. They haven't learned a thing."

She winced at the mention of my parents.

"I know how far you've come," I said. "I know how hard it was for you to put that awful experience behind you and make this beautiful life here. But maybe you shouldn't have tried so hard to forget. You've found money and power and—and your art, too. But it's all so cold. You have to stop running away from the past, Lex. It's not too late."

"I have to go."

A dam burst in me. "I can't lose you!"

"You don't need me any more, Nora. Not like you used to."

She stepped away. "Michael, these suitcases—"

"He won't," I said. "I won't let him."

I blocked his way, but Michael had turned to stone.

I seized her hand. "Lexie, I'll go to the police with you. So will Crewe. We'll find you a lawyer who will understand that you've got all these issues, that you were a victim, too."

"No," Lexie said, clipped. "I'm not weak."

"It's not weakness. Your cousin hurt you and it's affected everything since! He shut you off. He made you feel helpless."

She yanked out of my grasp and put her hands over her ears. "I can't go to jail, Nora! It would be too awful, trapped like that. I wouldn't survive."

At last, Michael said, "It's not so bad."

Lexie turned away from me to stare at Michael. He had gone very white, as if he'd been punched. His voice sounded strange.

Gently, as if speaking to a child, he said, "You need time to think, Lexie. To figure out your life. A prison isn't such a bad place to do that."

I caught my balance on the newel post and gulped back a sob.

He said, "Can you live with what you did, pushing your partner to his death?"

Lexie wobbled, too. She flinched as if she were the one being pushed until her back hit the balcony rail. She put her hands up to fend off a blow or the thought that she must forever remember that awful moment when she lost her head.

Michael said, "You don't just forget. But if you do your time? It can be a penance. And you come out of it absolved, with a new life. A second chance."

He took a breath. "Look how Nora loves you. If you run away, you'll lose that. And listen, I know what it's like to live alone, without that kind of love. It's worse than any prison."

"Stay, Lex," I said.

She began to cry. I took two tottering steps and wrapped my arms around her.

We held each other, clinging. I tried to give her what strength I had left.

"I'll be with you," I said. "Every step of the way."

"I don't think I can face it."

Michael said, "Talk to the lawyers. See what they can work out for you. It's not the end."

"I don't know," she said.

I said, "Lexie, don't you want a normal life?"

"I don't know what that means," she whispered.

"Then you've got to find out."

"I don't know . . ."

She wept in my arms, messed up her makeup and her hair and sobbed until she couldn't breathe. It was a storm that left her too weak to stand. We helped each other to the sofa. Michael brought her a glass of water.

Lexie regained her composure at last. Withdrawing inside herself, perhaps. "Okay," she said to Michael. "I'll talk to your lawyers. I hope they're as good as I think they are."

Michael made the call. Lexie found me something to wear in her closet. I took a hot shower and put on her clothes.

Cannoli himself came. He was courtly. She was self-possessed. It was a kind of summit, almost ceremonial.

They spoke for several hours. Michael listened and contributed, stepping outside onto the deck to take phone calls. Cannoli telephoned for another associate, who arrived at one a.m. in a suit and tie.

Almost sure she was convinced not to run, I curled up on Lexie's bed after that, too exhausted to think straight.

When Michael came in at dawn and shook me awake, I felt as though I'd slept only a minute. But I sat up quickly, afraid.

"Call Crewe," he said. "She should see him this morning."

So I telephoned Crewe, who arrived looking frantic. Michael went out for groceries, and the two of us cooked breakfast for everyone—eggs and bacon and the works.

Crewe came into the kitchen later, and when I hugged him, he wept.

I had known Lexie. We played with dolls together—cutting all Barbie's hair off and tearing her clothes so she'd look more like Madonna—the strongest woman we knew.

School, parties. Little spats. Sneaking champagne at high school graduation. The bond I felt for Lexie was stronger, perhaps, than the ties to my own sisters.

I sat with her in the hospital the night she saw the rape counselor. While we waited, we played tic-tac-toe on her hospital gown with a textbook highlighter from my school backpack.

She had rescued me so many times. Picked me up after Todd's death, consoled me after my miscarriage.

But I had never been able to protect her from the demons she bottled up inside.

We all accompanied her to the police station. On the afternoon of the Fourth of July, I kissed her good-bye as they took Lexie Paine into custody.

"She shows the world her strength," I said to Michael. He had driven us to his house on the Delaware, and we stood on his deck as the darkness gathered. "But she's always been vulnerable. And afraid. Even Crewe couldn't break the barriers she's built around herself."

Michael held me.

"Her cousin broke her collarbone when she was eleven, did I ever tell you that? And he raped her a couple of years later." I drew a ragged breath. "Now I feel as if she's dead."

"She's not dead." He kissed the top of my head. "She won't be inside for long. A manslaughter charge like the one she pleaded to—it's only going to be five years, max. She'll be out in three."

It was no consolation.

The trees shivered overhead. The Delaware River rippled and murmured before us. The Delaware, shallow as it flowed before Michael's house, was a peaceful river. If I threw a leaf onto the water, though, it would rush down to the Chesapeake and out into the ocean, gone forever.

I said, "When did you know? That she killed him?"

"I had a gut feeling. The things she said, the way she pushed Crewe away. I knew she wanted to handle something alone."

"Like you," I said.

He tightened his arms around me.

But I turned in his embrace and looked up into his face. "Were you being truthful with her? About paying the price and being absolved? About a new life?"

"Yes."

"You weren't going to help her run away, were you? Please tell me that."

"When she asked me to get her out of the country, I thought about it. But I knew it would be wrong. I was going to try to talk her into sticking around. I couldn't have done it the way you did. You saved her."

"It doesn't feel that way."

In the sky overhead, a flicker of lightning flashed, and a moment later the thunder rumbled. The oppressive summer heat seemed to rush down upon us hotter than ever, and then it broke as the first drops of rain hissed on the deck beneath our feet.

But I said, "You're going to jail again, aren't you?"

"Yes," he said. "I'm sorry, Nora. I have to admit I'm an accessory to the truck theft. The only way my father will agree to go quietly is if I take some of the blame, too. And maybe it's right."

I felt the rain sting my cheeks. We let the rain fall around us, though. Cleansing, perhaps.

Chapter 24

After the weather broke and a few days of rain washed the world clean, my family voted to go to the beach. Libby insisted I come, too. We packed an enormous picnic. It took three cars to transport everyone and all our junk. The day was warm and clear with a brilliant sun.

We staked out a spot on the sand and spread quilts before the weekend crowd got too huge. We opened umbrellas and checked that the coolers had plenty of ice. We could smell popcorn and seawater on the breeze. Daddy bought a box of taffy, popped a piece into his mouth and immediately pulled a crown off one of his molars. I took Maximus down to the water and held his arms while he squealed and splashed his pudgy feet in the waves.

The twins went off to look for dead fish and desiccated crabs. Lucy dug a hole near the water's edge and spent the afternoon burying things. Rawlins and Shawna rented boogie boards and plunged into the ocean to be alone with each other in the crowd. Max took a nap in my arms.

All morning, Emma sat, ominously silent, in a beach chair. She dug her toes into the sand, wearing black sunglasses that hid her eyes from the rest of us. She drank can after can of ginger ale and didn't say much. Her brooding made us all nervous.

When she pulled a T-shirt over her head and sauntered off to find a bathroom, Libby whipped off her sun hat and leaned toward me. "Actually, Emma handled the whole episode very well. Except for lighting the Haffenpepper girl's dress on fire. And Hart's a quick thinker. I give him all the credit for stripping off the dress before anybody got hurt."

"Did Hart propose to Eva Braun's daughter?" I asked.

"He did, but then there was all that screaming. I'm surprised you didn't hear it, Nora. Anyway, Hart's a free man. The beer heiress never wants to see him again."

"Did Emma tell him? About the baby?"

"Yes, she did. And he took it badly, but I don't think that will last. Mark my words, Nora, there's something happening between those two. Of course, I'm not entirely sure they like each other much. And there are dozens of issues to be settled. But the sexual tension is electrifying!"

Jacque Petite sat up on his elbows on the quilt where he'd been sunbathing. His back was already beet red despite several layers of sunscreen Libby had lovingly applied. His electric blue Speedo had inched downward to reveal some dazzling white skin of his surprisingly perky bottom. He slid his sunglasses up onto his perspiring forehead and smiled. He was always smiling, of course. Except when he was giggling with my sister.

He said, "I think it would be very hard to enjoy good sex with someone you didn't love just a little bit."

Libby patted his cheek. "Yes, my darling, I agree completely."

I said, "I heard a rumor Hart may make a bid for what's left of the Paine Investment Group."

"Really? Would Lexie let that happen?"

"I don't think she has any say in the matter."

"Won't she be blown to bits if she loses the firm?"

"She's lost it already," I said quietly. "But after she's released, it will be interesting to see what she chooses to do with her life."

"Darling," Libby said to Jacque. "Did you bring any of your incomparable chocolate-covered strawberries, by chance?"

"You think I might forget your second-favorite treat, my pigeon?" He cast an appreciative glance down the flirty skirt of her bathing suit and gave her knee a squeeze. "I brought champagne, too. You said we have celebrating to do."

"Yes, Nora's promotion!"

My family applauded.

I acknowledged their approval with a seated bow. "Thank you. But it's not exactly a promotion. Just an assurance that I'll be allowed to stick around for another year. Especially if I can continue to come up with good video material for the paper's Web site. And the editors want me to help everybody choose content."

"That sounds very creative. Very promising," Jacque declared.

Daddy piped up. "We're very proud of you, Muffin."

"Does it mean you won't be available to look after the children?" Libby asked. "Because Jacque and I were considering a trip to the islands soon."

Jacque said, "Why don't we take them with us?"

Libby looked prettily astonished. "With us?"

"Certainly! I love children. And yours are all so interesting, dearest. We could have a glorious time."

"Well . . . I suppose we could do that."

From the other end of the quilt, Tierney interrupted. "Should we be worried about Henry? I think Lucy's got him buried up to his neck over there. What if the tide comes in?"

We all looked over at Lucy's construction project. The whole family was pleased to see she had replaced her imaginary friend with a real person. We hated to break the spell by interrupting.

Daddy said, "As long as he's still breathing, I think he'll be okay."

Tierney said, "He's supposed to take me to the airport later, that's all. My flight is at nine."

I said, "You could stay another week, Tierney. You don't really need to rush back to your business, do you?"

"Yes, I do. For so many reasons."

"Son," Daddy said, "you're a member of the family now. I hope that means you'll be inviting us to visit you soon."

"Uh—"

"And, of course, we expect you home for all holidays. I carve a mean Christmas goose, you know."

A diplomat, Tierney tipped up his mirrored sunglasses and said, "Thank you. I'll take that invitation under advisement."

I hid my smile. I had seen a glimpse of the Blackbird genes in Tierney. Perhaps part of his reason for fleeing us so soon was that he could tamp down the spirit yearning to break free inside him.

Daddy said, "We do a very festive Thanksgiving, too. I presume all our tax issues will be settled by then. It's only a matter of paperwork now, I'm sure. Nora sets a lovely table. She's a miracle-worker with centerpieces. That is, if she doesn't decide to house-sit for those peculiar friends of hers. What on earth would you do with yourself if you move into the city, Nora?"

"Walk to work?" I said.

"But think of all the joys of family living you'd be missing!"

I was thinking precisely of those dubious joys when I told Daniel and Eric I'd look after their home, but I changed the subject. "Tierney, did you find an investor for Amazon Chocolate?"

He settled down on the quilt again to sunbathe. "My friend the loan shark came through," he said lightly. "A silent partner, I guess you could say. Amazon Chocolate's going to survive."

Mama had been sharing the big umbrella with me, reading from a book with a tattered brown cover. Suddenly she gave an exclamation and sat up. "Here it is!"

"Here what is?" Daddy inquired.

She planted her forefinger onto the yellowed page. "Exactly the ceremony we need to have for Emma!"

Emma's shadow appeared over us, and she blocked the glare of the sun. In her hand was another can of ginger ale, fresh from a vending machine. "What kind of ceremony?"

Mama's sequined sunglasses sparkled. "A godparents' incantation! At least, I think that's what this is. My translation from the Inca text might be off."

"You're reading an Inca text?"

"No, Nora, this is an interpretation by the famous mentalist Charles Merriman—with footnotes in Incan symbols. I'm sure you've heard of him. He was a famous nineteenth-century Jesuit who left the order to become a scholar in metaphysical beliefs of ancient cultures. That was before he turned to magic acts to make a few bucks. Of course, he lived out his days in a mental institution, but that was after he wrote this brilliant book."

"Sounds like a bestseller to me," Emma said.

Mama took off her sunglasses and pinned Emma with a disapproving glare. "Don't you want your baby to have all the advantages? You know, a healthy appreciation for spiritual well-being begins in the womb, Emmaline."

Michael woke beside me and lifted the paperback book off his face. He squinted up at my sister. "Emmaline?"

She kicked his ankle.

Mama clapped her hands together smartly. "We need volunteers! Spiritual godparents, anyone?"

"I nominate Nora," Libby said in a shot.

"And Mick," Emma added. "If he's going to make fun of me, he's got to pay a price."

He laughed. "Sure, Emmaline."

Michael's skin had turned a delicious shade of bronze in just a couple of hours. Stretched out beside me, he looked like a Roman god, but he appeared to be unaware of the effect he had on passersby. He rolled over on one elbow. "What do I have to do? Wave a palm frond at a virgin or something?"

Mama frowned at her book. "Let's see. First there's

something here about embracing the cosmic forces with an open heart and then . . ." She flipped a page. "Ah, do both of you solemnly swear to uphold peace in the universe and—and—oh, dear, I've lost my place. No, here it is. In the perpetual motion of the sun, moon and stars, you must take each other's hand. Go on, do it!"

Laughing, I reached for Michael's hand.

"In the sight of all who gather here, do you vow to forswear all others?"

"Okay," Michael said.

"And pledge to remain joined despite all tribulations—and—let's see here, tempests in storm-tossed seas?"

"Of course," I said. "Whatever that means."

"And you must revere this joyous bond every day of your life together, in sickness and in health, as long as you both shall live?"

"Wait a minute," Michael said. "This sounds—"

Mama picked up the pace, rapidly bulldozing over his objections. "Do you love this woman above all others?"

"Yes, but—"

"And you, Nora, do you vow to spend the rest of your life bound in happiness to this man?"

"Mama—"

"Do you?"

"Yes, I do," I said as Michael's hand tightened around mine. "But—"

"Then, by the blessings of this gathering, I hereby declare that you—"

She flipped the page and said, "Oh, dear. I think this is the wrong ceremony. It says we can declare that you are joined for life. Does that mean . . . ?"

"Kiss her quick," Jacque advised Michael. "Just in case it's for real."

"Mama, what have you done?" I cried. "The Blackbird Curse!"

My mother closed her book with a snap. "Whatever do you mean, Nora?"

"The family curse! All the Blackbird women—our husbands die!"

"Don't be silly, darling. That old curse only counts when the father objects to the marriage. Or if the ceremony takes place during a leap year. And there's something about Halley's comet, too, but I'm not sure about that part." She put her sunglasses back on and settled contentedly into her chair. "Your grandmother Blackbird was never very clear."

"Daddy?" Libby said. "Do you object to this marriage?"

"Well, I keep hearing rumors about a jail sentence." My father put on a stern face. "Just what's that all about, young man?"

"I can't lie to you, sir. I'm going away for a little while. It'll give me a chance to think about the kind of life I want to make for your beautiful daughter. But I expect to be back in time for that Christmas goose."

"And what are your prospects, may I ask?"

"Prospects?"

Tierney was laughing. "The newspapers say he's taking over a whole family business."

"Is that true?" I asked hotly. "Is that why yesterday's newspaper suspiciously disappeared?"

"Nora—"

"Sorry, Mick," Tierney said. "I thought she knew."

"It's just a few loose ends," Michael assured me. "Hardly anything at all. I can take care of it from inside, no problem."

Michael kissed me, and I hesitated only for a moment before kissing him back. Libby brought out the chocolate-covered strawberries, and Jacque popped the cork from a bottle of chilled champagne. Emma gave me a hug, and I think she meant it.

Daddy proposed a long-winded toast that ended with, "It's wonderful to have a plumber in the family!"

After we drank champagne from paper cups, Michael pulled me down to the edge of the water, and we waded into the surf. Children shrieked and splashed around us. An elderly couple stood ankle-deep nearby. I saw Rawlins catch a wave, showing off. Watching him from her boogie board, Shawna caught sight of me and waved. I waved back.

Michael said, "So this is it? As close to married as we can get?"

"We'll talk about it. When I come to visit you in jail." I took his hand as a wave splashed against our knees. I looked at the horizon and breathed deeply of the sea air.

Michael said, "You okay?"

I tipped my face up to him. I had learned to love many people in spite of their flaws. Somehow, that realization made me ready to have my own family now.

"Yes," I said. "Let's be happy."

Make sure you haven't missed earlier high society high-jinks from the Blackbird Sisters, listed here in the order in which they were originally published.

How to Murder a Millionaire

From riches to rags . . . Nora Blackbird has found a job as a society page columnist for a Philadelphia newspaper. This down-and-*almost*-out debutante is happy to reclaim her place within the city's elite, while trying to keep under control the antics of her two kooky sisters and her attraction to the sexy son of a New Jersey crime boss. Then, on her first party assignment, she stumbles upon the murdered body of the host—a millionaire art collector and old family friend.

Dead Girls Don't Wear Diamonds

When a high society jewel thief winds up drowned at the bottom of a pool with a tacky garden gnome tied to her ankles, Nora must swing into action to save her old flame, Flan Cooper, from a murder charge. But then a politically ambitious millionaire with hushed-up secrets, a dotty grande dame with a penchant for polo teams, and a cat fancier who keeps a gun with his silver tea set all steer suspicion onto Nora herself.

Some Like It Lethal

When Rush Strawcutter, the husband of a wealthy dog food heiress, is found bludgeoned to death in a horse stall at an exclusive hunt club, Nora is as surprised as anyone. Her surprise turns to shock when her sister Emma is discovered nearby, unconscious and badly bruised. Worse still, the evidence points toward a devious blackmail scheme—with Emma as the main suspect.

Cross Your Heart and Hope to Die

Nora's next journalistic assignment: the unveiling of the most miraculous bra in fashion history. But before she can hand in her uplifting story, her boss is found shot execution-style and trussed up in expensive panty hose—an Abruzzo family trademark. Now Nora must find the killer before her innocent lover takes the rap.

Have Your Cake and Kill Him Too

Murder is always distracting, especially when the victim is the tycoon owner of Cupcakes, a spectacularly tacky sports bar known less for its hot wings than for its hot waitresses. Nora trails a secretive politician, a shady former rock star doubling as a pastry chef, and a dangerous aristo-brat on the verge of stardom. And even as two hot men vie for a long-term place by Nora's side, she learns she's in a delicate condition. . . .

A Crazy Little Thing Called Death

Nora has agreed to wed Mick Abruzzo, son of New Jersey's most notorious mobster. Now she has to help him survive the Blackbird Curse. But Nora's superstitions are eclipsed by some ominous news: ex-Hollywood starlet Penny Devine has disappeared—presumed dead—and it's revealed that Nora has inherited her extensive couture wardrobe. The only way for Nora to keep her name clear is to snoop among the snooty . . . and sniff out the truth.

Also Available
from
Nancy Martin

A Crazy Little Thing
Called Death
A BLACKBIRD SISTERS MYSTERY

Nora Blackbird has made the society
pages yet again. The impoverished
Philadelphia heiress has agreed to wed
Mick Abruzzo, son of New Jersey's most
notorious mobster—if he can survive the
Blackbird Curse. Because anytime a
Blackbird sister remarries, the groom is
bound to die...

**Available wherever books are sold or at
penguin.com**

The Bestselling
Blackbird Sisters Mystery Series
by
Nancy Martin

Don't miss a single adventure of the Blackbird
sisters, a trio of Philadelphia-born, hot-blooded
bluebloods with a flair for fashion—and for
solving crimes.

Also Available:

How to Murder a Millionaire
Dead Girls Don't Wear Diamonds
Some Like It Lethal
Cross Your Heart and Hope to Die
Have Your Cake and Kill Him Too